A Sky So Hollow

THE STARDUST DUOLOGY BOOK TWO

CRAIG MONTGOMERY

~

For Karen,
who showed me that loving and being loved was worth the fight.

GLOSSARY & PRONUNCIATION GUIDE

I believe that the reader is right when it comes to pronunciation. This is for those who may care about how the unfamiliar words were designed to be spoken.

Names:
    Belen (bell-in)
    Brissa (bree-suh)
    Eman (ee-mah-n)
    Faus (fah-s)
    Malia (mah-lee-ah)
    Orrin (or-rah-n)
    Stallastis (st-ah-lass-tiss)
    Talleah (tuh-lee-ah) / **Tal** (t-æ-l)

~

Places:
    Novilem (noh-vil-em) - city inside of a moon
    Ouranos (or-uh-noh-s) - planet that Novilem orbits

Celestery (suh-les-stir-ree) - where the Estellar governs

Creatures:
    Tektranos (tech-trah-nos)

Terms:
    Estellar (es-tell-ah-r) - council that governs Novilem
    Preitan (pray-tan) - seated member of the Estellar Council
    Enotis (ee-noh-tih-s) - political movement
    Exoria (ex-or-ree-ah) - group of people exiled to the Surface
    Fosergatis (foh-sir-gah-tee-s) - the magic in Novilem
    Sedrivani (seh-drih-vah-nee) - the source of aether
    Kanos (kah-noh-s) - the source of corrupted aether
    Telos (teh-los) - title given to someone with access to all twelve houses of aether

CAST OF CHARACTERS

Casper - from Earth, brought to Novilem as the new Telos
Helix - (*Capricorn*) protégé and grandson of Preitan Brissa
Talleah - (*Leo*) disadvantaged mother of a Gemini
Hector - (Leo) Talleah's partner and captain of a crew at the
Academy

Agnes - former Telos of Novilem who was exiled
Belen - (*Sagittarius*) Helix's crewmate
Brissa - (*Capricorn*) head preitan of the Estellar Council
Danielle - Casper's girlfriend from high school
Daphne - (*Gemini*) child Casper meets his first day in
Novilem
David - Casper's father
Eman - (*Aquarius*) leader of the Farseers
Faus - (*Cancer*) Helix's crewmate
Gloria - (*Virgo*) Helix's crewmate
Malia - (*Libra*) Helix's crewmate

Orrin - (*Capricorn*) Casper's tutor and steward of the Estellar

Hector - (*Leo*) Talleah's partner

Jacob - (*Taurus*) elder preitan of the Estellar Council

Peter - (*Aries*) Helix's crewmate and childhood friend

Theo - (*Gemini*) elder preitan of the Estellar Council

This story contains some difficult material. I have done my best to approach these topics thoughtfully, but I encourage you to take care of yourself.

This is a non-exhaustive list of content warnings:

Graphic
Violence, blood, death, dead body, animal death, homophobia, outing, parental abuse

Moderate
Body horror, drug use, panic attack/disorder, cursing

Minor
Vomit, injury details

This is the second novel in a duology. While both stories are intended to have their own complete arcs, this story relies on the groundwork laid in book one, A Circle of Stars. For those who have read the first novel, but it's been some time. Below is a brief overview of the events that occurred.

Previously in The Stardust Duology

Casper Bell, an eighteen-year-old boy, was having a rough go of it. In the last week of his senior year of high school, his teammate assaulted and outed him. His religious parents did not take well to the news, kicking him out onto the streets of Chicago.

Luckily (debatable), before he can process being unhoused, a pack of demonic coyotes attack. He's saved by magic wielding strangers, who then abduct him to their home, called Novilem, on the other side of the universe. Novilem is a city carved into the stony center of a moon orbiting an Earth-like planet.

Casper learns that Novilites use magic through an energy called aether. Aether moves at different frequencies and when a person takes their first breath, they attune to the frequency during that period. Thus, his abductors all care very deeply about their astrology sun signs. Oh, and Casper is going to be their Telos. A person born at a special converging point in the wavelengths of the universe which gives him access to all twelve star signs' abilities. He represents the unity of the houses and is expected to become a figurehead.

It doesn't take long for Casper to notice that this seemingly utopian city isn't as shiny and perfect as it seems. The city is governed by a council of leaders, called preitans, from each of the twelve astrology houses. Four of which are assigned as elder seats, who, from Casper's perspective, seem to rule the city with an iron fist.

One more so than any: Preitan Brissa. Brissa is spiky and none too happy that Casper is in Novilem. But more importantly, she has a heartbreakingly handsome grandson named Helix.

Helix Stallastis is many things: A Capricorn, captain of a crew at the Academy, the grandson of the governess of Novilem, but definitely not a prince. He and Casper cross paths at a family gathering in Brissa's villa and the sparks tingle at their first meeting. Casper is nothing like anyone Helix has ever met, and Helix is the first boy that Casper feels safe enough to flirt with. It doesn't hurt that he is really, really hot.

When we meet Talleah, Helix is seeking her out for information on ramal, a hallucinogenic drug being traded against the council's orders. After his childhood best friend was exposed smuggling ramal into Novilem during their crew's missions, Helix wants to know why and how the drug is being produced and brought into the city.

Talleah is a cook and runs a very popular food cart that is located on the promenade outside the Celestery, the council's giant, shiny pyramid where they run daily business. She doesn't have information to help Helix, but we soon learn that her choice of location is no coincidence. Talleah has a daughter, who was taken away from her. Daphne, born a Libra, started using magic that can only Geminis can use.

When the council discovered this, they removed Daphne from Talleah's care and placed her with the Geminis, who live in a large cave behind the Celestery. The council has kept the Gemini segregated from the rest of the populace for nearly 80 years. We learn later that his is a reaction to the part Gemini magic played in a bloody uprising the last time a Telos was born.

Desperate to get her daughter back, Talleah seeks out a group called the Enotis, a political movement that aims to free the Gemini and have those who have been exiled by the council return to Novilem.

By the time Casper's ascension festival arrives, where he is to be paraded in front of the public and announced as their new Telos, he has learned enough to be wary of the council and unsure of his best path forward. Although he knows that Brissa will punish him harshly for stepping out of line, he plans to speak out at his ascension to inform the public that they are being manipulated.

However, he isn't given the chance. His ascension is crashed by the Enotis, who are enacting a coup, and in an attempt to remove the power that Casper's presence represents, they prepare to teleport him to the dangerous Surface of the planet Ouranos. Knowing that Casper will die if he's sent to the Surface alone, Helix slides into the jump circle. Seeing her grandson risking his life for an assassination attempt that she secretly has backed, Brissa tries to pull Helix out, but the magic is cast and Casper and Helix arrive on the Surface with half of Brissa's body.

On the Surface, Casper and Helix fight to stay alive while the horrors of Ouranos give them a run for their money. Casper, facing a never-ending onslaught of adversity since we met him, is crashing out. This brings out the negative side of his personality and Helix struggles to coexist with him. Meanwhile, Talleah, having helped the Enotis, is trying to use the chaos to get to Daphne. Only, when she gets to the Gemini caves, there is no one there.

After a few harrowing days, Casper and Helix are found by the Exoria, a group of exiles sent to the Surface as punishment for crimes considered too egregious for reconciliation. Among the Exoria are Agnes, the former Telos who was at the center of the bloody uprising 80 years prior, Peter, Helix's childhood best friend, and Orrin, Casper's assigned mentor and steward to the council whom Helix previously considered Brissa's right-hand man.

In an attempt at justice the Enotis feel they were denied, they handle social issues in a public forum. Thus, Helix finds himself on trial for telling the council about Peter's smuggling and having his whole family exiled. To defend himself, Helix has to expose the council's, namely Brissa's, lies. He informs them that Brissa was trined, meaning she had access to three houses of aether.

Using Gemini and Pisces aether, Brissa was able to manipulate people with the touch of her hand. Having been a powerful woman, Helix had always thought her influence was earned from her strength, but he had felt the push of her magical persuasion enough to be disillusioned. This was how she had made him share with her the information about Peter. Helix never intended to betray his friend, but Brissa used aether to coax it out of him.

With the hypocrisy of the council's actions laid bare, it's only fair that at this moment a battalion of acolytes (people who enact the council's wishes, think cops and/or clergymen) launch an attack on the Exoria. Casper and Helix fight with the Exoria and during the fray, Casper taps into the aether channels of Ouranos.

It's too much power for him to handle and he doesn't know how to cut it off. The aether takes over him in what is known as a supernova. When he is seconds away from losing himself to the aether, Agnes jumps into the sky with an astrolabe, a magical device that is designed to help the wearer connect with aether. She isn't sure what will happen to him, but it being a Capricorn astrolabe should limit the amount of aether that he is channeling to that single house. Casper chooses to try the astrolabe instead of letting himself slip away into the light, and it works.

When the boys return to Novilem, the city is on rocky footing. The attempted coup has created a frenetic energy, and the council is on high alert. Having discovered the extent of their deceit, and the machinations of Elder Preitan Jacob specifically (the Taurus preitan who previously gave Casper the mega creeps), Helix suggests they confront the council publicly, hoping to use the lingering unrest and the outrage of the public when they learn of the council's lies to pressure them into reform.

It seems like it might work. The gathered populace is backing Helix's argument and the elder preitans are crumbling. It's at this moment that Jacob dons a power suit, grabs Casper, and launches away. Once they are in what looks like Jacob's laboratory, he gives his big villain monologue. He hated Brissa for always besting him and treating the council like they all belonged to her. More importantly, he believes that Novilem has been stagnating too long. Without space to expand and opportunities for their people, he believes that Novilem will collapse. And Brissa stonewalled his every attempt to advocate for growth opportunities.

So, with her gone, he plans to take things into his own hands. He has used his Taurus aether to make a battery of sorts. One that can absorb and use aether much like a person does. The catch is, the machine absorbs aether by channeling it through a person. Jacob latches Casper to the machine and begins to funnel massive amounts of aether through him. Having nearly supernova'd on the Surface, Casper is too familiar with the feeling that overtakes his body.

So, when Jacob reveals that his plan is to teleport the

entire populace of Novilem to the Surface in order to force them to create a habitable space on the planet, Casper diverts the aether being gathered. Outside the window of Jacob's lab he can see that they have teleported a giant, two kilometer tall, residential tower to the Surface.

The change in mass affects the gyroscopic mechanism used to generate a livable gravity in the city (if you don't recall, the city is on the inside of a moon). The city turns on its side, literally.

Helix arrives and frees Casper from the battery machine. Jacob makes a break to escape and they chase after him, fighting on the side of one of the remaining residential towers. Casper defeats him, but when the boys turn their back to check on each other, Jacob slips away.

Disaster sort of averted, the city begins to mend its wounds. The people teleported the Surface with the tower are returned to Novilem. Helix, having learned of Brissa and the council's deceptions, lends his voice to the argument of the Enotis, advocating for the people to be reunited. The council agrees to work toward reintegrating the Gemini and allowing the Exoria to return.

Talleah has a tearful reunion with her daughter. Casper and Helix made it through everything in one piece and are more fond of each other for the journey. It was a fight hard won and they are happy about it.

If only Jacob hadn't escaped...

Aetherium Astrologica
on the houses of aether

Pisces
emotional aura and influence
Nevafosi
Allagi
Strathero

Aries
strength and speed
Kardiafosi
Kyrio
Strathero

Taurus
Material manipulation
Somafosi
Myalfosi
Allagi

Aquarius
astral projection and divination
Myalfosi
Strathero
Kyrio

Gemini
Mind bonding
Nevafosi
Kyrio
Strathero

Capricorn
regeneration
Somafosi
Kyrio
Allagi

Cancer
borrows aether through touch
Kardiafosi
Strathero

Sagittarius
aether empowerment
Kardiafosi
Allagi
Nevafosi

Leo
aether production and strength

Scorpio
Light manipulation

Virgo
Healing others

Libra
Teleportation

Telos

Kyrio
Strathero
Allagi

Ouranos

Novilem

aether of the...
Myalfosi △ Mind
Nevafosi △ soul
Kardiafosi △ heart
Somafosi △ body

art by Ellie Spain

CHAPTER
ONE

Helix Stallastis approached the train platform with heavy feet. It was an hour past Split rise before he peeled himself away from Casper's bed. He would have lingered longer, but if he left Malia waiting, she would bail on him. It was not the first time Helix wished he had one of those cell phones Casper told him about.

A cycle had passed since Jacob's attack on the city, which the people were calling the Turning. With each passing day, Casper seemed more preoccupied with when he would return. A permanent line was forming between his brows. The council assumed Jacob was hiding away in the missing tower, though their Aquarius could not see inside to confirm.

"You're late," Malia said. Her trademark bob had grown out to shoulder length. She wore it gathered into a hair tie on the back of her head, her face more open than he had ever seen it.

"Sorry," Helix said. "I got a little tied up."

"Really?" Malia's brow lifted. "I took star kid as a vanilla type."

"Stars above." Helix covered his face with his hands. "I won't dignify that with a comment. And he doesn't like when you don't call him Casper."

"Considering the spell he has you under, I could call him the dick wizard if you prefer."

Helix glanced around the empty train platform where they were meeting. The lobes of his ears pinched with heat.

"If you think anyone in this city hasn't seen the two of you giving each other sweet eyes," Malia said, "I've got bad news for you."

A pod arrived at the platform and Helix took the first ride. Anything to escape the conversation. On the other side of the translucent pane, Malia rolled her eyes, grinning.

Novilem looked depressed as the track brought him in an arc across the city. He worried the subdued energy was a new norm. There was as much to mourn as there was to celebrate with the fallout of Jacob's uprising, the return of the Exoria, and the release of the Gemini. And then there was the sickness—the reason he was visiting the Farseer grotto.

He observed the empty space where the western tower should be until his pod rounded the corner and new construction replaced his view. A group of Taurus was quick at work building homes for the displaced citizens and new populace.

His pod came to a gentle stop at the border of the crop fields. Nestled into the wall of Novilem, just beyond the farthest border of the city, a burst of wild nature hid the entrance to the Farseer grotto. Excitement trickled through his chest. This was his first time approaching it. No one, not even the Estellar council, was allowed inside. The Farseers had an emissary that would attend to the council upon request, but the Farseer's service to the Estellar was contingent on them being allowed to exist independently.

"This is a waste of time," Malia said when she joined Helix at the bottom of the train platform.

Part of Helix agreed, but if anyone had information on what was causing people to get sick, it would be the Farseers. And as much as he tried to pressure the council to take the illness more seriously, they were not concerned enough to prioritize the issue. Theo had made sure of that.

"Got a busy day ahead of you?" Helix asked.

"Yes, actually. I had an entire afternoon planned of leaving well enough alone."

Virgos could clear corruption sickness. They knew this from handling the infections of crew members coming back from the Surface. So, the council arranged for the sick to be tended to and kept their focus on the business of getting back to normal. But people didn't get corruption sickness in the city, thanks to astrolabes. They not only made aether easier to attune to, they also filtered out corrupted aether. As far as he was aware, these were the first cases of people getting sick inside Novilem.

Lentils, beans, potatoes, and more variation of greens than Helix could count spread out in beautiful rows around him. The temptation to remove his sandals and feel the stamped earth path they were following nearly over-whelmed him. He rarely visited the other side of the Split. There was a quiet energy there that beckoned him. An invitation to rest that was at odds with the buzzing energy inside his mind. As they reached the end of the rows of vegetation, lush greenery extended from the dirt. Berries and flowers colored two rows of bushes on either side of an arch of tree branches, narrowing the field of view to a small cave opening partially obscured by leaves.

As they neared the grotto entrance, Helix noticed two guards stationed with long wooden staves in hand. Their presence was not only unexpected, but alarming. Armed guards were certainly not the norm, even at the Celestery.

"Better than your best behavior," Helix said to Malia. Then to the guards, "May the stars bless and guide you." Neither of the men answered. Their orange robes indicated they were Leos. The Farseers adhered to sign coloring for even their daily attire.

The guard on his right gave him a once over. "You may not enter the grotto."

"I'm aware entrance to the grotto is forbidden," Helix said. "I'm here to request the wisdom of the Eye."

The guards looked at each other before the same man spoke. "You are a child. The Eye only communes with the Estellar."

"I am young," Helix said affably. "But I'm actually Junior Preitan Helix."

"Junior?" the other guard asked.

Malia snickered behind Helix. It took effort to ignore her. "Yes, I have a junior title, but I still serve the council."

The man shrugged. "You still may not enter the grotto."

"Do you think the emissary might come out to speak with me?"

"The Eye does not—"

"Would you just ask?" Helix said in a hurry. "It is important I speak with her."

The guards looked at each other silently again. The one who spoke nodded, and the other guard disappeared behind the cascading leaves toward whatever mystery lay behind them.

Helix and Malia waited in uncomfortable silence under the watch of the remaining guard. When Helix was nearly ready to turn around and call the attempt a wash, he heard footsteps returning toward them.

A woman wrapped in vibrant mint green emerged from the low-hanging branches covering the entrance. A long scarf held her hair back from her face. Billowing sleeves covered most of her golden-brown skin.

"We are graced by the presence of the Eye," Helix said, bowing his head low.

When she spoke, her voice was rhythmic and deep. Her vowels were long and sing-songy, a holdover from her mother tongue. "I know your family well and felt you might make a fuss of this, so I came to address you myself."

Eman was preparing to turn them away.

Helix should not know her name. She was the Eye. The envoy for the Farseers, who spoke on their behalf when communication was required between the Estellar and the grotto. But Brissa had complained a little too loosely one evening when he was younger, and he remembered liking her name. Helix dug his nails into his palms to bring his mind back to the present. Since losing her, thinking of his grandmother turned his mind morose.

"The city has only just begun to recover from the Turning," Helix said. "Now sickness spreads. Clearly you have concerns about this." Helix gestured to the armed guards standing beside her. "Do you know what is causing our people to fall sick?"

She studied Malia and Helix in equal measure. "Who is this?"

"Malia." Helix placed a hand on Malia's shoulder. "A friend and my crewmate."

Eman's face remained a flat plane, but her eyes were bright and curious. "The council has not beseeched our input. Why is the young Stallastis here?"

"Because I'm worried about my people."

"Yes, you've said," she replied. "Why are you here on my

doorstep? A child. Instead of an Aquarius requesting my presence, as is custom, according to our agreement with the Estellar."

She was not giving way. Helix could sense the door closing on the conversation. He wasn't here with the support of the Estellar, and from the look in her eye, he suspected she knew as much.

"Please," Helix said. "There have been 40 cases of infection in the last week. There were 15 the week before. Whatever is happening, it's getting worse. The Farseers have always guided Novilem with wisdom in times of need. We need you."

"Do you know what wisdom is?" Eman asked.

"Yes?" Helix wasn't sure if she was asking for a definition or confirmation.

She smiled, but it was not out of amusement. "You do not. Because you cannot know. You come here seeking wisdom because somewhere in that young mind of yours, you have recognized that your people have lost theirs. That silly council of yours has abandoned their history."

Helix grew hot at the insult. Then, realizing a part of him agreed with her, shame flooded his chest. His ears burned red.

"Yes, you are aware."

"Hurt my pride all you want," Helix said. "I am here to help my people. The sickness is getting worse, and they deserve to know why. Can you help or not?"

"The people know nothing," Eman said without bothering to hide the sharpness in her tone. "We have precious little time. More fear among the city will be a problem."

So, she knew something. Her mouth was open to dismiss them.

"Things are changing," Helix said. "We are trying. The council has added two democratic seats."

"I am aware, and I disapprove. I will not give you what you seek. Information will only cause more suffering. What comes, comes." She shifted the length of her skirt away from her foot and turned. "I came here to deny you personally out of respect for your family." She took a few steps back toward the curtain of leaves and turned her head to the side. "Stars bless you in the coming days, Helix."

He watched the Eye until she disappeared into the cave, his chest caving in a bit more with each step. This was his last idea to get around the council's persistence at ignoring his concerns. He had been beside the council through his entire adolescence, and yet only at nineteen had they finally managed to make him feel like a child. The thought of returning to the Celestery only to be dismissed, to feel the growing distance between him and Theo...

No, he did not have it in him. As he and Malia made their way back to the train, Helix only wanted to see Casper. To crawl back into his bed and hide in his arms.

TWO

The streets of Novilem hummed with life. The Split was about to lower and people were busy with end of day tasks. Looking around, Casper couldn't shake Theo's warnings of lingering political unrest. Despite the council pretending the city had moved on from the Turning, the tension on the streets never fully dissipated.

He rounded the corner down a thin alley to take a shortcut he had become fond of. There were pockets of the city running in strips that broke away from the large street connecting the Estellar grounds to market row, and Casper had found delight in seeing the small spaces. His Greek was still abysmal, but hearing the conversations of families from open windows as he walked by made him feel part of the people.

The council awarded Casper a home. A fact he had not yet wrapped his head around. It was a proper estate with a small garden in the hillside villa neighboring where Helix's family lived. It was everything he needed. Two rooms, a living area, and a kitchen with aetherized gadgets he hadn't yet learned how to use. Like most of Novilem, it was built of the dark stone of the moon they resided in, and it was well-appointed with colorful rugs and light curtains on the windows.

It was a beautiful home, and he was working on believing it was his. Because to his dismay, having a home had not fully grounded him. Things that are given can be taken away. After all, a month ago he was shot down to the Surface and left to die. He knew better than to trust the Estellar had quelled decades of damage in a few short weeks.

The buildings lining the alleyway grew closer together until the walls were shoulder width apart. This was Casper's favorite part. He felt like he was finding a secret path. On his walks, he would often turn a corner he had never seen before to find what mysteries he could discover, but today he had no time to waste.

A semi-regular part of his week was going to the library to speak with the public. Theo had coached him on every-thing from talking points to posture. Sometimes Casper could tell the people gathered didn't speak enough English to follow along, but the council was more concerned with his showing face than anything. That standing-on-the-edge fear of saying the wrong thing sometimes squeezed his throat. Memories of the angry mob surrounding the dais of the amphitheater would crowd his mind instead of the faces filling the library. But so far, the events had all gone off smoothly.

He exited the alley to a meandering side street. He couldn't help but think about the hands of Taurus past that carved the stone underfoot with decorative lines. The build-ings were squat and covered in ornate facades. It was a charming neighborhood. The curves and worn edges of the buildings were cozy. Across the way was a cafe with its doors wide open and a semi-circle of small tables spilling out into the street. It called to Casper's soul. He wanted nothing more than to find any excuse not to show up at the library. It was only a matter of time before he said the wrong thing and excited another political storm. Theo wasn't nearly as harsh as Brissa, but he had no less exacting standards.

And Casper had so much more to lose.

He turned from the warm embrace of the cafe and followed the street toward what he thought was the main road, hoping the way ahead would lead him directly to the library. He neared the end of the road, confirming his sense of direction was correct. Then he had to reach out to the building beside him to steady himself. His vision went dark. He sunk to the ground as his body gave out. And with a tug, his consciousness was swept away.

It felt like he was dreaming. He floated over Ouranos, its swirling atmosphere occluding the world below. Then he was on the Surface. A three-legged creature with spiked feathers and a large beak lay on the ground. Its stomach looked as if it had burst open from the inside. The plants surrounding it were covered in dark berries. Its branches sagged low under the weight of the fruit. A few had split and were leaking black goo.

He turned away and an expanse of black stone stretched up in front of him. The missing tower. He blinked, and then he was inside. The world was upside down. His neck ached with strain. He was cold and hungry.

Someone was speaking in Greek. The words were quick and angry. The click of footsteps tapped against the stone underneath his back. He was scared. Time was running out.

His arms were chained, stretching them away from his body. He tried to pull in aether, but it still hurt. It always hurt.

The Greek ranting stopped as the footsteps neared. The world turned upright, and he could see he was in a small, circular room. He was nauseous. A shiver rippled through his body.

He was lifted from the floor. Shadows crept up the walls. He saw stringy gray hair first.

"No, please." The voice wasn't his, but it came from him.

Jacob turned to him, looking him dead in the eye. He smiled and his eyes lit up with that sickly yellow glow that haunted his dreams.

"Hello, you," Jacob said.

Casper rose with a jolt. The surrounding alley was spinning as he slowly came back to consciousness. He was cold and clammy.

A man who was too close exclaimed, "You are ok!"

The edges of a figure came into focus. He was leaning over Casper and helping him to a seated position.

Who did Jacob have imprisoned? They were so afraid. So defeated. Whoever it was, they had been captured long enough they couldn't track how long it had been. And then there was the plant he had seen outside the tower. The corruption on the Surface was getting worse.

"Are you ill?" the man asked.

Casper's vision was clearing up and he recognized the man's acolyte robes. Great, just what he needed. An acolyte reporting this straight to the council.

"I'm fine," Casper said. "I must have forgotten to eat lunch. Got a little lightheaded."

The man grabbed Casper by the arm and helped him to his feet. Casper turned, locating the way back home. Theo wouldn't be happy, but he was in no condition for pageantry.

"Thank you for checking on me," Casper said. He started off at a brisk walk before the acolyte could interject. He was too shaken by the experience he just had to deal with council nonsense.

The worst-case scenario had been confirmed. Jacob was hiding out in the tower. And he had recognized Casper in whoever's body he was holding hostage. Something was wrong. Very wrong.

CHAPTER
THREE

The next morning, Helix woke feeling content. Pretzeled in Casper's arms with the first rays of morning light slipping over their bodies, he smiled. Not because he was supposed to. Not because it was what a good grandson would do. He smiled because something deep in his core called for it.

He traced gentle circles on Casper's uncovered shoulder. Soft locks of Casper's dark hair tickled his chest. A lingering scent of gelandra shampoo, sweet and spicy, filled his nose.

Habit bit at the back of his mind, telling him to get going. But he quickly quieted the thought. There were no drills to run. The council offered to dismiss his service to the Academy in honor of his and Casper's efforts to save Novilem, but Helix refused. He wasn't ready to move on, and he couldn't abandon his crew. But the council placed them on a hiatus from running missions anyway, as a forced recovery period. So, even though his body woke like he had responsibilities to attend to, he allowed himself to relax in the bliss of a quiet morning.

He savored the scent of Casper, kissing his forehead. He traced the planes of his face, cherishing the calm there before the worrying began. It seemed like Casper could always find something to worry about.

Casper stirred, rolling off Helix with a yawn.

"Morning, starlight," Helix said.

Never a morning person, Casper grunted.

"I'll make breakfast."

Helix rose from bed, dressed, and walked down the hall to the kitchen of Casper's home. The council provided Casper with a house in the western villa. It was a grand gesture, but Helix suspected it was an effort to keep him close. The Enotis had been awarded their two seats on the council, and indeed the people had been given a voice, but the council's grip on Novilem wasn't shaken overnight.

The Enotis had made a project of cleaning up the slums. The Gemini were welcomed back into their family homes. A quiet had settled on the city, almost like it was actively healing. Helix would have been tempted to believe that it was, if not for the corruption sickness that began to spread in the Turning's wake.

He was working at the kitchen island when Casper shuffled in from the hallway and offered him a lazy smile. He sat in the eating area. A large glass door let in the morning light from the garden on the eastern side of the house, lighting Casper's face. Helix brought a plate of sliced fruits and toasted bread to the table.

"Tea?" Helix asked.

"Yes, please."

When Helix joined him at the table with two warm mugs, Casper spoke around a mouthful of bread.

"I could get used to you making me breakfast."

"I'd say you already are."

Casper winked at him as he popped a strawberry into his mouth. Helix still officially lived in his family home in the neighboring villa, but a couple nights a week had turned into more nights than not of Helix staying over at Casper's place.

"You could just move in," Casper said playfully.

"No, I can't, and can we please not have this conversation again?"

"I know everything with us has moved fast. But you're here all the time, anyway."

"I'll tell you what, you manage to wake up before me and make me breakfast and we can talk about this again."

Casper playfully narrowed his eyes. "You don't play a fair game."

"Well, you sleep like you're dead." Helix laughed.

"We both know why I sleep so hard."

Heat spread across Helix's chest. Memories of them sinking into soft sheets flooded his mind. He shook his head. "I want to actually leave the house today."

Casper smiled mischievously. "Alright." He took another piece of fruit on his way to the hall. Halfway there, he turned over his shoulder to look at Helix and slid his tunic over his head.

"Later," Helix said.

"Of course," Casper called from down the hall. "I'm just changing."

An hour later, they were still lying naked on the bed. Casper seemed particularly reluctant to get up. Helix rose onto his elbow. Casper's eyes were only half open. These were Helix's favorite moments. When Casper's mind was quiet enough for him to relax. His smile appeared more easily, and those adorable wrinkles next to his eyes showed up.

Then the world seemed to come down on him and his face fell flat. He shut his eyes and his grip on Helix tightened.

"What's on your mind?" Helix asked.

Casper sighed. "Theo's going to be upset with me."

"What did you do this time?"

Annoyed, Casper nudged his arm. "That's not funny."

"I'm sorry." Helix caressed his back and pulled his body a little closer. "Talk to me."

"I skipped an appearance at the library last night."

Helix waited a moment, but that seemed to be the end of it. "Correct me if I'm wrong, but disobeying the wishes of an elder preitan is not something you usually fret over."

Casper laughed through his nose. "You're not wrong."

Helix craned his neck to get a look at Casper's face. "What is it?"

Casper's mouth twisted to the side. "Something happened to me on the way there."

"Something like?"

"I think I had a vision? It was like a dream, but not really. Or maybe it was not *my* dream. I wasn't in control. It was almost like using Aquarius aether."

Helix pushed himself against the headboard, sitting up slightly. "A vision of what?"

Casper slid to his side, his eyes drifting to the corner of the room. Then he described a vision of being chained up and tortured by Jacob on the Surface.

"Then I was back here, lying on the street in Novilem." He covered his face with his hands. "Fuck. With an acolyte waking me up. The council's going to know I fainted in the street."

"Do you think it could have been an episode?" Casper

experienced flashbacks sometimes of the abuse his father put him through.

Casper shook his head. "No, it was real. Or like, not the same as that, at least. I don't think it was actually me chained up in that room."

"But it was your body?"

"I don't think so. The voice wasn't mine."

"How is that possible? It would require an immense amount of Gemini aether to connect to someone on the Surface from here."

Casper shrugged. "I don't know, but unfortunately, I was right. Jacob's up to something."

"The Aquarius haven't been able to see inside the tower, but we can't know what we don't know. Right?"

"What a comforting thought."

Helix grabbed Casper's hand and laced their fingers together. The distraction of their morning in bed was gone, and the tense focus of his eyes meant he was slipping back into what was becoming a constant state of worry.

"Not every problem is yours to fix," Helix said.

Casper gave his fingers a squeeze. "This one is."

Helix braced himself, knowing he was opening up an old argument. "We need to take this to the council."

To Casper's credit, he didn't roll his eyes, but he did pull away. Helix felt the absence of his touch as an ache.

"The council has made it clear what is expected of me," Casper said. "Do my song and dance at the library or wherever they point me. You know how Theo has been."

Theo, who consoled Helix and Casper both when Brissa was so harsh on them, had been alarmingly more and more controlling since the political landscape had stabilized.

"What does not telling them accomplish? Jacob will still be out there doing Jacob things."

Casper covered his face with his hands and sighed loudly. Through his fingers he said, "I keep waiting for life to become normal again. But it's never going to be normal, is it?"

Helix rolled a little closer and wrapped his arms around him. "Probably not. No."

Casper melted into his embrace. "We have to tell them, huh?"

"We don't have to do anything. But I think we should."

"Fine. But *when* Preitan Horace calls me a busybody, you owe me."

"Yeah? What will I owe you?"

"I haven't decided yet."

Helix smiled, knowing he'd give Casper anything.

The white marbled surface of the Celestery shone particularly bright in the late morning sun as they approached. Casper eyed the building with hesitation. He didn't like talking to the council. It was clear they viewed him as erratic and uncontrollable. He'd done nothing except parrot their stories to the public since the Turning, and still, they treated him like a ticking time bomb. It's not like he asked to be the Telos. He was doing his best to be a comforting presence for the Novilites that came to see him, but every time he stood in front of the council and felt the pressure of their collective gaze, it reminded him that he was an eighteen-year-old boy.

But Helix was convinced that between the Eye's cryptic warning and Jacob being Jacob, the Estellar would have to take action. So, Casper followed him inside with a tightness in his chest.

"And what would you have us do with this information?" The Aries preitan was the first to offer comment after a long silence following Helix's report about the vision and the Eye's warning. A contingency of Casper's. His idea, his problem. Helix had to do the talking.

"I didn't come with a course of action in mind," Helix said.

"That much is clear," the Leo preitan said.

Casper watched the muscle in Helix's jaw tense as he clenched his teeth. From his vantage point, he could see Helix's own concerns with the council a little too clearly. They weren't taking him seriously. Casper surveyed the stern faces looking down at them. Cold, indifferent—superior. Helix looked to Theo, who should have been his guaranteed ally in the room.

"Thank you for sharing your concerns," Theo said. His eyes shifted to the door. An instruction to leave more than a dismissal.

The back of Helix's neck broke out in a sweat.

"Are you ok?" Casper asked.

Helix was determined to make them listen, but they weren't giving him a chance, and Helix was shaken. Casper had never seen him so thrown. He sighed to himself. It wouldn't be as fun breaking his own rules, but he couldn't stomach doing nothing while the council completely dismissed Helix.

"There are more people sick every day," Helix continued, a note of desperation in his voice Casper was sure only he could hear. "It can't be coincidence. Why aren't our astrolabes blocking corrupted aether? Our friend's mother has been ill since the Turning. The Virgos haven't been able to help her at all."

Theo remained unmoved. "We've seen corruption sickness before. This isn't new."

Casper stepped forward. "Even so, Jacob literally turned the city on its side. How can you pretend he isn't a threat?"

"I think you've grown a taste for being a hero," Theo said. "And I'm starting to worry you're letting your title get to your head."

Casper grimaced. "This isn't about my pride."

"It very much is. I don't think the two of you have had enough rest to recover from the Turning. Maybe some time away would help you gain perspective."

"Preitan—"

Theo raised his hand, silencing Helix's rebuttal. "If you think aether is causing so much trouble, with the sickness and your... vision, then you can take a break from it. We'll assign a crew of acolytes to escort you to Earth. Try to think of it as a restful vacation. Maybe pick someplace tropical. I've read they really enjoy beaches on Earth."

Helix stepped toward the table. "Preitan Theo—"

"That is an order," Theo said. "You will now leave the council to attend to our actual business of the day."

Casper was going to reply, but Helix grabbed his hand and pulled him toward the exit. His face was flushed, his eyes tracking the floor.

"Fighting more won't help," he murmured. "They're done with us."

Casper returned to his home with Helix, where they both stewed in their frustration until frustration morphed into anxiety, at least on Casper's part. Helix's frustration morphed into a baffling acceptance that only frustrated Casper more. "Our first chance of finding out what Jacob is doing, and they act like I'm just getting a big head. I *wish* someone else could do something about Jacob. What happens when I leave? What if he comes back while we're gone?"

Helix opened his hands in a hear-me-out gesture. "What if a vacation could be fun?"

"You do realize that jumping across the universe is dangerous, right?"

"We've never missed," Helix said. "It's a point of pride for Novilem."

"Jacob is torturing someone on the Surface. I'm literally the only person who can get any information about what is going on inside the tower. I don't want to take a fucking vacation."

"What if Theo has a point?"

He glared at Helix.

"Look, it has been a lot," Helix said. "I know I feel it. Even without running missions recently, I feel worn out. Yes, things are still not fixed here. But they will never be fully fixed. There's always going to be a problem."

"So, we should just fuck off and let shit hit the fan?"

"No. The acolytes will protect the city. Like they're supposed to."

Casper was pacing. "Jacob still has that machine he used to suck the aether out of me. And we have no idea how it works. He doesn't use aether like anyone else. You saw how powerful he is."

"He was powerful because he stole your aether."

Casper stopped in his tracks. "Oh my god. He has Agnes."

"What?"

"Jacob has Agnes. That's who was in my vision."

"Did you remember something else? Did you see her?"

"No, you're right. He was powerful because he stole my aether. So, if he doesn't have me, of course he would go after the other telos."

Helix's mouth twisted to the side.

Agnes had not returned to Novilem. The Estellar claimed she died on the Surface. What if their story was fabricated to cover up her absence? They wouldn't bat an eye at not having to accept another telos into the city. Why hadn't he tried to contact her?

"I know that look in your eye."

"We have to do something."

"Cas... I hate the idea that Jacob might have Agnes, too. And you are going to hate hearing this, but there's nothing we can do about it right now. We leave for Earth tomorrow."

He was very correct. Casper did hate hearing that. Even if it was largely true. The council had issued an order. They were going to Earth. But they weren't strangers to not following the council's orders.

"Why are you falling in line with them?"

"I'm not falling in line. I'm accepting reality. And maybe there was some truth to what Theo said."

Casper winced. "Ouch." He had never wanted to be a hero. Hearing Theo speak of him so nonchalantly had hurt.

"Not about your character. About the rest." Helix cupped his face, fingers sliding along the hair behind Casper's ear. "You haven't stopped since you came to Novilem."

"Since I was *kidnapped*. You like to forget that I was stolen away from an alley after being nearly mauled by demonic coyotes."

Coyotes and giant walls of black smoke that were both a result of corrupted aether. On Earth.

"I thought we'd established that no kidnapping meant no us, and therefore the kidnapping was the least of the bads."

"It was a capital T trauma, regardless."

Helix pulled him into a hug, and Casper could feel that he wasn't winning this fight. Helix wasn't on board with defying the council. But if they were going to give in to the council and take a vacation, it didn't have to be in vain. There was corrupted aether on Earth. Maybe not having the council breathing down their neck while they tried to figure out what was going on with the corrupted aether would be a boon.

Helix kissed his forehead. "When we get back, I will go to the Surface to look for her myself if I have to."

"Fine. Yeah. We'll be good little boys and take our time out."

"Oh." Helix narrowed his eyes.

"What?"

"I didn't think that would work."

Casper smiled at him coyly. "You know I'm a sucker for forehead kisses."

Helix rolled his eyes. "I'm not going to question it because then you'll change your mind. So, Chicago?"

"We can go anywhere. Why do you want to go back to Chicago?" Casper asked.

"What's the name of that holiday Americans celebrate for the winter solstice?" He rubbed small circles on Casper's back.

"Christmas," Casper said.

Helix pulled away. His eyes grew with excitement. "Yes! We should go to Chicago for Christmas."

Casper frowned. "Why would we do that?"

"Because it would be fun."

"Christmas is about family," Casper said. "And spending a lot of money on presents. We can't exactly show up at my parent's house and expect a warm welcome."

"I've read about the jolly man and the flying creatures," Helix said. "It's not just about family."

"What has gotten into you?" Casper laughed.

Helix grabbed his hand. "I think you deserve to have a little fun." Casper winced, so Helix amended, saying, "We deserve to have fun then."

"Helix, I can see you're trying to distract me. I appreciate that. I really do. But it's just a holiday. We can celebrate whatever winter solstice Novilem has. We can pick somewhere else. Somewhere warm."

Novilem's orbital path around Ouranos was nearly 100 days off Earth's yearly cycle. But just like honoring the zodiac of their Earth ancestors, keeping the traditions of their holidays was important. And being inside a moon meant the reality of their celestial existence was kind of irrelevant. The sky was not available to them, so the people of Novilem held onto their memories through tradition.

"We will celebrate Novilem's winter solstice. There will be a festival. But that will happen after we celebrate Christmas."

Casper groaned. "Why are you like this?"

"Because I love you," Helix said. "And I want to know you. Even the parts you're scared of."

"I'm not scared of myself."

"Great!" Helix patted Casper's chest before sitting on the edge of the bed. "We'll go then?"

Revisiting the doubt that lingered in the back of his mind Casper said, "What happens if we don't?"

"You mean if we defy a direct order from the council?"

"They can't exile us. What's the worst they can do?"

Helix held out his fingers as he counted off punishments. "Demote your housing assignment. Revoke your restaurant privileges. Give you a curfew. I actually recall an instance where a guy wasn't allowed to leave his home for weeks because a nasty bug knocked out the Court of Gemini for a couple days."

"Ok, I get it. They can make life suck."

"They *will* make life suck. We have to go, Cas."

Casper thought for a moment then nodded. "Fine. We go to Earth. We'll even go to Chicago." He held up a finger when Helix smiled. "But while we're there, we will investigate the corrupted aether. Maybe we can learn something useful."

"There's not much aether on Earth to begin with."

"I was attacked by those corrupted coyotes. So, there's enough. If things are getting worse here, maybe they're getting worse on Earth, too."

"If it will get you to agree to the jump, then sure. But we're still going to Christmas."

Casper rolled his eyes.

"Non-negotiable."

"Fine." Casper was annoyed but added playfully, "We can Christmas."

The cold was immediate, all-consuming, and painful. It started in his toes. The bones ached like they were being squeezed at every joint. Within seconds, his eyelashes and nose hairs were frozen.

"Dust me," Helix said with a clattering jaw.

"I told you it was going to be cold," Casper said.

"Yes, well, when I agreed to your plan, I don't think I knew what cold actually was."

Helix danced in place. The many layers of cloth wrapped around his feet padded each step, but they did almost nothing to combat the crisp bite of the Chicago winter. It was late in the evening on Earth and the shroud of dark sky seemed to amplify the cold.

"This happens every year?" Helix said. "And you complained about Ouranos?"

Casper exited the alley they jumped into and checked the street before crossing.

"Show me a bloodsucking snake made of rocks, and we can discuss the relative horrors of our planets," Casper said. "A thick coat and a pair of boots deals with the cold."

"Earth has many terrors," Helix said. "Volcanoes, tsunamis, earthquakes, there are almost 30 different species of spiders that are deadly to humans."

Casper whipped around. "Spiders are off-limits. We don't talk about spiders."

Helix laughed.

Casper did not. He turned around and crossed the street, hugging his middle and tucking his hands into his armpits.

"Wait, seriously?"

"Seriously!"

"You have fought off keiona with your bare hands, but you're scared of spiders? Aren't they really small?"

"Shut up, Helix." Casper didn't face him. He focused on the roofline of the house they were approaching.

"Fine, I won't talk about spiders."

"Thank you."

A metal fence surrounded the house. Black paint flaked off in random places. A soft light was glowing from a window on the far side of the house. The gate screeched when Casper pushed it open.

"Shit."

Casper's curse seemed to echo in the thin winter air. He moved forward and slipped into the front yard. Helix followed him, his steps more like hops as he tried to reduce how much contact his feet made with the frozen concrete.

Helix remembered the home from their last visit to Earth. It felt even more foreboding, lit only by a florescent streetlamp and shrouded in the bitter winter air. For all Helix knew, it could be the source of this cold, the hatred in that building sucking the life out of the city surrounding it.

"Maybe this isn't a good idea," Helix said.

"It's a little late to back out." Casper was already scaling the side of the house. He crested the roof and rolled his body onto the dark shingles.

"What if we get caught?" Helix asked.

Casper didn't answer.

"Can you handle seeing them?"

"Helix." Casper's head popped out, hanging over the roof. A small halo of light glowed around his face from the light shining through the alleyway behind the house. "Parents and spiders. No-go zones. Now come up here before you're too stiff to manage the climb."

When Helix made it onto the roof, Casper had a window pried open. He slipped a leg inside and writhed in through the opening. Helix placed one of his numb feet in the window and nearly fell as he tried to roll inside like Casper had. Casper's arms wrapped around him, catching him before he could fall.

"Careful," Casper whispered.

The warmth of the house was glorious, aside from a gust of chilly air seeping into Helix's back. He turned around and pulled the window closed. It fell shut quickly with a loud snap.

Casper grunted through clenched teeth; his hands closed

in fists. They both stayed as still as possible, listening for a response in the house. After a few moments passed with no stirring, Casper let out a heavy sigh.

"It gets stuck when it's cold," he said.

Helix nodded, but he was distracted by the room surrounding them. The wall in front of him had shelves filled with shiny figurines standing on top of podiums.

"What are these?" he asked as he picked one up.

"Trophies…" Casper's eyes fell to the floor.

"Like memorabilia for winning a competition?"

"They're soccer trophies," Casper said.

"There are so many."

"There aren't that many."

"You won all of these?"

"My teams did," Casper said. "I played soccer for twelve years. It adds up."

"This is incredible!"

Casper was blushing. "It really isn't. It's embarrassing. I can't believe my parents still have them." He took the trophy from Helix's hands and placed it back on the shelf.

There were posters on the wall with colorful illustrations of creatures Helix had never seen before. "And what are these? Our texts don't speak of animals on Earth that look like this."

"Those aren't animals." Casper's cheeks were solidly red. He turned to a small closet in the corner of the room. "They're called Pokémon."

"What is a Pokémon?" Helix asked.

"It doesn't matter."

"Casper." Helix pulled him away from digging through the hanging clothes. "This is probably my only chance to see your childhood room. Indulge me a little?"

"You promised me I couldn't die of embarrassment, right?" Casper thumbed the back of Helix's hand.

"You haven't yet, which I think is a testament to how true that is."

"Uggggh." Casper's shoulder sagged as he let the word slide out on a long breath. "Fine."

"What's your favorite thing?" Helix asked, turning back to the room.

Casper stepped toward a wooden dresser. He opened the top drawer and dug around, pulling out an oval-shaped piece of metal. He handed it to Helix. There was a large animal imprinted on the front of it. Helix wracked his memory, trying to recall the name.

"A bear?" he asked.

"Yep," Casper replied. "It's a smashed penny. There are these machines at theme parks that will flatten out a penny and imprint it with something as a way to remember your visit to that place. I made that one when I was eight. My dad took me to the zoo on the first day of summer break. It was just the two of us. He was really happy that day. So was I."

"Cas—"

"No parents. No spiders."

"That's not fair. You brought it up."

"And now I'm closing the discussion." He turned around and stepped back toward the closet. "We need to grab winter clothes and get out of here before someone wakes up."

"A bit late for that."

"Fuck," Casper said.

There was a young woman standing in the doorway. She had Casper's warm brown hair, but her eyes were light blue. She also had Casper's nose, and the corner of her eyes half closed the same way his did when he smiled. Or cried. A tear slid down her face. She swiped it away with the back of her long-sleeved shirt.

"Who is this?" she asked.

"I'm grabbing some warm clothes and then I'm leaving," Casper said.

She stepped into the room like she was going to approach him but stopped when Casper flinched.

"I thought you died," she said almost too quietly for Helix to hear.

Casper tossed a massive coat at Helix. It crinkled as he grabbed hold of it, the material deflating under his fingertips like it was stuffed with clouds.

"You can keep thinking I did if it makes it easier for you."

"Jesus Christ, Casper. It's been almost six months."

"And now you're taking the lord's name in vain?" Casper said. "Things have changed."

More tears were rolling down her face.

"I'm Helix." He wasn't sure why he introduced himself, and when she glared at him with obvious disdain, he regretted the decision.

"Where have you been?" she asked.

"I don't owe you anything," Casper said. He slipped his arms into a thick coat and slung a pair of boots at Helix. "We're leaving."

"Casper, wait," she said.

"Jess, I'm not interested in having a conversation with you." Casper stomped his feet into his own pair of boots. "You told me to run away. I ran away. Conversation over. Have a nice life."

"Mom is going to leave Dad."

"Good for her," Casper said.

"Cas," Helix said.

Casper shook his head at Helix, so he backed off and worked on getting his overly wrapped feet into the boots.

"I'm sorry," Jess said. "I'm—"

"Cool," Casper said. "Thanks for the apology. Are we done?"

She stood frozen in place. The only part of her moving were the tears falling freely down her cheeks. She turned and left the room, closing the door behind her.

"It sounded like she was really sorry, Cas."

"I'm not interested in her feelings."

Casper helped Helix get into the puffy jacket and buttoned the front.

"Let's go," Casper said.

They climbed out of the window, and when Helix was fully out, Casper intentionally let it slam shut.

The cold air grabbed at Helix's exposed skin, but Casper was right. The coat and the boots did help keep the ache of it away. Helix wondered what it would take to do the same for the pain Casper carried in his shoulders as he climbed down the side of the house.

FOUR

They spent the night in a comfortable hotel on Lakeshore Drive near the Gold Coast. Casper was surprised to find out that Helix had US currency with him. Apparently, the Estellar had a vault of funds for their trips to Earth. If he had known that he would have just bought them some winter gear in the light of day instead of breaking into his family's house. He would have done anything to avoid seeing the look on Jess's face when she saw him. How dare she act like he had hurt her?

When he woke up, Helix was already dressed.

"Were you watching me sleep?" Casper asked.

"I'm excited!"

Casper rolled onto his stomach and covered his head with a pillow. He responded with a grunt.

"I have coffee and a donut for you," Helix said.

Casper poked his head out from under the pillow. Helix was holding a paper cup out to him.

"You are the nicest person who has ever lived." Casper

sat up and accepted the coffee. It was hot and deliciously sweet. "Oh my god. I miss coffee."

"Drink up. I want to Christmas," Helix said.

Casper laughed. "Ok, let's Christmas then. But we're making a stop first."

After grabbing a prepaid smart phone, they started with Casper's favorite Chicago Christmas tradition, the Christkindlmarket. The outdoor market was themed to look like a small village in the mountains of a European town. Entering the Daily Center square felt almost like entering another world. That probably had as much to do with the crowd of bodies one had to squeeze through as the decor and holiday spirit.

Grasping Helix's gloved hand, Casper squeezed through an imparting sea of people and finagled their way to some of the craft booths. They would have to fight their way to the snacks later.

"Dust me," Helix said. "Is that Santa!?"

Casper looked around for someone in costume, but Helix skipped to a booth with an array of wood carvings. There was everything from log cabins to dragons, but Helix picked up a small figurine of Santa Claus. One hand was placed over his belly and his face was alight with laughter.

"He is just as jolly as I'd hoped."

Helix's face mirrored the joy on the small figurine. A wide grin, his eyebrows lifted high, the sparkle of Christmas magic in his eyes. There had been a handful of moments like this over the last couple of weeks that swept Casper away. Watching Helix get enraptured by something. The awe of him made the world disappear. Helix could be so intentionally present that Casper sometimes was intimidated because he didn't know how to show up the same way. But when a moment caught him by surprise and Casper could watch that spark of joy exist so innocently and honestly inside of him, Casper fell even more in love.

"Do you want it?" Casper asked.

Helix's eyes fell to the ground bashfully. "It's not for children, is it?"

"Santa is for everyone," Casper said. "If it makes you happy, it doesn't matter."

"Ok." Helix smiled.

Casper noticed the booth also offered custom ornaments. He was handling the money since he was the one familiar with Earth, so he leaned in to pay for the figurine and ordered an ornament. Luckily, Helix turned away, so he could keep it a surprise. Casper would circle back to the booth later to pick the ornament up.

"They make all of this without aether?" Helix asked.

It was slow going walking down the lanes of the market because they constantly had to navigate around groups of people, but Helix was not deterred from seeing what every booth had to offer.

Casper chuckled. "No magic. I assume some of this stuff is machine manufactured. But some things look hand crafted."

Seeing how earnest Helix was, Casper pushed aside the pesky part of him that wanted to rush through the market so they could start investigating. Right now, Helix was having fun.

They meandered around the market until Casper's frustration with the crowd overwhelmed him and he pulled Helix over to the section with food. The Christkindlmarket had a lot of German snacks like schnitzel and potato pancakes, but Casper had his eye on the prize.

"Strudel is the best," Casper said. "The cherry is my favorite."

"How many favorite foods do you have?" Helix said.

"I've never counted."

Helix smiled. "But there should only be one. That's the point of a favorite."

"I won't be limited by semantics. If it's a favorite, it's a favorite."

Someone walked by with a steaming mug in the shape of a small boot.

"What is that?" Helix asked. "It's so cute!"

"They have hot chocolate and mulled wine. You get to keep the mug as a souvenir."

"Let's do that."

Casper shook his head. "We can't have wine because we're underaged and I don't like the hot chocolate. If we're going to do hot chocolate, it should be the best."

"A favorite." Helix was grinning.

"Always."

At the strudel booth, Casper ordered cherry for himself and apple for Helix. When they came out, steam rose from the pastries into the chilly air. Casper's first bite was euphoric. He hadn't had a sweet pastry treat in months. Flaky with tangy cherry filling, it was absolutely a favorite. Helix was chewing a bite of his pastry quietly. The deep line between his brows that meant he was thinking hard was present.

"What do you think?"

"It is hot fruit in bread," Helix said.

Casper laughed. "I guess it is. But it's delicious, right?"

Helix's mouth twisted to the side. He took another bite and after a moment said, "It is quite sweet."

"Do you want to try mine?"

Helix accepted Casper's strudel and took a bite. His eyes lit up with the same sparkle he had when he found Santa.

"Yes!" He held the cherry strudel in the air. "This is delicious."

Casper took the apple strudel from Helix's other hand. "You can have that one."

"No. Casper, it's your favorite."

"And now it can be yours, too. I'll have the apple."

Casper took a bite and savored the tart apple filling. "See, this one's mine now. You can't have it back."

There was a slight redness in Helix' cheeks from the cold, but it spread just enough that Casper knew he was blushing.

"Thank you," he said.

"Come on, I want to find something."

Casper swung back to the ornament booth and forced Helix to promise he wouldn't look as he gathered the piece he requested. Then they shuffled through the crowd to the other side of the market where the indoor huts of glass Christmas ornaments were.

"Here!" Casper said, pulling Helix to a booth outside the area.

"What are these?" Helix asked.

The booth had an array of Christmas decor, but what Casper was seeking was right in front of him. A miniature Christmas tree made of wood and plastic. He picked it up and showed it to Helix.

"What is it for?"

"We decorate these trees as a tradition. People who celebrate Christmas put them up around holiday time. They're usually a lot bigger than this, like at least six or seven feet tall. And then we hang ornaments that we collect on them."

"We should get one and decorate it," Helix said.

"Funny you should say that."

Casper paid for the miniature tree and handed it to Helix. Then, out of the bag of goodies he was carrying around, he grabbed the ornament he ordered. He handed it to Helix and studied his face to capture his reaction. The sparkle returned to his eyes and Casper felt warm and tingly, despite the cold that was starting to bite through his warm winter gear from being outside for so long.

"Casper, it's beautiful."

The ornament was a five-pointed wooden star. Its surface was decorated with a minimalist winter scene of snowflakes and trees. In the center were large swooping letters reading C & H.

"I love it," Helix said.

Before Casper could respond, he heard someone call out to him. He froze in place, his neck heating under a wave of anxiety.

"Oh my god, Casper?"

He turned around to find himself face to face with his ex-girlfriend, Danielle. She crushed into him, squeezing him in a tight hug. Slowly, his arms fell around her. His heart was hammering in his chest. Sweat broke out on his brow and under his arms.

"What on Earth are you doing here?" she asked.

Helix chuckled over Casper's shoulder. Danielle's wide eyes bounced between the two of them.

"Helix, this is Danielle." Casper kept his eyes locked on the ground, unable to take in how either of them were reacting. "Danielle, you might remember Helix... my boyfriend."

Danielle was moving as soon as Casper finished talking.

She wrapped Helix in a hug, saying, "It's so nice to re-meet you!"

Which was nice. Or alarming. Casper couldn't make out which. She was so hurt when he was outed.

Helix was unfazed, returning her hug. "I've heard so much about you."

Danielle did something between a chuckle and a sigh. Then she turned her focus back to Casper. "We have been so worried about you. Like… seriously. Started to believe we might actually find your body in a ditch kind of worried."

"Sorry. I needed to get away."

"And now you're back?"

"Not really, no. Just visiting." He grabbed Helix's hand. "Showing Helix where I'm from."

"We are Christmasing," Helix said gleefully.

"Well, that sounds fun."

It felt good to see Danielle smiling. To remember how easy being around her was. It washed away a bit of the pain Casper remembered from their separation.

"Could I join you? I can't say I have ever Christmased."

Casper's stomach dropped. After appeasing Helix's wishes, he was hoping to shift over to investigating an area with a few recent reports of strange events with wildlife. Making up stories about the last six months wasn't going to get him anywhere on finding out if the corrupted aether was still on Earth.

But Helix and Danielle were both looking at him with excited eyes. What a wildly odd duo.

"Of course, yeah," Casper said.

Nothing bad can happen from my ex-girlfriend hanging out with me and my alien boyfriend. It's fine. This is so normal.

∼

While waiting for the train, Casper did a quick search on the prepaid phone for something they could do. He couldn't stomach ditching Danielle, but he needed her to not stick around too long. A bar on Halstead was hosting a drag brunch, which was perfect. She may have been more open to Casper having a boyfriend than expected, but Boystown would surely put her off. It was only a block away from a reported coyote attack a couple of weeks ago. So, maybe after brunch, he could initiate their goodbyes and still do a little investigating.

A coyote attack didn't mean they were demonic dark aether coyotes like the ones that attacked him, but it was the most recent odd event he had found. When Casper suggested the drag brunch, Danielle surprised him again with her enthusiasm. Helix was clueless but agreed anyway.

A CTA ride up to Boystown later, Casper was in his first ever gay bar. His boyfriend sitting on one side of him, and his ex-girlfriend sitting on the other. So normal. Everything was fine.

"Ladies, gentlemen, and those of us in-between, I am your host, Capri Corn."

The crowd exploded with applause. Capri Corn was decked out in a canary yellow sequined dress and her hair was easily three feet tall. Stars were painted along the arc of her brows.

"Like a Capricorn," Casper said, leaning over. Helix's eyes were glued on the stage, and he was cheering with the crowd.

"Yes!" Capri Corn called back. "I'm a Midwest girl who knows how to shuck. Listen folks, tonight we have a special first appearance of Chicago's very own superhero drag queen. Let your nerdy little hearts run free because she's giving nostalgia and comedy to help you laugh the pain away. Please welcome to the stage, Blue Jean Gray Dragon!"

Casper joined the audience in cheering as a vision in blue showboated onto the stage. Tall, and in six-inch midnight blue heels, she had to duck to stop her silver-blue hair from catching on the stage lights. She wore a metallic blue jumpsuit that sparkled under the spotlight. The collar of her top stood straight up, framing her face. Her lips and eyes were painted in the same shimmery blue as her outfit.

When the cheers quieted down, she pivoted, turning her back to the crowd, revealing decorative blue jean pockets on her backside. Casper laughed with the crowd. When he looked over at Helix, his mouth was agape, and his eyes were wide.

"She is so shiny," Helix said.

"Hello and welcome! I am indeed Blue Jean Gray Dragon." Her voice was lively and warm. "For those of you who had an ounce of self-respect and social lives as children, that's an X-Men reference wrapped in a Yu-Gi-Oh reference, and no, I will not elaborate further."

She presented a long leg, sliding her hand along the shimmering fabric of her pants and then smacked her blue jean pocket. "All that matters is that I'm blue and fabulous."

Laughter rolled through the bar.

"The first thing you need to know about me is that I'm married, but for the right price, I'm also very single. And that's called what? Capitalism."

She walked to the end of the stage, eyeing the crowd, and very obviously paused on Helix.

"Speaking of being negotiably married, who is this smoke show?"

Blue Jean pointed at Helix and a spotlight from the stage twisted to illuminate him. The bar broke out into cheers.

"That's what I'm saying." Blue Jean fanned herself with her hand before covering her eyes to get a better look. "Superman, Scarlet Witch, and Space Ghost Coast to Coast, you are beautiful."

Then Blue Jean noticed Casper and Helix were holding hands.

"Wait, are you in love?" Her voice jumped up an octave. "Aww. They're so young and beautiful. I live for this gen-z finding young love like the straights do situation. But if you ever want to discover that life has more to offer…" She mouthed the words *call me*. "I'm kidding." She winked at Helix. "Unless? No. Ok! Ok! Calm down, everyone. They're very in love."

She turned back to observe the crowd. "I mean this with full offense. Why are all of you so young? None of you are going to understand my references."

The crowd laughed easily.

"Why don't we start things off with a volunteer?" Her voice lilted up, trying to elicit excitement.

Casper shrunk back into his seat, going as far as moving into his Libra trine and trying to find some aether. He wasn't above pocket stepping out of the bar to avoid being in the spotlight.

"Come on up, darling." Blue Jean pointed into the audience on the other side of the bar. "What's your name?"

The spotlight was on the opposite side of the room. Casper sighed in relief and relaxed in his chair.

"You ok?" Helix asked, placing a hand on Casper's knee.

"We can go if it's too much," Danielle said.

"All good. Just didn't want to go on stage." He squeezed Helix's hand and interlaced their fingers. Then the volunteer spoke, and Casper's heart skipped a beat before kicking into double time.

"Conner."

Casper's eyes shot to the stage and there he was. In a rainbow tank top so loose his nipples were visible, his former soccer teammate was standing center stage. His former teammate from their very Christian private school. Where Conner had assaulted and outed Casper, getting him expelled and kicked out of his home.

Helix's grip on his hand tightened. "Ok, you're definitely upset. What's going on?"

Casper was sweating. The edges of his vision lightened. He couldn't get enough air into his lungs.

"Let's go," Danielle said.

She stood up. Then Helix stood up. Casper's body was stuck. He was cold, but he was sweating, and the blast of the heater against his face made him dizzy. Hands pulled him up and then the world came back into focus when Blue Jean looked him straight in the eye.

"Are you ok, honey?"

Beside her, Conner turned. He took in the three of them and his face paled.

Casper still felt out of body, but the words came anyway. "He assaulted me and outed me at school." Was he going to throw up? "So, I'm gonna go."

Danielle and Helix were ushering him away. The bar ignited with noise. Casper tried to get a look at the stage, but bodies were standing, blocking his line of sight.

"Yes, see him out. Thank you." Blue Jean's voice broke through the chatter over the speakers.

Their way became blocked as people moved to make way for two men pushing Conner toward the exit.

"Where is our friend?" Blue Jean said. "Can the house come up?"

The lights flared on. Bodies shifted and returned to their

seats until Casper was exposed. Helix and Danielle both paused. Blue Jean looked directly at them, mic in one hand, the other shielding her eyes like a visor.

"I'm sorry all this attention is on you, baby. You can leave if you need to. But you are safe here." The crowd cheered raucously. "And you hear this. The only reason that troll laid hands on you is because he knew you were out of his league. Look at who is on your arm now! Gucci. Tom Ford. Prada. You're a winner, baby!"

The crowd cheered. There was so much love in the space being made for him. He wanted to let it in. To feel that support. But his body was shaking. He was leaning more and more on Danielle and Helix's grip to keep him standing. With no need to be told, they continued to shuffle toward the exit.

"Take good care of him," Blue Jean said. Then she turned her attention back to the crowd. "First days, am I right?"

Wrapped in their layers and back in the cold, whipping winds of winter, the world started to feel more solid.

"I'm sorry," Danielle said.

"There's no way you could have known he would be here," Helix said. He brushed Casper's coat arm. "What do you need?"

To melt into a puddle and stop existing.

He thought about the coyote attack, but he couldn't convince himself to bother. He wanted to leave before he saw Conner somewhere on the street. "I just want to get out of here."

Danielle pulled her phone out. "Why don't you come over to my place? My parents can make dinner."

"We can also go back to the hotel room," Helix offered.

"You wanted to Christmas." Casper sighed, feeling guilty that his emotional baggage was getting in the way.

"I want you to be ok," Helix said.

"I will be." Casper turned to Danielle, who was buried in her phone texting. "You sure it's ok?"

"Definitely." She gestured with her phone. "My mom already said yes. She's excited to see you."

"Nothing more Christmas than a family dinner," Casper said.

"Great." Helix smiled at Danielle, then turned, widening his eyes at Casper in a silent question.

Casper squeezed his hand. "It'll be fine."

Danielle being Casper's ex-girlfriend was a little strange for Helix. But she was nice and didn't seem to harbor any animosity toward Casper or himself. Still, having dinner with her family was unsettling. Casper hadn't fully recovered after seeing Conner and was employing his usual tactic of refusing to speak about the situation.

It was Helix's first time seeing a full home on Earth and his impression was that it was very full of things. It was pleasant, but his eyes felt overwhelmed. They seemed to be very fond of pictures. They had decorated every wall and surface with photographs and paintings.

Kate and John, the parents, were youthful and overly concerned about Helix's comfort. They had offered him something to drink three times before dinner was served. Danielle had fluctuated between friendly and shy throughout the afternoon, depending on whether or not she and Helix had made eye contact. Here she seemed to settle in and open up. She and Casper laughed easily over seemingly innocuous things.

The conversation rarely moved past pleasantries. Helix let Casper do the talking, since he had to construct a narrative of their vagabond life. A plan Casper whispered to Helix on the train between Christkindlmarket and the bar. Since Helix didn't know anything about locations or even names of other cities, he wouldn't be able to lie about their travels.

"So, how do you support this lifestyle?" John asked at the dinner table.

He was asking Helix. His eyes were earnest and watching him intently as Kate reached for a dish of green vegetables.

"Well..." Helix searched his mind with panic for any profession he was aware of that would earn currency on Earth.

"We both had a little bit of money saved," Casper said. "And, of course, we're really lucky that Helix's parents are supportive. They gave him the van we use to get around."

"Those live-in vans are so neat," Kate said. "I would love to see yours."

Casper laughed nervously. "Yeah, we'll have to bring it around to show you another time. We left it parked outside the city and took the CTA in. With all the parking restrictions, we didn't want to get a ticket."

"You can park it out front of our place anytime you like," John said. "We have a parking permit for our street you can toss on the windshield and be good to go."

"That's very kind," Casper said. His eyes fell to the table, and he reached for a dish containing something fluffy and white that they referred to as mashed potatoes.

"Are you going to spend the holiday with Helix's family, since..." Danielle fell off before she finished because Casper noticeably winced as she spoke.

"Yeah, we are," Helix said. "But I wanted to see the city's

festivities. Casper has so many fond memories he's shared with me."

"And where is your family?" John asked.

"The northeast," Casper answered quickly.

"Yeah, they're kind of spread across the east coast." Helix smiled warmly.

"Ahh," John said, like he discovered something. "That makes sense. Is that Italian I see about you?"

"John," Kate said, leveling a sharp glare at him.

Helix assumed he was referring to his light brown skin and features. Their whole family had the same pale complexion as Casper.

"Greek actually," Helix said.

John nodded with an appeased look on his face. Helix wondered what that kind of lineage would mean in this world. He toyed with the idea of asking John what his astrological sign was, but that would be a dangerous conversation to step into. They'd likely never believe that Casper and Helix could use magic, but Casper was already on edge. He wouldn't risk toying with the conversation and making Casper even more nervous.

"Your Christmas tree is beautiful." Helix opted to steer the conversation away from the personal. Casper looked like he was going to melt under the pressure.

"Thank you," Kate said proudly. "Decorating it is my favorite part of this season."

"I don't know, Mom," Danielle said. "I think shopping is your favorite."

John pointed his fork, loaded with a slice of roasted meat, toward Danielle. "That, I agree with."

Kate laughed and her cheeks turned slightly pink. "Stop it, both of you."

Casper was chewing, watching them with half a smile.

Helix knew him well enough now to recognize the shadows hiding behind his eyes. The longing that snuck up in his lingering glances. The way his body slightly leaned away from Helix and toward Danielle's family. It hurt a little to see, even if he understood. This was the world Casper had known for 18 years. He imagined this was probably the life he had planned for himself.

He slid his thigh to the side and brushed up against Casper's leg.

Helix's thigh bumped against his and Casper made the effort to smile at him. His heart was both full and achingly empty. He was happy to see Danielle and her family. It was so comforting to be welcomed into their home. And it also felt like his chest was being stabbed by an icicle. He hadn't had a warm, happy dinner with his own family in years. He couldn't get the heartbreak on Jess's face out of his mind. His mother was... no. He glared at the Christmas tree across the way, focusing on the minor details of the ornaments to clear his head.

"Casper?"

John was talking to him. Casper blinked away the blur of potential tears and returned his attention to the table.

"I'm sorry," he said. "I spaced out. What was that?"

"I asked if you have heard from your folks."

"Dad..." Danielle rolled her eyes, then addressed Casper. "We don't have to talk about it."

Casper cleared his throat. He went to answer, but the words wouldn't come, so he shook his head. Helix rubbed his shoulder tenderly.

"They'll come around," John said.

"And you'll be ok if they don't," Kate said. "Helix seems wonderful. It's clear you've grown close."

"Thanks," Casper managed to get out.

He tried to imagine his parents coming around. What would that mean? A dinner like this, where they gathered around a table and Casper would have to suffer thinly veiled disgust while they pretended like having his boyfriend in their home didn't fly in the face of their beliefs? Jess's words played in his head on a loop again. *Mom is going to leave Dad.* Did that mean that his mom wanted him back? Jess had looked so sad. If they were capable of changing their thinking enough to want Casper back, could his dad?

The ache in his chest became overwhelming. Shoving thoughts of his family to the back of his mind, he tried to feel anything else. He spent the rest of dinner giving small smiles and head nods. Helix picked up the slack in conversation, and from the pitying glances Danielle and Kate gave him, Casper knew they suspected he was tapped out.

When they were clearing plates from the table, John suggested a game of cards.

"We should get going," Casper said.

"Are you sure?" Helix asked. "A game sounds fun."

"We have a really long drive to get back to the coast before Christmas Eve," Casper said. "But thank you so much for having us. Honestly, this has been so special." Even though his chest felt empty, he meant it.

Helix stepped a little closer and spoke quietly. "Are you sure, Cas? You deserve to enjoy this."

Casper fought back the cry that choked him. He closed his eyes. "Yeah... um. I really need to go."

Helix squeezed his hand. "Ok."

Casper hugged Danielle first. "I'm sorry," he said, the tears breaking through. "It's too much."

"I understand," she said. "Take care of yourself."

Casper waved at her parents and turned to get his layers on as quickly as possible. Helix shuffled around the room, thanking Kate and John. He heard Danielle exchange some words with Helix as he was buttoning up his coat. "Take care of him," was all he could make out.

"I'll wait outside," Casper said to Helix when he joined him in the foyer. "I need some fresh air."

The cold shock of air against his face offered sweet relief. A tear in the corner of his eye crystalized. The sun had set nearly an hour ago, so the street was lit by only streetlamp. When Helix joined him on the sidewalk, Casper's breathing started to even out. Helix wrapped an arm around him in a side hug and leaned in to kiss him on the cheek.

"I'm ready to go back," Casper said.

"Hey, what's going on?" Helix asked. "You seemed to be having a nice time."

"I did have a nice time. I just... it hurts. To be here. And I think I need to not be here now." His face prickled under the streaks of tears that fell.

Helix wiped them away with his gloved fingers. "Ok. Let's go home."

Casper felt the pressure first. Like the feeling before his ears popped on a plane ride as his body adjusted to being somewhere it wasn't meant to be. He spun around. The dark street offered no evidence of unwanted company, but the sensation didn't ease. His heart beat faster in his chest. His breath shallowed.

Helix squeezed his hand. "What's wrong?"

Casper desperately searched the blurry edges of the streetlamps on Danielle's road, looking for any inky, moving edges.

"I can feel it." His voice was thin.

He wasn't ready. He probably would never feel ready. But not now, especially. Not here. In spite of the freezing air pinching at his cheeks, he felt sweat on the back of his neck.

"There's no one there." Helix pulled at his arm, urging them to continue toward the train.

Casper didn't budge. His gut said to run, but he couldn't bear not knowing. What if he really was here? Was he following Casper? Or was there another reason he was on Earth?

"It's Jacob," Casper said. "I can feel him."

A voice spoke from the darkness. "Cas?"

His breath caught painfully in his throat. That wasn't Jacob. Fear and hope warred inside of him. This was the worst-case scenario, and yet a small voice in the back of his mind—the one that imagined sitting around a dinner table with his family and Helix—whispered, *What if?*

He and Helix both jumped when a large dog crashed against a wooden fence down the street, barking. Helix whistled. The signal for the acolytes, who until now were giving them the illusion of privacy, to close in.

Casper's eyes burned against the cold air as he stared at the street. Was that a ripple of aether? A figure emerged, illuminated by a cone of light about ten cars away. A man with rounded shoulders in a black puffer jacket. Too tall to be Jacob. But that feeling didn't leave Casper's gut; the feeling that something was wrong.

Then the man lifted his gaze from the sidewalk and looked directly at Casper with a piercing blue gaze that he often saw when he closed his eyes. Every naive fantasy that had crossed his mind evaporated when those eyes brought memory to the present. Casper turned on his heel and pulled Helix into a quick walk.

"What's going on?" Helix asked.

The train station was close. But nothing was stopping him from following them onto the platform. The acolytes would have to be enough to keep him away. He would get them to block the turnstiles.

"Casper!"

The authoritative boom of his father's voice halted him in his tracks. Helix's hand slipped away before he realized Casper had stopped walking. Years of freezing up in his father's presence had apparently left a mark on his body.

"Who is that?" Helix came back, looking over Casper's shoulder.

Shuffled footsteps grew closer. Every kick on the salted concrete accelerated Casper's heartbeat.

"My dad," Casper said.

Helix's face fell flat, his brows casting a shadow over his cheeks in the harsh light. Casper inhaled sharp air, filling his body with any trace of Libra aether he could find. He needed to feel like he could get away. Then he turned and faced the last person he wanted to see.

"David," Casper said.

His father's cheek twitched. He wasn't close enough to touch, but he was still too close.

"Where have you been?" David asked.

Helix stepped slightly forward. He wasn't as tall as David, but under their winter layers Helix was definitely the stronger of the two. Something small cracked inside Casper's chest. No one had ever stood up to his father for him.

"How did you find me?"

"John texted. Said you were having dinner at their place."

That smarted. He had trusted Danielle's parents. Apparently a little too much.

"What do you want?" Casper was proud that his voice

didn't waver. Tears were still threatening, but he couldn't make space for them. They wouldn't stop if they started.

"It's been months!" Was *he* tearing up? Or was that just his eye twitching? "We haven't heard a word from you."

"You kicked me out." Casper didn't mask the bite in his voice. "That doesn't exactly scream, *keep in touch.*"

"Your mother is inconsolable." David stepped forward. Helix lifted a hand to stop him as Casper stepped back. David's jaw flexed. That was always the first tell that he was nearing the edge of his self-control. "Who is this?" All signs of concern slipped away as his voice went sharp. The second tell. When Casper paused before answering, his lip snarled upward. The third tell.

This was the same man he remembered. Losing Casper hadn't spurred some change in him. The faint hope in Casper's chest that this encounter was a sign his family was growing died.

"My boyfriend," Casper answered him.

David scoffed, his arms flapping against his sides. "Of course he is."

"We're going to leave now." Casper met Helix's gaze and nodded in the direction of the train.

"No," David said and slammed into Helix.

Their bodies crashed into a parked SUV. David pressed his forearm into Helix's chest, pinning him against the car.

"Dad, get off him!"

Helix threaded his arm through David's and around his shoulder and, rolling to the side, flipped him onto his back. The scratch of him sliding against the salted sidewalk echoed throughout the street.

"What the fuck is wrong with you?" Casper approached his prone body. His father looked at him, then quickly away.

Casper stumbled, backing away. There was a yellow glint in his eyes.

"Why are you always so much trouble?" David put a hand to the back of his head.

"Look at me," Casper said.

David was crawling back to his feet but paused to look at Casper. The yellow glow was unmistakable. Casper turned to Helix. "Do you see it?"

Helix glared at David and sighed. "Yeah."

"What do we do?"

Casper noticed the shapes of the acolytes nearby. Close enough to step in if needed.

"I don't know," Helix said.

David grunted as he stood back up. "What are you talking about?"

Casper checked again. The glow flared a little as he made eye contact with his father.

"We can't leave him here like this," Helix said.

"Absolutely not," Casper said. Helix was studying David, but when he looked at Casper, it was with pity. "Helix, no."

"It's too dangerous," Helix said.

The council was still trying to figure out the corruption sickness, but the biggest sign that it had progressed too far was glowing eyes.

Helix was still angled to protect Casper from his father. "If he's showing symptoms, he could spread it."

For a fleeting moment, Casper wondered if they should kill him. But despite how much his father's presence made his skin crawl, he wasn't interested in stooping to that.

"Give me your phone," Casper said to David.

"What? Why? What the fuck is going on?"

Casper approached him, reaching for his jacket pockets. David tried to push his hands away, but Casper quickly found the phone and pulled it out. When David moved to get it back, Helix shoved him away as Casper stepped to the side. He opened the messenger app and started a new message to his mom and sister. A group chat opened after he filled in their names. Casper's heart kicked in his chest reading their last messages.

Jess: I saw some kids playing soccer in the park today. I miss him.

Leanne: Me too. Wherever he is, God is taking care of him.

David's response was there searing itself into Casper's brain.

God only protects his flock.

Casper tapped out a message and hit send. There was no way to explain what was happening to his mom and sister, but he did his best. Then he returned the phone to his dad.

"What is going on, Casper?"

"Unfortunately, for both of us, you're coming with me."

"Where?" David asked.

"Circle up," Casper called to the acolytes in the street. "Change of plans. We're leaving."

"Are you ok?" Helix asked him.

"No," Casper said. "But I'll live."

"Who are these people?" David demanded.

Casper cringed, remembering his own panicked questioning when the Novilites first found him. The acolytes formed a circle, joining hands. Casper grabbed Helix's hand and the woman's next to him. Two acolytes took hold of his father.

"Dad," Casper said. "Shut the fuck up. You will want to hold your breath."

. . .

Casper felt the familiar pinch in his gut of the jump starting. David's shouted response to him cut out as the world slipped away. When the hard stone of Novilem appeared underfoot, everyone sagged, while David crashed to his hands and knees. He emptied his stomach violently and obnoxiously loud. Of course he would be performatively sick, so everyone would know how bad it was.

Casper paced the length of the small room in the Celestery they jumped into. Helix looked like he wanted to comfort him, but Casper shook his head.

"You good?" he asked.

Casper shrugged, gesturing at David's mess. "Peachy."

David collected himself quickly for having made such a show, then swiftly shrunk in on himself as he looked around, finding dark stone walls and colorful drapery instead of the frigid city street outside Danielle's home. He turned to Casper and stood to approach him, but Casper backed away.

"Where are we?" His voice was pleading. "What just happened?"

Casper didn't respond. This would shatter his father's entire worldview. He complained about evolution pushing kids away from God, what would the existence of magic do to him?

Then he remembered the look on David's face when he kicked him out. The lines of disgust carving him into something sharp and unknown. Casper wrapped his hand around his forearm where he could feel the ache of David's grip. Let him be the one to have a mental breakdown for once.

"We just teleported farther away from Earth than you can fathom." Casper moved into his Libra trine and pocket-stepped directly in front of him.

David jumped backward, the blood draining from his face. He looked around at the acolytes surrounding him.

"Where have you brought me? What have you done to my son?"

"They gave me a place to belong when you kicked me out on the street. So, maybe sit with that before you start pointing fingers."

"What the fuck is going on?" David yelled, his voice pitched up in desperation

"Alright." Helix signaled to the acolytes. "Straight to quarantine. He's sick."

The Acolytes moved in and grabbed hold of David. He struggled, trying to pull himself free. "Get your hands off me!"

It was a strange experience. Part of Casper enjoyed watching him melt down. Knowing that his father's pride would finally take a blow made him feel vindicated. But another part of him felt horrible watching Acolytes drag him off to a prison cell when he had no idea what was going on.

"I can't tell if you're smiling or if you're going to cry," Helix said.

Casper grabbed his hand and pulled him to start their walk home. "Me neither," he said.

CHAPTER
SIX

Talleah's heart skipped a beat every time Daphne pocket stepped to the top of the playground equipment, but she couldn't hold back her smile when she squealed in delight as she slid down. Hector draped his arm over her shoulder, his hand warm against her skin. Dozens of children swarmed around the playground, moving in tiny packs. Over the past month, she had watched their little groups form. She encouraged Daphne to try making friends, but she always seemed more comfortable playing alone. Talleah's heart was heavy, wondering if her time isolated with the Gemini had robbed her of precious years building easy friendships like children are supposed to do.

"I'm not ready for this to end," Hector said.

The council granted a bereavement period for the families affected by the Gemini segregation. Their work orders were paused to allow time for them to reconnect. A grieving period as much as it was a reunion. In a week, Hector would return to complete his final year of service to the Academy. Talleah had not decided if she would return to her food cart.

"I still think we should petition the board of the Academy. You've given them so much more than is required already," Talleah said.

Hector laid his head on her shoulder and sighed deeply.

"I know," she said. "You are choosing to go back. I will support your decision. But... I also think you've served your time."

"Has the economic board responded to your request?"

"No," Talleah said, melting a little into the bench. She requested an extension to her bereavement. It had only been a cycle. It was too soon to spend the majority of her days away from Daphne. She would start at a new school soon, and there was so much time to make up.

"She is going to be ok," Hector said.

Daphne's squeal pealed through the air as she spiraled down the slide. Three older kids were running straight for the landing pad. Daphne was going to collide with them. Talleah shot to her feet and cried out to her. Two of the children reached the bottom of the slide right as Daphne's ankles breached its edge. Talleah's chest squeezed tight, anticipating their collision, and in the next moment Daphne was on the opposite side of the playground, running and giggling.

Restraining herself from shoving children out of the way, Talleah ran to the other side of the playground.

"She's fine," Hector called after her.

"Mommy!" Daphne said as she approached.

"I think it's getting too crowded," Talleah said, more fear and frustration in her tone than she meant to convey.

Daphne's eyes fell to the ground. "I'm not ready to go yet."

In the days following the Turning, they could have the park mostly to themselves. Then they had to shift to going in the morning. It wasn't long before the city returned to its usual rhythm. Most public spaces were filled as long as the Split was up.

It was difficult to find any breathing room outside their home. With the loss of housing from the missing western tower along with the release of the Gemini and the return of the Exoria, there were just too many people. Hector had to give up his apartment, moving in with Talleah before they had planned. It was never a question of if they would combine their homes, but life had frozen for Talleah when Daphne was taken away. Every piece she could hold in the same place was kept where it had been. The idea of things moving too much and there not being enough space for Daphne to come back to what she left behind was unbearable. With her back, it was a slow and painful process to let things move again. Having Hector move in early was ultimately a minor inconvenience considering the families that were sleeping on the streets, but it was still an adjustment period for their home.

A child crashed into her rear, almost knocking her over. She took a long, slow breath to soothe the rage that kindled suddenly in her throat. A tear fell down Daphne's cheek.

"I'm sorry," Talleah said. "We'll try again tomorrow morning."

"Can we at least get a pastry?" Daphne's voice was quiet.

Talleah took her hand. "I think that's doable." Hector approached them, studying Talleah's face. "Would you mind taking her for a pastry?"

"You aren't coming?" Daphne asked.

"I need a few minutes to myself," Talleah said.

Hector took Daphne's hand, still looking at her. "Need anything?"

Talleah softened a little knowing the fullness of the question: a pastry, a hug, for him to punt the rowdy children across the playground. He'd do anything for her. She shook her head. "I'll meet you at home. I'm just going to take a walk."

At odds with herself, she turned to leave the park. Every moment with Daphne was a gift. Choosing anything else felt like shredding a piece of herself away. But she couldn't shake the frustration rising inside her chest. Her patience was unusually thin as of late. Moving helped, and soon enough, she found her legs were bringing her toward her food cart on the Celestery's promenade.

The last thing Casper wanted to do was check on his father. But after a night of not really sleeping, David's presence in Novilem felt like a wraith haunting his every thought. His attention was pulled to it no matter how he tried to distract himself. The Estellar was holding David in the cellblock behind the Celestery. Those who developed corruption sickness were being treated in a clinic uptown, but because his dad was infected on Earth, they weren't taking risks in mixing him with other infected people.

Casper hoped it was something the Virgos could mend. The glow of his eyes had been faint. Maybe it wasn't that bad. He could get better and go right back to Earth. Would that make him the first person to return to Earth from Novilem? Would the council let him go back? Casper couldn't make room for the possibility they would say no. David needed to be back on Earth as soon as possible.

"Do you want me to come in with you?" Talleah asked.

He crossed paths with Talleah on the way to the Celestery building. Helix and Casper accompanied her on visits to her mother at the clinic as often as they could, so she insisted on joining him. He reached out, and they grasped hands. His breath was coming in shallow gulps. Her touch was warm and comforting. Part of him wanted to have her company, but it would only confuse him to have more of his two different worlds colliding. To be known how Talleah knew him while his dad tried to excavate the pliant, damaged child he had molded... it was too much.

"I won't be long," Casper said, squeezing her hand.

He followed a portly acolyte down the hallway and too soon Casper found himself face to face with his father.

"Son," David said.

The acolyte unlocked the cell and walked far enough down the hall to imitate privacy.

David sat on a small bed, half his body under the covers. A collection of herbs and tinctures were arranged on a thin shelf next to him. The cell smelled of earth and spices. Casper stood near the doorway, eyeing the bench opposite the bed. He didn't really want to take a seat. He didn't really want to be there at all.

"They fix you up?" Casper asked, gesturing at the medicinal tinctures.

"They're working on it." David's eyes fell to the smooth fabric covering his legs. "This corruption business is pretty stubborn, it seems."

Casper couldn't recall a time when his father was fully ill. He'd caught a few head colds from Casper in grade school, but it was strange to see him... *feeble*. Casper's ears rang. His jaw was clenched shut. The urge to turn and walk out the door consumed him.

"Have a seat?"

His father's voice was calm, welcoming. He hadn't spoken to Casper that way in years. With a sigh, Casper crossed to the bench and sat. His heart was kicking double speed in his chest. He watched the door. Glanced at his cuticles. Anything to keep from looking at his father directly in the eye.

"The Lord works in mysterious ways," David said.

Casper's chest tightened. Scripture, sermons, and lectures from his father twisted around him. Months had passed since the day David threw him onto the streets of Chicago. He had a whole new life in Novilem. And yet, sitting under his father's gaze made him feel ten and powerless. The only thing he wanted less than to hear his father's diatribe about religious doctrine was to find out how angry he would be if Casper pushed back.

"I've been praying for you."

"I can't do this." Casper stood and stepped toward the hall in one motion.

"Don't go."

The words stopped Casper in his tracks. Because it wasn't the angry shout he was expecting. It was soft. So soft it could be sincere.

Casper turned back to him but remained standing.

"How sick am I?" David asked.

The glow had faded away from his eyes, but the deep lines of a lifetime of disdain were still there.

"I don't know," Casper said. "We're still trying to figure the sickness out."

It was a long and exhausting explanation. Casper considered risking the use of Gemini aether to bond their minds and show his father that they were in a subterranean lunar city on the other side of the universe. But that would also mean learning about every horrible thought his father had about him, so he opted for the old-fashioned and much longer way of using words. As Casper expected, the longer they talked, the less agreeable David became.

"Will it kill me?"

Casper's heart ached, then he felt whiplash from how quickly his gut filled with disgust for feeling sympathy for his father.

"We don't know," Casper said.

There were only a handful of cases that had advanced beyond the healing capabilities of a Virgo. None of those patients had died, but it certainly seemed like it was heading in that direction. Casper thought of Talleah's mother and how withered she looked.

David beat his fist into the mattress he was sitting on. His flashes of anger had grown more frequent during their talk. Not abnormal for his father, but the sporadic bursts were also symptoms of the sickness. The infected lose the ability to mitigate emotional reactions. Once it advanced beyond repair, people were prone to impulsively act on their basest instincts. Greed, lust, fury. The loudest emotions seemed to take over the driver's seat.

Casper wondered how long his dad had been sick. How much of his behavior had been derailed by the sickness? He quickly shoved the thought away. He wouldn't be excusing anything his father did to him.

"Well, now I know," David said with surprising clarity and acceptance. He met Casper's gaze with clear eyes. "I want to go home."

Casper squirmed under the pressure of his hope. He wanted to take pleasure in denying his father of something. Of finally being the one with the power in their relationship. But it didn't feel good. In fact, it felt awful.

"You can't go home. Not while you're sick. You could hurt people."

"Then fix it!" The lines over his brow creased. "If you've got all those powers you talked about, make it go away."

"It doesn't work like that."

The fury was building. Casper shrunk as his father postured to take up more space. When David stood from the cot, Casper rushed out the cell door, closing it behind him. David slammed his hands against the bars.

"Let me out!"

The force of his voice rattled Casper as it echoed down the long hallway of the cell block. The acolyte rushed forward and locked the door. Casper's mind hollowed out. There wasn't enough air. He broke into a cold sweat. The corners of his vision went fuzzy. He walked toward the exit.

"Casper! Let me out!"

Casper's shoulders crunched with tension as his father's voice hit his back, the sound smacked against him like a physical force. He ran, trying to focus on his feet pounding the stone. Eyes locked on the door ahead.

"Casper!"

He was crying when he entered the large hall of the Celestery. He fell to the ground in a heap. Hands landed on his shoulders in a comforting touch.

"Hey, it's ok," Talleah said. The coo of her voice smoothed the sharp edges in Casper's mind a little. "Come here." She guided him to a bench and sat with him, grasping his hand in hers. "I'm right here."

The tears flowed freely, and Casper let them. It took so much energy to carry this thing between him and his father all the time. And as painful as it was to face how broken their relationship was, it was a relief to set the burden down. He cried into Talleah's shoulder, and she caressed his hair.

"I know," she said.

And for the first time, Casper felt like someone really did

know. Her mother was also sick. Their relationship was even more fraught than Casper's relationship with his father. What a gift it was to not be alone in the weight of his grief.

He wrapped his arms around her, letting relief buoy him.

"Thank you," he said. "For being here." A cry shook out of him. "For understanding."

"Sometimes family that you build stands stronger than the family you're given." Talleah pulled back from their hug and wiped Casper's cheeks with her thumbs. "And sometimes the family that you're given teaches you how to hold on to the family that you build."

The world went blurry again behind his tears. "Yeah," he said.

He pulled her back into a hug and held on like his life depended on it.

Talleah gave him an extra hard squeeze. "Let's have a family dinner tonight. Daphne missed you while you were gone."

There were so many things to do, but clearly Casper wasn't functional enough to do them, and dinner sounded nice. Family sounded like comfort. Maybe, with a little comfort, he could get back to finding out what Jacob was up to.

Casper let go of Talleah. "Yeah, dinner sounds nice."

CHAPTER
SEVEN

Casper's life was in a never-ending tailspin. Before he could leave the Celestery grounds, an acolyte delivered a message stating that Theo expected him to return to his public facing duties by the end of the week. This news made him feel like he was wearing a coat three sizes too small. His father was here, in Novilem, sick with corrupted aether, and the council expected him to stand up in front of strangers and talk about their efforts toward reform.

He knew the cost of spreading fear firsthand. He woke up from nightmares about his ascension regularly. A crowd of eager faces listening to his every word, and the chaos that broke out when he turned their attention to the council's lies.

There would be no facing the public. Theo was being horrible to Helix, anyway. He wasn't exactly inclined to remain in his good graces. He needed to focus his energy on getting his father back to Earth and figuring out how to save Agnes from Jacob.

Helix slipped his fingers between Casper's as they neared the restaurant for family dinner.

"Casper!" Honeyed curls bounced around Daphne's face as she skipped forward, crashing into Casper's legs.

He reached down and hugged her back. "Are you taller?"

She giggled, looking up while still bear hugging him. "Nooo."

"Then I must be shrinking."

"I saw you last week," she said. "I couldn't have grown that much."

"Hey, I was on Earth. Really, really far away. You never know what could happen."

"Maybe you got shorter on the jump back," she said with a laugh.

Helix chuckled, measuring Casper with crinkled eyes. "Yeah, I thought you seemed a bit smaller."

"Hey now, how did this turn into picking on me?"

"Because you're very easy to make fun of," Talleah said.

"Not you too," Casper replied.

She leaned in and kissed him on the cheek. "It's good to see you smile."

Helix embraced her in a quick hug. Daphne released her grip on Casper and reached back for Hector's hand as they entered the building.

"Two cross universe trips within a few months and you're still standing," Hector said.

Helix smiled. "A good night's rest and some Capricorn aether does wonders."

"Let's sit," Talleah said. "I'm hungry."

Casper's stomach grumbled. He had missed dinner the night before, having crashed as soon as he got home, and couldn't find his appetite after seeing his father that morning. He pressed down the ache that filled his stomach, refusing to let thoughts of David linger in his mind. Tonight was for the family he was building. He forced a smile onto his face.

Daphne took Casper's hand, leading her through the restaurant, weaving through tables of cheery patrons. At every table, someone's eyes would go wide when they noticed Casper, but he kept his gaze on the path as much as he could, acting like guiding Daphne took all of his focus. People had begun to leave him alone more often than not, but the gawking remained. He wondered if this was what famous people felt like back in America. Like they were always being studied anytime they were in public.

A few deep breaths helped him leave the peering eyes behind. When they arrived at their table, Casper grabbed a chair facing the wall so he wouldn't get distracted by curious patrons peering over.

"I want to sit next to Casper!" Daphne said.

"Then I guess this chair is for you." He patted the chair next to him. Casper had grown very fond of Talleah and Hector in the weeks since the turning. They checked in on him and Helix and they were quick to humor when in the right mood. But his friendship with Daphne was what made his heart sing. She was the brightest light in the room, and it didn't hurt that she constantly picked him. This little circle was the one place he was comfortable enough to crave the attention.

Helix took the seat on Casper's other side and leaned over, kissing him gently on the shoulder. The aroma of fried bread and heady spices filling the room made Casper's mouth water. The chatter of the surrounding tables returned to a normal volume. He heard English and Greek spoken in equal measure. He had started practicing Greek with Helix, but he wasn't even close to being able to follow along at a conversational level.

"How was your trip?" Hector asked.

"Really good," Helix replied. "Except for the end, I guess."

"Let's stick to the really good parts," Casper said.

"Did you see any dinosaurs?" Daphne asked.

"The dinosaurs are only in museums now. They lived a really long time ago," Casper explained.

Daphne twisted her mouth to the side as she turned her attention to unfolding the cloth napkin in front of her.

"How are things back here?" Casper asked.

Hector turned to Talleah and she deflated with a sigh.

"Novilem is the same as it's been." She watched Daphne refold her napkin into a new shape. "The housing issue is out of hand. Every day feels like a breaking point and the Estellar is pretty much as careless as ever."

"They aren't careless," Helix said. "The two demos seats have been very vocal about the issue."

Talleah laid a hard glare at him. Casper nudged Helix. It became clear early on that discussing council business turned heated quickly, but neither of them could ever go long without talking shop.

"Careless or willfully negligent," she said. "Your choice."

"Both of you," Hector warned, his voice low. "Fight on your own time. This is a family dinner." He reached over and brushed Talleah's arm gently. "One you don't have to prepare yourself, might I add. Let's put some effort into enjoying it."

She smiled at him and laid her hand over his. "You're right. We can complain about the woes of life another time."

"Lord knows you will," Casper said, earning him a hearty laugh from Hector.

Helix tucked a twist of curls behind his ear. His neck was

rouged with heat. Talleah had riled him up a little too easily. He was probably going to need a few moments to collect himself.

"Speaking of housing," Casper said. "Are you finally all moved in?"

With Daphne back in their custody, it only made sense that their little family combined into one home. With the influx of Exoria and Gemini returning to the city, Talleah and Hector felt they should forgo tradition and move in together before marrying. It was only a matter of time before they went through with the wedding, anyway.

"Unpacked and everything," Hector said.

Talleah was smiling. "It's a bit tight, but we'll make it work."

"My room is across the hall from the bathroom," Daphne said.

"I bet that makes getting ready in the morning really quick," Casper said.

"Yeah, and Mom and Dad are right next to my room."

"We'll have to come over soon so you can show me your room."

"Yeah!" Daphne squeaked.

"What about you two?" Hector asked.

Helix's eyes perked up and he almost choked on the sip of water he just took. "Too early."

"He might be ready when we're thirty," Casper said.

Helix rolled his head to the side. "I'd move in with you tomorrow, but..."

"Timing matters," Casper finished the statement. "I know."

"I don't think it's a bad idea to take your time," Talleah said. "We sure did."

"Yeah, we did," Hector said. "Maybe don't take as much

time as us. What are your plans now that you're back?" he asked. "Your crew is still on hiatus?"

"Yes," Helix said. "Starting to feel like the council won't be lifting the order."

"There are worse things than not running dangerous missions on the Surface," Casper said.

"You've served your time," Talleah said. "And you have your work with the council, right?"

"The council has been... difficult," Helix said.

Casper rubbed the back of his tunic to comfort him, and Helix leaned into the touch. Seeing the curiosity on Talleah's face he quickly shifted the conversation back to Daphne's new room and let her distract the table.

Dinner was delicious, the company was perfect, and for a moment Casper was able to forget about the world outside the restaurant. It was just him, his boyfriend, and the best friends he'd ever had.

Daphne said something silly. Laughter came easily, and Casper found some hope that things could be like this. Life could be good. Once he stopped Jacob.

EIGHT

Seeing Brissa's chair empty at the Estellar's table still stung. Theo had kept his word, installing two democratically elected seats for the Enotis. They were titled as demos rather than preitan, given their role of representing the public. Cesia's seat had also been filled. A qualified and willing candidate had not yet been selected from house Capricorn or Taurus. Preitan Naomi had ascended to an elder role, and the table had decided to hold off on assigning the other two elder seats until the remaining preitan seats were no longer vacant.

Helix's position as junior preitan had run its course since the council once again sat at 12 seats. He was no longer allowed a vote, as he would serve as a tiebreaker and that was deemed too much power for a 19-year-old to wield.

Two additional chairs were added behind the half-moon slab of stone and, out of respect for Theo, Brissa's chair was left untouched. Looking at it, Helix remembered the first time he entered the council hall. How Brissa had smiled at him as he ran his hands along the smooth surface of the table. She had encouraged him to sit in her chair as she explained to him what she did for work.

His heart ached as he wondered how much of it was his own volition to follow in Brissa's footsteps and how much she had influenced him to follow that path. He bit his cheek to distract himself from the pain of wondering how much he didn't know about his yiayia.

"Absolutely not," Theo said. His sharp tone pulled Helix out of his grief. "If all twelve houses are not present, how could we possibly think that our voices are being heard with any sense of equality?"

Demos Bennet, the more vocal of the two Enotis seats, responded matching Theo's energy. "I think it's a bit of a farce to cling to the idea that the council has ever presented equal voice to the houses. The fact that there are elder seats flies in the face of equality."

"That's a fundamental misrepresentation of the function of the elder seats." Theo's face was ruddy with heat.

"The people want to know that their concerns are being prioritized by the council," Demos Mirta said.

She was young, probably half the age of the youngest preitan, but that wasn't what surprised Helix about Mirta being allowed at the table. Her central role in the Enotis's actions after Marcus's death was more of his concern. And her stubbornness and short temper. She caused a lot of fuss the first week of the Demos seats being added, trying to usurp every conversation. After being threatened with a vote to depose her, she put effort into tempering her words, which is how Bennet became the more vocal of the two.

Helix attended meetings as often as he could since the Turning. Council business had been focused largely on city-planning to house those previously forced to the slums and the returned Exoria. Without the power of a vote, there really wasn't a reason for him to be there, but he had a burning need in his chest to do something; to help. The only thing that felt right was being close to the table.

The conversation devolved into bickering, per usual as of late.

"What about the Gemini?" Helix spoke over the back and forth. When enough heads had turned to him, he pushed on before he could be silenced. "I've been studying democratic structures employed on Earth. They collect opinion from their populace to inform their decisions. The Gemini are particularly suited to gathering public opinion."

"That's a fantastic idea," Demos Bennet said.

"What do the populace understand about governing matters?" the Cancer preitan asked.

"They wouldn't make decisions on how we govern," Helix explained. "It would be the council's work to figure out the function of governing while considering public opinion. Giving the people a voice on what we do here will help them feel satisfied."

Theo was watching Helix carefully with a flat expression. He couldn't tell if his pappous was proud or if he was in trouble. A too familiar experience as of late.

"I don't like the idea of the table being beholden to the public," Preitan Naomi said. "What happens if we act against their wishes?"

"Isn't this the same reasoning behind the demos seats?" The Sagittarius preitan gestured at Bennet and Mirta. "We've already made adjustments to give the people a voice."

"Which is not enough," Mirta said. "There is still much unrest in the city. We are nearing a cycle out from the Turning, and we've only managed to properly house a quarter of those displaced. Hundreds have ended their work for the Academy. We have acolytes stationed in the central park to suppress the fighting that has been breaking out."

"Tensions are high because we have been through a time of stress," Theo said. "Things will settle."

"Things will settle when the people's needs are met," Mirta said. "How long do you expect them to sleep in the streets?"

"What else is there to do?" Theo stood from the table. The room went still. It was an unspoken understanding that power positioning was taboo. Losing Brissa had done strange things to Helix's calm, collected grandfather. Whether by grief, denial, or some volatile mixture of the two, Theo had developed a habit of trying to fill the void of Brissa's presence. "The Taurus are at work building as quickly as they can, in spite of the fact they keep falling sick with dark aether. You speak in ideals, but we live in reality. It does no good to bring hopes and dreams to this table. What can we do today to make things better for the people of Novilem?"

The room remained silent. Theo ran a hand over his white beard.

"It does not matter that the Gemini can expedite communication and the collection of public opinion," he continued. "If we give the people a choice in where or how they are housed, it will exponentially slow down the process. What if they choose a new location? Or they want to live in an established neighborhood? Do we move families out of their current homes to make room for them?"

Helix's stomach clenched. This was not his kind and understanding grandfather. In moments when Brissa was hard, Theo offered comfort. To see him cling to the old ways, grandstanding in her absence, was bizarre and heartbreaking.

"Preitan Theo," Helix said. "If giving the people a voice

creates a sense of satisfaction, even if it prolongs the solutions we can provide, wouldn't their happiness be worth the effort?"

Theo's eye twitched as he listened to Helix. "Helix, you are dismissed from the table. Please leave the hall."

"Preitan—"

"Now."

Theo didn't meet his gaze. He was staring at his hands as he leaned against the table. The other preitans were split between looking at Theo and watching Helix as he stood from his offset chair. Heat pricked at the back of his neck. Brissa had never dismissed him from a room. Not even as a child. He could barely stomach the idea, but worried that he was losing his pappous, too. The table remained silent until the door to the hall closed behind him. He leaned his head back against the closed door and, like anytime he relaxed his mind, he wished for his yiayia.

CHAPTER
NINE

On the first and fifteenth of every cycle, the Demos held space for a public forum. Talleah attended regularly. She shuffled into a row near the top of the city park amphitheater, making sure there was easy access to an exit. She pulled Daphne onto the bench next to her, rubbing the side of her arm in a hug. Hector sat on the other side, sandwiching their daughter.

Previously, she had left Daphne home with Hector. Her nerves were too wrecked to have Daphne near a space as charged as the forums. But Talleah couldn't bear being separated recently. As safe as she tried to convince herself their home was, it was unbearable to let Daphne out of her sight.

Hector pulled a notebook out of the satchel he carried and handed Daphne a marker so she could draw. Daphne took it happily and turned around, placing the book on the bench. Talleah leaned over and kissed her head.

"Moooom, I'm drawing."

She met Hector's eyes, and they smiled. It felt normal. It felt right.

The rows of the amphitheater were filling up. Down on the dais, Demos Bennet and Mirta were readying to start the forum. Despite Mirta being given a seat as a demos, Talleah had a hard time thinking of her with respect. Her former hotheaded crewmate may have found her way onto the council, but she would always be a wildcard to Talleah.

The chatter in the space died down as Demos Bennet called for silence. A couple dozen acolytes were stationed at regular intervals amongst the aisles and standing along the perimeter. The feeling of being watched was prominent, and from the shifting eyes of the people surrounding them, Talleah could tell she wasn't the only one who noticed.

The council had assigned heavy patrols of acolytes in the streets after the Turning from Split rise to Split fall. They were taking no chances of civil unrest brewing, but the over-correction had an unexpected consequence. No one wanted the acolytes to step in, and the pressure to not be corrected pushed people to be more and more insular. Even here, where she would expect the lively conversation of people gathering to share opinions, the crowd was making barely any sound.

Novilem was built on trust. Even their economy functioned solely on a system of trust. Trust that your neighbor was doing their part. Trust that there would be enough food at the market tomorrow. Trust that the council's boards would balance everyone's best interest when assigning housing and work. The presence of the acolytes monitoring their every action in public spaces destroyed any concept of that trust. It was eroding the cornerstone of Novilem that Talleah believed was worth fighting for.

"Thank you for joining us today," Demos Bennet called out to the crowd once. "Demos Mirta and I are happy to take note of your thoughts and concerns. We will be sure to take them to the rest of the council for proper consideration. We'll start by addressing reoccurring concerns that have been presented to the council and then we'll open the floor for individuals to speak. Please remember you are not to approach the dais at any time. And if everyone speaks, no one is heard. The person speaking before you may very well have a similar concern."

Meetings usually remained orderly the first half hour, then devolved into a cacophony of yelling, at which point Talleah would slip away.

Bennet gestured to Mirta. She lifted a ledger and began to read, projecting her voice through the amphitheater. "The first buildings of new construction on the outer rim of the city are nearing completion. As a reminder, if you are currently unhoused, you need to ensure you are registered on the waitlist.

"It has been twelve days since the last public disturbance. This does not meet the council's requirement of a full cycle of peace. The curfew will not be extended."

The crowd groaned collectively. Mirta's face was very nearly expressionless, but Talleah recognized the hint of a scowl. The irony of the rule breaker turned to rule enforcer was nearly comical. Her mind slipped back to cycles prior when she and Mirta stood on that same dais and Theo connected their memories. Sometimes Talleah wondered if Mirta's memory could be trusted. She had spent years denying negligent action in the face of their crewmates falling to their death. But was she ever capable of taking accountability? Of even considering that her juvenile antics could have ended their crew's lives?

Talleah's attention went back to the forum when the first Novilite spoke.

"I am a Virgo," the man said. "I'm currently serving at the clinic treating the corruption sickness."

The place where Talleah's mother was being treated. She knew it well.

"We saw ten new cases the week we opened our doors. Yesterday alone, we saw ten new cases. We're on track to treat nearly 200 people before the cycle ends. I think the council needs to consider establishing a second clinic. Our space won't be able to handle the intake of patients soon."

"Why are the cases of infection increasing?" A woman called out from the crowd. It was the exact question Talleah had.

"Please refrain from speaking unless you hold the floor," Bennet replied.

Talleah flinched when a man behind her yelled out, "Let her speak!" She had to restrain herself from turning around to yell back at him. The anger flooded through her with shocking speed. She steadied her breathing, trying to calm herself. She was unsure what exactly upset her. She agreed with him. She was glad someone spoke out, but she was fighting the urge to bear her teeth and yell at the man.

Daphne was still content, using the bench as a workspace for her art.

The woman stood from her seat and the crowd acquiesced space to her. Bennet rolled his eyes, gesturing to the woman to speak.

"The sickness spreads every day," the woman said. "What has the council discovered about it?"

Bennet and Mirta exchanged a silent glance.

"It remains treatable," Mirta said. "The clinic has proven entirely effective at clearing the infection."

"For how long?" The woman was not placated. "If the

spread continues to grow exponentially, how long until our Virgos cannot keep up?"

"The council has allocated every possible resource to investigating the illness," Bennet said. "We don't have new information to share, but I promise it's our main priority."

The woman started to reply, but Bennet cut her off. "Thank you for your comment. I'm very sorry, but I can't let the entire forum be derailed by this concern. I understand your fears, but we are already putting every effort into addressing the illness. We have noted the suggestion of establishing another clinic to get ahead of the growing number of people experiencing symptoms."

For a moment, Bennet's efforts worked. The crowd fell back, considering his words. Talleah was already bent over, telling Daphne it was time to go. The calm wouldn't last. She nodded to Hector, and by the time they rose from their seats, dozens of people were yelling. With the acolytes stationed, it wouldn't derail too far, but Talleah's nerves couldn't handle the fervent energy of an angry crowd.

The noise of the amphitheater fell behind but was no less audible as they made their way through the park grounds.

"Not much has changed," Hector said.

Talleah hummed a noncommittal agreement. In a way, he was right, but she also couldn't deny that deep inside, she believed that everything had changed. They were all just doing a lot of work to pretend that wasn't the case.

"You ok?" Hector asked.

She wasn't. The fury that burned below her skin was alarming. And her growing eagerness to let it out worried her, but she couldn't explain something she didn't understand. A part of her wanted to open up to him. Hector would support her. She knew that. But she was also afraid that speaking about it would give it more power, and she wasn't sure she could keep it at bay if it kept growing.

"Yeah," Talleah said. "Tired. Let's go home."

He rubbed her arm, and she leaned into the comfort of his touch as the heat in her chest drained away.

Casper's back garden was beautifully laid out. It was small but had distinguished zones that he really enjoyed. A dining area for six, three rows of raised planters where he could grow produce, if he learned how, and a sunken seating area with a fire pit. He and Helix were curled up on the rounded bench of the circular lounge around a flickering fire.

"You haven't talked about seeing your dad."

Casper tensed. He had very much been enjoying pretending like his father wasn't in a Celestery jail cell. "There's nothing to say."

"Cas…" Helix gently massaged his hand. He opened his mouth to speak but changed his mind.

"He's the same," Casper said, not hiding his frustration. "He's sick, and he's here, and I can't wait until we send him back to Earth. What else is there to say?"

Helix pulled his hand back. The fire was small, but it may as well have been blazing for how hot Casper's skin was. He started sweating.

"You keep doing this," Casper said. "Why won't you leave the dad thing alone?"

Helix puffed out a quick breath. The shift of his eyes and brow pressing together indicated he was measuring his words. "Because it's bothering you."

"Of course it's bothering me."

"Then why won't you talk about it?"

"Because there's nothing to do. He can't go home until he isn't sick, and the Virgos can't clear his infection."

"I'm not talking about finding a solution."

Casper huffed. "Then what do you want?"

Helix dropped his face into his hands.

"What is it?" Helix's silence was worrying. He was so seldom at a loss for words.

Helix shook his head. "We don't have to talk about it now. I don't want to argue."

Helix pulling away made his head feel like a kicked beehive. He was surprised at the anger that came up. "Is that why you won't move in?" Casper asked. "Because we've been bickering?"

Helix sat back and looked Casper in the eye. "I've explained that I'm not ready."

"But you haven't explained why."

Helix grew tense and visibly frustrated. "Living together is more than sharing a roof. It's sharing your life. Your space. Your time. We're young. We barely know how to take care of ourselves. So, of course we don't know how to properly take care of each other yet."

The buzzing quieted and he deflated. There was a hole inside his chest. A chasm of space and suddenly Helix felt like he was standing on the other side of it. "I don't understand why we can't learn how to care for ourselves and each other together."

"Why is this important to you? What does me moving in mean to you?"

Casper folded in on himself. A pinch of red flushed his cheeks. "It just is."

Helix hummed. "You can ask for time to consider the question if you need. But I'm going to need an actual answer."

Casper leaned over, burying his face into Helix's shoulder. His sigh rumbled against Helix's tunic. "It's bad enough to have feelings. Why do I also have to be perceived experiencing them?"

"That's the pain of being known."

"Like you know anything about the pain of being known. You're the most comfortable-in-your-skin person I have ever met."

"Why wouldn't I be comfortable in my skin? It's my skin."

Casper leaned back and shook his head, smiling. "It's another Earth phrase. It means confident and like present in your body."

"You are not present in your body?"

"Less so by the second. My soul is currently ascending to another plane. I don't need Aquarius aether to leave my body." He tapped the side of his head. "This puppy is capable of many magic tricks. Blitzing off into the black abyss is a specialty of mine."

"Isn't a puppy a small dog?"

Casper rolled his eyes. "Not the point."

"Does that help? The abyss? Does it make you feel better?"

"Momentarily? It helps me feel less. Which makes remaining alive more bearable. But better? No. It doesn't help me feel better."

"You spend a lot of energy trying to change the way you feel."

Casper laughed. "Doesn't everyone?"

Helix shook his head.

"Shut up."

Helix smirked.

"I'm serious, Helix. You can't be telling me that most people are just ok with the emotions they feel."

"Not ok with them. Life is often a series of uncomfortable emotions. But they don't last. You feel them and then they go away."

Casper laughed again. Helix narrowed his eyes.

"What kind of magic are you talking about?" Casper asked. "Feel the emotion and it goes away? Emotions are sticky. When they show up, they get all over everything and then your mind spirals about how loud they are, and you find a way to distract yourself until another feeling arrives."

"Stars. They really did a number on you, didn't they?"

"You're telling me that your feelings go away on their own?"

Helix nodded.

Casper didn't understand how that was possible. He couldn't recall a single instance where an emotion left him alone after it arrived. Usually, his body freaked out as soon as he felt something and would not stop panicking until he could explain why he felt that way. Which was not always apparent, so he was better off trying to figure out a way to feel something else. He stared at the dancing flames in the pit and quietly said, "They just show up and then go away?"

"I'm starting to understand why you're always irritable."

Casper pushed Helix. "Hey! Don't say things that are devastatingly true."

Helix laughed. His eyes moved to his sandals, and he

chewed on his lip. "It scares me. That you're so out of touch with your feelings. That's what I was not wanting to say before."

"Oh." The chasm in his chest opened again. The implications of Helix's words landed heavily. This impasse they kept hitting in their communication was his fault. The reason Helix kept bringing it up was because it made him uncomfortable. Which also probably meant that Helix wouldn't feel comfortable moving forward in their relationship until that discomfort was addressed.

"Well, fuck," Casper said.

"I don't hold it against you," Helix clarified. "I understand why it's so uncomfortable for you. But I can't ignore that sometimes your emotions are volatile. And while that is valid for what you are experiencing, it's not the foundation that I want us to be on when we make decisions about something like living together."

Casper melted further with every word. He considered using Taurus aether to scoop the stone from underneath him and sink deep into the bedrock of Novilem.

Helix rubbed the length of his thigh. "I can see you're uncomfortable. I've been nervous about bringing it up."

A terrible thought made Casper go rigid. The words spilled out of his mouth before he could consider them. "What if I can't change that? What if this is just who I am?"

"You are not your emotions," Helix said softly.

"But they matter enough to make you question us."

"I'm not questioning us."

"I mean... yeah, you are. You said I'm too volatile for us to move forward."

Helix looked pained. "That is not what I said. Please don't stretch my words."

Casper twisted, sliding away on the bench so they were

face to face. "You literally said we can't move in together because of my emotions."

"I said it was part of my consideration. We haven't even been together for a year. I don't think it's unreasonable for me to not be ready to move in."

Casper was in a spiral. Things with Helix had been good from the start. Casper was so enamored with every single thing about him, and outside factors had never slowed down enough for him to consider that they weren't on the same page. What if Helix didn't see a future for them? What if this tornado of emotional distress that never slowed down lived inside his chest for the rest of his life? Could wounds as deep as his heal? Or would he be an emotional wreck for the rest of his days? Would they survive if the wedge he was now realizing was between them grew larger and larger?

He looked at Helix, tears filling his eyes. Warm, solid, stable Helix. He nearly cracked, feeling the love in his heart turn conditional.

"Hey, hey." Helix reached out to him.

Casper almost pulled away, terrified of the pain that would come from Helix disposing of him. A primal, hot instinct in his chest begged him to storm away. To protect what little of his heart remained. Helix's hand grabbed his gently. His fingers rubbed back and forth as his gaze searched Casper. There were too many tears now for him to see through.

"Where'd you go?" Helix asked.

"I..." Casper choked on a cry, desperate not to showcase his vulnerability. "I don't want to lose you." It was barely a whisper, but Helix's grip strengthened. He had heard.

He allowed himself to be pulled into Helix's arms. He was shaking against his chest when they finally embraced.

"I'm not going anywhere," Helix said.

"I don't deserve you."

The admission shocked Casper as much as it seemed to shock Helix. They both froze. The ache of his words stopped the tears for a moment. Helix, still holding him, tensed before squeezing him harder.

"You deserve everything," Helix said.

Casper buried his face in his shoulder.

"Where are you right now?" Helix's voice vibrated against Casper, the depth of it touching every part of the ache in his chest. "There is nothing about what you're experiencing that isn't understandable. I'm sorry that my fear sounded like doubt. There was probably a better way to voice my feelings. Honestly, I was a bit scared of exactly this."

Casper smarted at that. He felt bad that Helix hadn't been comfortable to share how he was feeling because he was afraid of how Casper would respond. But louder than that was the shame. Seeing how much his past was holding their relationship back hollowed him out. He pulled away from their embrace, wiping his face. A panic had taken place of his need to cry.

"Cas?"

Helix sounded worried as he pulled away. Casper turned, unwilling to meet his gaze. The backdoor to his house was a few paces away. He desperately wanted to run inside and slam the door, locking out all of the loudness inside him.

"I'm going inside," Casper said.

"Yeah, we can do that."

Casper stood but didn't turn around. "I think I need some time."

"Oh." He didn't need to see Helix to know how crestfallen his face was.

"I'm sorry," Casper squeaked out, his throat constricting.

He shuffled into his house, sliding the paned door closed.

There was a couch nearby. Some part of Casper managed the work of lowering himself onto its surface, and then he braced for the waves of emotion that rocked through his body. He stifled the wail that lodged in his throat, worried that Helix might not have left the garden. He was visible from the backyard, but Casper refused to see if Helix was checking on him.

The grief was larger than their conversation. It tapped deeper, connecting to more pains and hurts than Casper could name. Why was life so hard? The question became a central thread in his shaking cries. Why was it always so hard?

Helix watched Casper through the pane of his back door. He was laid out on the couch, hugging a pillow as he shook, weeping. Helix ached to go inside and hold him. To try wrapping Casper's pain and tears in his arms. He stood there at the door for too long, weighing whether he should or not. Ultimately, he believed it was best to respect Casper's wish to be alone.

The conversation had fallen off the rails so quickly. Which, in its own way, was a validation of Helix's point. Casper's battle with his past was an obstacle to their ability to deal with conflict. As Helix exited the garden through the side gate, his concern for Casper waned enough to feel his own emotions.

He was frustrated to feel so alone. He wasn't sure Casper had even been able to hear what he was trying to communicate. So quickly, he had disappeared into his own distress. They hadn't experienced many disagreements, but the few that had occurred pointed his mind toward a pattern. Casper hadn't learned how to hold space for his own discomfort while also making room for Helix's.

The moment Casper discovered his fear that he couldn't change replayed in Helix's mind. He had turned younger before Helix's eyes, the honesty of his fear revealing the wound of a child.

A wound inflicted by someone who was currently being held in a cell. Helix was already making his way to the Celestery when he realized where he was going. The large, white pyramid rose proudly overhead as he entered the grounds. The circular skylight carved through its center almost felt like it was looking directly at him. Like the council had an eye watching over the city.

Up the stairs and around the building, Helix made his way to the entrance of the holding cell block. Novilem's civil disputes were generally managed swiftly. The Court of Gemini could read the minds of involved parties and make a decision within moments. So, the cell block was rarely used. But in the wake of the sickness spreading, it had been a useful place to quarantine people like David, who were sick but not in need of more intensive care yet.

The guard accepted his reason for visiting and allowed him inside. The shift in energy was immediate and palpable. Although light gems lit many cells and the length of the hall, the space was dark. The shadows felt deeper. The air hung close and was thin in his lungs. Helix could feel his heartbeat in his neck.

David was awake in his cell, sitting on his cot with his back against the wall. His eyes narrowed when he recognized Helix.

"What do you want?" David asked.

Helix wasn't entirely sure what an honest response to the

question was. He arrived at the cell by feeling more than logic. "Answers."

David didn't respond and his dark gaze didn't shift.

"Do you need anything?" Helix asked. "Food? Water?"

"Your people have tended to me. Even if their idea of caring for a sick stranger they forced across the universe is keeping me prisoner."

"The sickness is contagious."

"So I'm told."

The weight in Helix's chest was just as heavy as when he left Casper's garden. This was the man that had berated his boyfriend for years. Broken his spirit and made him doubt himself. Helix felt his cheeks redden with heat.

"Why don't you love him?"

If David was caught off guard by the question, he didn't show it. His narrow eyes were locked on Helix. His breathing was steady.

"I do love my son."

"Dust off. You abused him for years. Kicked him out of your home. That is not love."

David sneered. "Watch your mouth."

Helix nearly rose to the bait. Hate calling to hate. It would feel good to lay into David. It would feel good to release the frustration and pain that he carried with him every day since the disaster of the ascension festival on a deserving target.

"Do you have any idea how much you've hurt him?"

David's cheek flinched and he finally lowered his gaze.

"Casper is good. He is funny and smart. He is considerate and kind. He cares about everything so deeply. I've never met anyone who puts as much thought into his actions and words. And..." Helix coughed to clear the cry that filled his throat. "It fills my heart with rage to know that his consideration is born from trying to appease you."

David snarled, showing too many teeth.

"I will heal him of you. Until there is no shadow left to make him flinch. Until your memory is nothing to him. As insignificant as a scraped knee. His life will be full of love."

David's hands gripped the blanket beneath him, knuckles going white. "And his soul will be damned."

The unguarded disgust on David's face was unsettling. Helix had not encountered a hate that cheerfully worn. It carried the pride of a battle cry, but he was speaking of his son. What kind of evil had wrapped around this man's heart to make him hate his own flesh and blood?

Now Helix was the one snarling. "We're going to figure out how to rid you of the corruption. And then you're going back to Earth. But not before you apologize to Casper."

David scoffed.

"You'll do it from under my sandal, if necessary," Helix said. "But you will apologize."

David burst from the bench, rushing the bars of his cell. "You will regret speaking to me this way." His eyes glowed. The sickly yellow hue was more prominent than it was a couple days ago on Earth. He was progressing.

Helix faced him down, hiding none of the fury that spun in his chest. "I'm not afraid of you."

David's eyes flared brightly. "You should be."

"Careful, David. There are worse places than this cell."

His eyes grew wide. Then he pounded his open hands against the bars. Helix quit the hall to the sound of David screaming obscenities after him, unsure of what he had accomplished but feeling better for it, nonetheless.

CHAPTER

ELEVEN

Casper couldn't move from the couch. He cried himself to sleep, falling into fitful dreams, until he noticed his arms were chained. The pain around his wrists was familiar.

It was half dream and half waking. He was once again inside the dark cloak of the tower. Every part of his body ached. The exhaustion was overwhelming. There was nothing but time and too much of it. A singular thought circled over and over in his mind.

Let this end.

Jacob would be back soon. It wasn't clear what he did when he was gone, and as mouthy as he was, he didn't bother to divulge. His ravings were disconnected and typically exercises in building his pride. His self-regard was comically overblown. It was best to act too tired to respond to his talking, else he might be prompted to deep anger. The acting wasn't hard. Sleep was nearly always a blink away.

But never rest.

A feeling that Casper recognized deeply, even if it wasn't

his own. His mind turned on the thought. What made it not his own?

"Who?" His voice was throaty and dry. It pained him to try speaking.

He shifted, turning his head to observe the room. Looking for the source of what felt like someone's presence. There was nothing to find except the workings of a makeshift lab. The altar where Jacob funneled aether through his body was too near.

Images filled his mind. It had happened to him only once. The Turning. And yet, nearly a dozen memories presented themselves of Jacob strapping him to the stone. The whirring of the machine was so present in his mind it felt like he was physically hearing it.

"Who?" It was a cry. "...are...you?" His throat scratched painfully at the words.

Braids swung as he turned his head to search the room again. They pattered against his chest. Longer hair than he'd ever had. He lowered his eyes. The finely twisted plaits of hair were unspooling from too much time spent neglected. But even so, the color of the braids in the dim lighting spurred his mind.

He could feel himself tipping toward a waking state. That liminal space where a dream became known, and it felt like the dream was created by thought as much as it was involuntary. He grabbed on to the memory of those braids. The gentle flash of firelight against warm brown skin. Square shoulders and a confident smile.

Agnes. He was right. Jacob had Agnes.

"Casper?"

He said his name, but it was her voice that spoke. Because he was not himself here. This was not his body. Not his pain.

Agnes? He formed words with his mind and felt his body flinch.

How are you here? Her response was frantic.

I don't know. Are you ok?

Casper, please. Help me. I cannot get free of him.

I'll tell the council that Jacob has you prisoner. We'll come get you.

Not the council. You. He's too powerful. It has to be you.

What is he doing to you?

His heart was pounding. Quick breaths dragged through his dry throat. Footsteps clicked against the stone. There was no time. He was coming back.

Kill me if necessary. But take me away from him. He grows stronger every time. I cannot bear it. The pain is too much.

He could feel the disturbance in the air as Jacob entered the room.

Hold on, Agnes. I'm coming.

A fist grabbed his arm, yanking him, and Casper shot up on the couch. His chest heaved with quick breaths. He was sweating. Morning light poured in from the window. He was in his home. At least his body was. Back on the Surface, his heart was still in the clutches of Jacob's rough hands.

Casper couldn't manage a jump to the Surface alone. Going to the council was likely a bad idea. They would dismiss him or worse, go to the Surface without him. Which meant he would have to face Helix. His heart crumpled. He was so ashamed about how he shut down in the garden. What Helix said made him feel weak and pathetic. Even worse was that it made sense. Casper knew he was a mess. It hurt so badly that Helix thought so, too.

By the time he got ready and was about to leave, there was a knock on the door. Nerves already rattled, he jumped at the noise. He opened the door to find Helix. His hair was pulled back in braids along his temples. He had been to see his family then. His mother often braided his hair while they talked. Casper's heart thumped in his chest when they made eye contact.

"Hi," Helix said.

"I was about to come find you."

"Leaving last night was really hard. I'm sorry I upset you."

Casper studied the stone at Helix's feet, following the silver veining down the path outside his front door. "Thanks. Can we maybe not talk about it? I don't think I'm ready."

"Ok..."

Casper didn't look up, but he sounded disappointed.

"Why were you going to look for me then?"

"I had another vision." Casper guided Helix into the living room and explained what he saw and about his conversation with Agnes. "We have to save her. Jacob is using her to get stronger."

"I agree, but we'll have to see what the council will do."

Casper sighed. "They won't help us. And she said it has to be me. He's too powerful."

Helix rubbed his forehead. "We can't go to the Surface alone, Casper."

"So, we go with your crew."

"Let's assume my crew agrees. Then what? We defeat more powerful Jacob alone?"

"We find a way to get Agnes away from him."

"While we can't use aether because it will make us all sick?"

"She is a telos. Just like me. If I were down there. If Jacob had me chained to that stupid fucking machine, you would come for me."

"Of course I would. But this is different—"

"It isn't. He's hurting her. And whatever he's planning, he's using her to accomplish it. We can't leave her there any longer. I won't."

Helix studied him. He took a deep breath. "Ok. We'll ask the crew."

At the Academy with Helix's crew, Casper made his case for going to the Surface. They all looked at him with some variance of incredulity. The only one giving his suggestion real consideration was Faus.

"She's in the tower," Casper said. "It was the same lab he took me to before the Turning."

"It does make sense," Gloria said. "The Farseers would be able to find him if he was anywhere else. The tower is the only place they can't see into."

"How many visions have you had?" Malia asked.

Casper fought the urge to fold in on himself. Asking for help felt so deeply vulnerable. "Two."

"It's been quiet for months," Belen said. "What if he's dead?"

"Don't the visions mean he's alive?" Peter asked.

"He gets those panic flashes all the time." Belen gestured at Casper.

Casper's chest caved in. Of the crew, Belen was still the coldest toward him. But talking about his panic attacks like he wasn't in the room was low, even for him.

"It wasn't a panic attack." Casper stared directly at Belen until he met his gaze.

"What does going down achieve?" Gloria asked. "If the whole tower is shrouded with corrupted aether like you say, and the Aquarius can't even see inside... won't we get sick by exposing ourselves to the corrupted aether?"

"What if we outnumber him?" Peter was fidgeting with a padded weight that was designed to be strapped onto an ankle for training. It flipped in the air in clean rotations before landing back in his hands. "Go in with an army of acolytes. Force him out of the tower. Boom. Problem solved."

Helix shook his head. "The winter solstice festival starts tonight. The council won't spare any acolytes. And even ignoring that, the council won't antagonize Jacob. I know." He shrugged at their frustrated grunts. "Whatever Jacob is up to, they want him to make the first move."

"Which is ridiculous," Casper said. "He nearly destroyed the entire city. His first move could kill all of us."

"Or he could be rotting inside that tower," Belen said. "Jacob has to be full of corrupted aether, right? Normal aether doesn't do the things he was doing. *If* he isn't dead yet, he's on his way out."

"We don't know that the corruption sickness causes death," Helix said.

"There's only one way to find out what's going on down there," Faus said.

"No," Belen said. "I'm not going to risk my life because the star kid has a hunch."

"Belen," Helix said. "Stop being a dick. Let's put it to a vote. Those in favor of going to the tower, raise your hand."

Casper raised his hand. Helix, Faus, and Peter also raised theirs. Belen's arms were crossed.

Then Peter dropped his hand. "Sorry. I thought about it and realized I don't want to go back to the Surface."

Malia and Gloria were turned toward each other. If they split their votes, it would be a tie.

"I don't want to be the deciding factor," Gloria said.

"Then vote with me," Malia said.

Gloria nodded, and both of their hands raised.

"Ok," Helix said. "Quick reconnaissance. That's all that is happening today. We go down, check out the tower. See if we can get a read on what Jacob is doing in there. Then we get back in time for the festival. Understood?"

The crew nodded, and Belen groaned before agreeing. But it wasn't enough just to know what Jacob was up to. He needed to be stopped. How many more people would be hurt if he was allowed to continue? Helix was staring Casper down, waiting for his acknowledgment. His eyes narrowed when he noticed Casper bristle.

"We can't risk the entire crew's lives. It's in and out or we don't go," Helix said.

Casper stopped himself from objecting. It felt gross to be on opposing sides with Helix, but he had to go to the Surface. He couldn't leave Agnes suffering. He couldn't bear waiting for Jacob to bring the fight to him. Every moment felt so dangerous. A step closer to catastrophe. If it took bending his trust with Helix to get ahead of Jacob for once, so be it.

Casper nodded. "Ok."

"The tower is near the valley on the southern cliffs," Helix said. "We're familiar with the area. I think we should jump to the valley and work our way up."

"Why not jump to the cliffs?" Faus said. "The clearing is massive."

"And the valley is hunting grounds for aetoth," Belen said.

"What's an aetoth?" Casper asked.

"Very large bird," Gloria said. "Mean and territorial. Scare the dust out of me."

"The corrupted aether is shrouding the tower," Helix said. "It's messing with the Aquarius sight. I don't trust that we won't accidentally jump into something we aren't prepared for."

"Faus is right," Casper said. "I saw how massive the clearing is, and I can sense the tower. We can go straight there."

"And what if we need to emergency jump on arrival?" Helix said. "We will take in the corrupted aether and cross our fingers we don't get sick?"

"Then we figure it out," Casper said. "Why jump into unknown danger when we have better chances facing the problem we're aware of? Jacob's not going to be waiting outside the tower for us. The clearing is safer."

"Star kid has a point," Belen said.

"Stop calling me that."

"Fine." Helix looked away from Casper toward Belen and Faus. "We will jump into the clearing. Get your gear and packs. We leave now."

Casper followed Helix as the crew walked toward the gear stash.

"What's wrong?" Casper asked.

"Nothing." His voice was clipped, which didn't lend an air of honesty to his answer. When he looked and Casper was still waiting for a real answer, Helix sighed. "I'm the captain of this crew. It's my job to keep everyone safe. I've run over a hundred missions to the Surface. Why are you questioning me about this?"

Casper felt the heat from his face reddening. He wasn't questioning Helix. He just happened to have his own opinions. How inconvenient of him. He wanted to storm off. He wanted to let his tongue loose. But Peter approached and handed a pack to Helix, making Casper realize this wasn't the time to hash out an argument.

"I'm not," Casper said.

"Ok," Helix said.

"Ok," Casper replied.

"Trouble in paradise?" Peter asked.

"Shut up, Peter," they both replied.

TWELVE

The tower loomed before them, menacing and dark. The black marbled facade was wet from a recent rain. It glistened in the low sunlight.

"If I die first," Belen said, "I don't want any of you at my funeral crying."

"So dramatic," Peter said, laughing.

"You didn't have to come," Helix said. "Hang back if you're scared."

Belen bristled but didn't reply.

"It feels…" Gloria was staring at the tower. "Bad. Why do the shadows cling to it like that?"

"You can see the shadows?" Casper asked.

Gloria's mouth twisted in a half smile and one eyebrow cocked up. "Yeah. You're seeing this too, right?"

Malia nodded back her response.

This was the first time someone else had seen the dark aether. What could that mean?

Faus took a few steps forward. "It gets worse as you get closer."

Casper felt it, too. Similar to using Pisces aether, there was a vibe in the air. An ache that pushed into his chest. Like the tower was warning them to stay away. He forged ahead. It was his idea to come and standing around in the tower's ominous aura wasn't going to help.

"What is he doing?" Belen asked.

"We have to see if we can at least get inside," Casper called over his shoulder.

"I'll go with him," Helix said. "Wait here."

He heard footsteps nearing and then Helix was at his side. Casper fiddled with his astrolabe, manually adjusting to his Libra trine. He didn't plan on pocket stepping with this much corrupted aether around, but it was best to be prepared.

Helix handed Casper a sheathed weapon. The handle was form fitted, molding to his palm comfortably. The protective covering was dark gray and tightly woven. Casper tested the blade, removing the sheath halfway to expose a bright orange blade with a mirror finish. "What's this?"

"An aetherized copper blade. Since we can't use aether."

"I've never trained with weapons," Casper said.

"It's better than going in unarmed. Point the sharp side away from you and make sure we keep our distance from each other if we draw them. They are very sharp."

They reached the entryway to the tower. The building was on a slight lean, so the doors tilted up toward the sky. Helix paused, staring at the stone. His forehead was creased the same way it did when Casper told him a joke he didn't understand.

Casper hovered his hand over the tower wall. It was his idea to come, might as well be him who figured out if the scary tower was dangerous. He laid his hand on the stone and the aura of dread closed in around him. It took active effort to stop his arm from reflexively pulling away. But it was ok. The astrolabe's barrier held firm, keeping the aether outside of him. The stone was warm to the touch, as if it had baked in the sun all day.

"It's fine," Casper said.

"You have got to stop touching things."

"Someone had to." Casper shrugged. He set his weapon on the ground and jumped to reach the handle of the door. It wouldn't budge. Casper's hand slipped from it when it didn't release, and he landed back on the ground.

"Locked."

"If you're going to suggest we climb to bust open a window, the answer is no."

"We're already here."

"Casper, we can't use aether and that window is nearly three stories up. What's going on with you today? You have a reckless energy about you."

"So, what? We leave? We've discovered nothing."

"But we're alive." Helix looked up at the tower, his nose crinkling as his mouth twisted to the side. "Maybe this wasn't the right call."

Jacob was right there. If they went back to Novilem, it was only a matter of time before he attacked again. Casper couldn't stomach pretending they weren't biding time until that happened. He bent over and grabbed his weapon.

Helix's eyes went wide. "Cas… Whatever you're thinking about doing. Just talk to me first."

"I can't go back without trying to help her."

"The whole crew is risking their lives to be here. We have to work as a team."

Casper could see the crew watching them. They hadn't seen how far-gone Jacob was. How horribly he was treating

Agnes. He leaned in and kissed Helix. They would all be angry, but it was the right thing to do.

"I'm sorry."

Helix was panicked. His eyes were glazed. "Please don't."

Before he could lose his nerve, Casper jumped through the wall. The hurt on Helix's face lingered in his vision for a moment before everything went dark. Casper fell a few feet, sliding on the slanted floor. It was pitch black aside from a few peaks of light beaming overhead from the upper landing. The feeling of something threatening sunk into his skin with more intensity. His arms and legs broke out in goosebumps.

The air was stale and smelled slightly damp. He rose to his feet and craned his neck, trying to get his eyes on the upper landing so he could make a safe pocket step.

Then he heard a sharp whistle. It pierced through the large receiving room. Casper felt him before he saw him. The presence of a predator. Sweat broke out under his arms. His breath shallowed. Every cell in his body begged to jump back outside the building. But this is what he came for. To see the beast. He wasn't going to hide.

"Has the boy savior come to finish what he started?" Jacob's voice echoed through the empty space.

Casper searched for him, his eyes straining against the dark. A quick gust of air swept his hair into his eyes. He spun and met the yellow glow of Jacob's eyes.

"What a pleasant surprise." Jacob pushed a hand against Casper's chest and a force flung him through the air.

He tasted metal when he slammed into the far wall. The force held him suspended, his feet dangling in the air. Jacob became visible in the darkness, lit by deep purple shadows that licked at the air around his figure.

"I thought I was going to have to come to you," he said.

"I'm not a patient person." Casper tried to pull his limbs free, but the force pinning him to the wall held strong.

Jacob chuckled. "No, you aren't, are you?" The pressure on Casper's chest crushed him into the stone, making it harder to breathe. "And so, you're here, and you're not going anywhere."

"What are you doing with Agnes?"

"Ah! A good question. You'll find out soon enough. But I am much more interested in how you can help me."

Jacob's smile turned Casper's stomach. He started to open his aether channels, but the slick, oily texture of corrupted aether immediately made him shut himself off.

"I won't help you."

"Having a hard time tolerating the dark?" Jacob asked. "Try to relax. It will only get worse."

Casper snarled. He grit his teeth, pulling for enough Libra aether to jump out of Jacob's hold. The energy that flooded his body was dense. Thick and heavy like mud to aether's air. His stomach convulsed and he reflexively emptied it.

Jacob threw his hands in the air. "No one listens to me."

Casper caught his breath. "Trying to destroy the city and murdering people will do that."

"Judge me all you want." Jacob rushed forward. "But you don't know what I know. You can't see what is right in front of our faces. The aether will not bend to our will forever."

"What does that mean?"

Before Jacob could answer, a stream of aether blasted through the wall. It seared into the other side of the room, then the beam of light sliced upward. The crew was cutting their way in. Casper readied himself to try pulling in aether again.

Jacob watched the beam of aether for a moment. He looked back to Casper with a snarl.

"This conversation isn't over," he said.

The world blinked and Casper was falling. Light punched against his eyes painfully. He coughed out a cry as he crashed onto the grassy ground.

"Casper!" Helix's cry came from the distance.

Casper climbed to his feet. His disoriented vision struggled to stay right side up. The crew had abandoned their attempt to get inside the tower, retreating toward him.

Helix reached him first. His eyes were wide, searching Casper for any sign of injury.

"I'm fine," Casper said. "I'm ok."

But he felt himself slide away as he said the words, a flash of white bursting behind his eyes as he slipped from consciousness.

Agnes appeared. This time Casper was looking at her instead of slipping inside her mind. Her head drooped forward, thick braids covering her face, but he recognized the square of her shoulders and the warm, reddish hue of her brown skin.

She was still chained next to the large stone table in Jacob's lab.

Helix crouched over him and cupped his face. "Casper?"

Casper looked at Helix, but he was seeing Agnes. Exhausted and sickly, she looked like the life had been sucked out of her. He recognized the shackles on her wrists. Aether locks. She was helpless.

More images came to him, flashing in his mind the same way memories of his father did. Violent flickers that made his whole body clench. Jacob chaining her to the slab. The horrible taste of a murky bowl of liquid. Jacob screaming in her face. The never-ending hours of darkness when he was gone.

He recalled that during the turning, Jacob had stated he took Agnes's aether. Then the Estellar claimed she had died on the Surface, and to Casper's horror, he had believed them. She had not died. It was worse than her death. She was alive the whole time, being used as Jacob's power source.

"What's going on?" Helix tapped his cheek.

Casper tried to answer, but a presence grabbed hold of his mind and pulled him away. His body went limp as his awareness was enveloped by piercing white light.

The bright presence welcomed him. Not with words, or even thought, but with knowing. There was warmth and safety and gratitude in the light.

"Hello?" Casper did not have a mouth to speak with, but he knew how to communicate with only his mind.

"It is good you are here." The light spoke without a voice. Language came to Casper's mind on a cosmic wind. Thoughts wove together and filled his mind as if they were aether. Energy, not sound.

"But you are not yet ready."

Casper couldn't see anything through the light, but it felt like he was moving.

"What are you?" Casper asked.

"The source. One half of the whole. Sedrivani."

The light dimmed enough so that Casper saw the tower from an eagle eye view. Perched below the cloud cover, the tower looked like a branch shoved into the ground. Roiling waves of inky black smoke surrounded the structure.

"One half? What's the other half?" Casper asked.

"You are not ready because you do not know."

Casper had no corporeal form to flail with, but he cringed as the planet's surface raced toward him. They zipped over to the cliff's edge. In the periphery, he could make out where Helix was cradling his body, but his gaze was forced toward the tower. It was filthy with corrupted aether. He could feel the weight of it even though he wasn't in his body. It was tangible, like a veil was laid over the tower. They stopped before crossing the threshold, but Casper could feel the draw of the darkness. The corrupted aether called to him, and he was surprised to find that he wanted to answer.

"What is Jacob doing?" Casper asked.

"Balancing the scales," the voice said.

"He tried to kill everyone in Novilem."

"His mind rests with the Kanos."

"I don't know what that means."

The presence forcibly placed Casper's attention on the tower.

"One aether."

"But that is corrupted aether. Something is wrong with it."

Casper couldn't ignore the feeling of being seen by the tower. The corrupted aether was as aware of him as he was of it.

"Aether is. Like earth or sky. There can be no wrong. And there will be balance."

"What are we doing wrong? I don't understand what is out of balance."

"You are lost. Cut in half. You must mend the severing."

"Great. Cool. How?"

The vision blurred. The tower faded into white, and Casper could feel himself waking.

"Wait! I don't know what to do!"

He came to with a startled breath. Helix's hand rested on his cheek. He kept his eyes closed, not willing to face a world that needed fixing. How was he supposed to tell the crew that a disembodied voice told him to "mend the severing?" Belen already thought he was losing his mind.

"Casper?"

Helix must have noticed his breathing shift. Reluctantly, Casper rejoined reality.

THIRTEEN

Helix caught Casper as he lost consciousness. His eyes rolled back before falling closed and his body went limp.

"Gloria!" Helix shouted.

She came to his side, placing a hand on Casper's neck. "His pulse is strong. What happened?"

"I think he's having another vision. His eyes went unfocused and then he passed out."

She placed a hand on Helix's shoulder. "I'm right here with you. He's come out of these before."

Helix didn't realize the panicked pace of his breathing until Gloria started guiding him through slow, methodical breaths.

He was still holding Casper in his arms when he came to.

"Casper? Are you ok?" Helix asked. The relief he felt at Casper coming back to him was overwhelming. Helix had to stop himself from keeping him in his arms as Casper pushed to sit up.

"Agnes is inside the tower," Casper said.

The rest of the crew were gathering around to listen.

"What's he doing with her?" Faus asked.

"The table." Casper's gaze was haunted when he met Helix's eyes. "He's been funneling aether through her."

"What happened when you were inside?" Malia asked.

"I saw him. He's… more powerful than before. I couldn't fight back because the aether was overwhelming. It made me feel sick when I tried to open my channels."

"Did he say anything?" Belen asked.

"He was just taunting me. When you cut through the wall, he tossed me out here."

Helix was listening, but his eyes were locked on the tower. Sunken into shadow the way it was, it almost looked like the structure had ripped through another dimension. The sunlight beaming on the plane around them seemed not to touch it, the shadows masking the stone from the light.

If Agnes was being used to feed Jacob aether, it was only a matter of time before he made another catastrophic move. He nearly teleported all of Novilem to the Surface when he had Casper in his clutches.

"We have to get Agnes out of there," Helix said.

Belen cursed in Greek. An old, filthy phrase that Helix hadn't heard in many years.

"Why are we always running toward danger?" Belen asked.

"I agree with Helix," Malia said. "Strapping Casper to that table is how the tower ended up here in the first place."

"He's had her in there for weeks," Faus said. "Wouldn't he have already done whatever he can do?"

"She's a person," Gloria said. "We have to try."

"He's torturing her," Casper said. "Has her chained. I've been inside her head. She's weak. Barely fed. Always thirsty."

"Sure, getting her out is the right thing to do," Peter said.

"But how? You said you couldn't use aether inside. We can all feel the corrupted aether from here. If we go in there, we're all coming out with corruption sickness. If we come out at all."

Helix addressed Casper. "Can you find out exactly where she is?"

"She's in his rooms. I saw the apparatus next to her."

"That was the seventy-third floor?" Helix asked Malia. They had traveled up the tower to rescue Casper during the Turning. She nodded.

Helix started counting floors.

"Let's destroy the tower and be done with it," Belen said.

The group balked at him.

"We've seen what Casper can do," he continued. "Jacob is clearly lost to the sickness. He's a danger to Novilem."

"But Agnes is in there," Gloria said.

Belen shrugged. "It's her or Novilem."

"We are not destroying the tower." Helix pinned him with a heavy gaze. "End of discussion."

"I'm not going inside," Belen said.

"Then I suggest you find someplace safe nearby to keep watch," Helix said.

Belen's eyes darkened as his brow sunk low, but he didn't challenge Helix further. He spun to the open field and scanned the horizon for high ground. When he stalked off toward the distance, the rest of the group visibly relaxed.

"He's been testy lately," Faus said.

"I don't know," Casper said. "He's always seemed like that to me."

Peter laughed. "That's because he doesn't like you."

Casper looked hurt.

"Don't stress about it," Malia said. "He doesn't really like anyone."

"What did I do to him?" Casper asked.

"You breathed," Gloria said, evoking a bark of laughter from Faus and Peter.

Helix's eyes locked on the seventy-third floor. It was dauntingly high. The facade of the tower was too smooth to climb manually. Malia or Casper could technically pocket step, but the possibility of a fall was too risky. If they couldn't access aether on the way down because of the corruption, they would never survive. And the issue of what to do once they were inside... Helix had no idea. Jacob's strange use of the corrupted aether left too many unanswered questions. Leaving Agnes was too dangerous, but every scenario he ran in his head was untenable, the risks too great to subject his crew to.

"I have to do it." Casper was staring at him. "It's the only chance we have of getting her out."

"That is absolutely not true," Helix said. "You said it yourself. You were incapacitated inside. If he gets his hands on you, that's two telos. Then we're in even worse shape."

"He threw me out," Casper said. "He doesn't need me."

"That doesn't mean he'll do it again," Gloria said. "We were blasting our way in. He used you as a distraction."

"So, let's blast our way in again," Malia said. "Blow a hole in the wall of the seventy-third floor and I'll pocket step in. I can grab Agnes and get out before Jacob can react."

"You might not be able to use your aether inside," Casper said. "I threw up when I tried."

"What other choice do we have?" Malia asked.

"I'll go with you," Helix said. "Just in case." Being a Capricorn, he was hardier against corruption sickness. He hoped that meant he could better resist the effects of being around the corrupted aether, too. "Casper, are you good to open up the way? If not, I can get Belen back over here."

Casper shook his head. "I'll do it. I'm going to check inside with Aquarius aether to make sure she's out of the way."

His eyes focused on the tower, then he went very still. "He's got her on the table. He's got that machine turned on." Casper lifted both hands and the air pulsed as energy started to build in his palms. "We might be too late."

"For what?" Faus asked.

That machine let Jacob funnel aether into Casper's body and steal it somehow. If he was doing the same with Agnes, he was about to use a massive amount of aether.

"We should go back to Novilem," Helix said.

A massive beam of energy shot out of Casper's hands. "We can't let him keep her."

The shadows hanging on the tower rippled against Casper's Sagittarius aether like there was a barrier protecting the tower. When Casper let off his attack, the tower was unscathed.

Helix whistled three times in quick succession. The signal for Belen to return. "Round up," he said to the group.

"We have to keep trying," Casper said.

"We don't know what he's about to do," Helix said. "And we can't get to him fast enough to stop him."

"He could kill her," Casper said.

"He might kill all of us." Helix grabbed his hand. "We've risked enough."

Belen came back to the group in a sprint. The crew was joining hands. Casper looked back at the tower.

"I don't want to pull rank on you," Helix said.

Casper looked back at him, hurt. Helix recognized the feeling because it was how he felt when Casper chose to jump inside the tower, alone. Casper's nostrils flared and the plane of his brow creased. When he opened his mouth to respond, the ground shook. Everyone crouched, covering their heads. Helix turned to the tower. The shadows swirled violently until the entire structure was a blur. He blinked and the tower was gone.

"Dust me," he said.

FOURTEEN

The winter festival was in full swing. Feast and fest abounded. To symbolize the heart of the winter solstice, the Split was lowered, and the city was lit by baubles strung across every roof and balcony. It was Talleah's favorite tradition. A night amongst the stars. And yet, as they walked the streets under the soft yellow glow of thousands of lights, she could not shake her discomfort.

She was doing her best to fake a cheery attitude. The baubles of light strung overhead and the smell of baked treats in the air were so dissonant from her inner world. Daphne was occupied listing off all the things she wanted to do, swinging both her and Hector's hands gently as she chatted away. The winter solstice was a time for reflection and gratitude. And shockingly, even with her daughter finally returned, Talleah was feeling unable to access anything like true gratitude.

The crowds stirred up something restless in her chest. Her patience was nearly gone. She had snapped at Hector to hurry up while he was helping Daphne pick out a dress. This quickness to anger was new, and she was beginning to worry it wasn't only emotional fallout from her mother being sick. Did Daphne coming home break something? It had hurt for so long. Why couldn't she simply enjoy having her back?

She pondered this, hanging back while Hector attended to Daphne as she rode a mechanical wheel that lifted people in carts to get a view of the city.

Daphne ran back to her. "That was so cool!" she said. "Do you wanna try it, Mom?"

Talleah smiled. "Let's walk around for a while. Then we'll find another one for you to go on."

Daphne reached out for her hand, and Talleah reached out to rub her back instead. Her head wasn't clear, and she knew that look in Daphne's eyes. She was going to read her to find out what was wrong.

Hector brushed a soft hand against her shoulder. "Do you need anything?"

Yes. Even if she didn't know what. She shook her head. "Tonight is for Daphne."

Just ahead, people gathered in front of a shop, their eager faces lit by the bright light pouring from its open doors. Six acolytes were posted on the street watching the flow of traffic. That seemed unnecessary, but the Estellar had been overly cautious since the Turning. With the Enotis disbanded, the chance of anything happening was low. She was of two minds. She was comforted that it was a little safer to have Daphne out amongst the crowds because of the acolytes' presence. But she also bristled at the idea that their people needed to be policed. The very presence of a watch heightened her sense that something bad might happen.

Talleah hung back with Hector by the door as Daphne ran inside. It was a toy shop. Colorfully decorated and filled to the brim with puzzles, trinkets, and figurines both soft and posable.

"Where's your head at?" Hector asked.

Talleah wrapped her arm around his, leaning her head against his shoulder. "Everywhere."

"You deserve to have fun, too."

She kissed the rounded muscle of his arm. "I know. I'm trying."

Daphne came running back swinging a stuffed doll with every step. "Mommy look! She looks like me."

The doll had curls of brown yarn falling halfway to its feet. Its skin was sandy brown, and it was dressed in a simple robe.

"So pretty!" Talleah said.

"I'm going to name her Giggles. Because she likes to laugh."

Hector swooped Daphne into the air, then tickled her. "That sounds like someone I know."

Daphne pealed with laughter. "Stoooooop!"

Talleah's smile managed to reach her heart. "It's about time to find Casper and Helix." They had plans to meet up before dinner. Talleah hadn't heard from either of them that day, which was strange. But it was worth making their way to their designated meeting spot anyway. "Let's head to the park."

By the time they reached the location, the immobile crowds blocking paths and slow shuffling bodies had eroded any patience Talleah had left. She was brimming with so much frustration she knew she wouldn't last the whole night. Which broke her heart. Daphne had been looking forward to the festival for weeks. So had Talleah, even if she suspected it was going to be difficult.

She was considering going home by the time they

reached the planned meeting spot. The last thing she wanted to do was pick a fight with a stranger in front of Daphne, and every bump and cut off was pushing her closer to that being an inevitability.

They found an open spot in the grassy field of the park. By the time they laid down a blanket and were settling in, a large group of teenagers parked themselves immediately to their left. Talleah's nerves were shot.

"You hanging in there?" Hector asked.

Talleah shook her head.

"What's wrong, Mommy?"

"I'm a little sad that Yiayia is alone tonight." She looked to Hector. "I think maybe I want to go spend some time with her."

Hector's eyes widened for a moment, but he recovered quickly. "You sure?"

"The crowds..." Talleah closed her eyes, taking a deep breath as the sound of laughter from the group next to them drowned her voice out. "I think I have to."

"Alright," Hector said. "I've got her. Go take care of yourself. We'll be home in a couple hours."

"I don't want you to go," Daphne said.

"I'm sorry. I'm just a little overwhelmed. You'll have so much fun with Daddy and your uncles. I'll see you soon, ok?"

She stood before Daphne could convince her to stay. "I love both of you so much." Hector blew her a kiss, and she hurried off, wiping a tear from the corner of her eye. She was annoyed that she couldn't shake the hot fury that was rattling in her chest. Which then made her angry with herself.

She placed a hand on her mother's arm, thumbing the gold bracelet she had worn since Talleah was a child. Her skin was cool and patched with mottled gray rashes. The unblemished sections were covered in webs of dark blue veins that were too visible under her almost translucent skin. She wiped sweat from her mother's brow with a cloth and wondered if today would be the day.

A full cycle of care with the Virgos and there was no improvement. There were no records of corruption sickness that progressed so far. Every breath seemed harder to take than the last.

She was holding her mother's hand, mulling over how stupid it was that she couldn't manage the discomfort of a crowd long enough to enjoy the evening with her family, when the ground shook. Half a moment later there was a shattering sound. Shards of stone fell from the ceiling in a sheet, pebbles piling in the room's corner. Then a wave of something passed through her. It wasn't air, and it wasn't aether. It was something hollow. Hungry.

Her mother choked, then gasped, alternating between coughs and sputtering breaths. Talleah left the room to find a healer, the ground still rumbling under her feet. Someone cried out from the entrance of the building. Talleah followed the line of bodies running in that direction.

She pushed her way outside and almost cried out herself at what she saw. Shrouded in a cloud of dust, filling what used to be empty space on the horizon, was the missing western tower. Suddenly, the wall of the clinic exploded beside her. Crashing through the rubble, a humanoid creature with leathery gray skin leaped into the air and unfurled giant wings of webbed skin, taking up a terrifying amount of space. It raised long legs up toward its center and flared a set of glossy black talons. A woman dropped to the ground, dodging the creature's grasp. It opened its mouth too wide and released an ear-splitting scream.

Talleah covered her ears with her hands as she dropped to her knees, staring in horror at the creature. Its profile was gaunt and skeletal. A handful of long strands of hair clung to parts of its skull. Its eyes were clouded and dull. Thick spit dribbled off its long tongue as it turned its head toward the towers in the distance.

As it took off, Talleah noticed the shine of a gold bracelet on its arm. Glittering pieces of Novilem's dark marble fell from the creature's back as it gained elevation. A terrible suspicion shuttered through her as she watched the creature fly off into the distance.

"Mom?"

FIFTEEN

Casper was almost used to the feeling of the world coming back to him in pieces. Almost. There was screaming, which felt too familiar. He was heaving in labored breaths between all the motion. Was he being carried? Little bits of his vision returned spun as his body was flipped over and laid on the ground. Hands cupped his cheeks. Through his spinning vision he caught pieces of Helix.

"Thank the stars. You're ok."

They survived the jump back from the Surface, but Casper clearly wasn't at full capacity after his vision. It hurt like he had taken a blow to the head.

"We have to keep moving!"

The voice sounded like Malia, but anything beyond Helix's face was too blurry to consider. Casper thought he might need to throw up. Helix grabbed Casper's astrolabe and held it in front of his face.

"There's no time. I need you to move into your Capricorn trine and get on your feet. We have to go."

Something screeched in the distance. Casper's skin broke

out in goosebumps at the sound. Whatever made that noise was angry, and too close for comfort. Casper took hold of the astrolabe and turned his attention inward. He thought of the warm, fuzzy presence in his chest that came with using Capricorn aether. His astrolabe twirled in his hands until the little rings snapped closed and energy burst inside his body. His limbs started working before his mind did, recovering quickly with the aether.

He rose to his feet and let Helix guide him into a jog. They were running away from the festival grounds. The screeching was coming from behind them. Actually, from both sides as well. Was it coming from the air?

"What is going on?" Casper asked.

"Not sure yet," Helix replied on a heavy breath.

"Are we running toward whatever is making that horrible noise, or away from it?"

"We're going to the Academy," Helix said. "It's our best chance of getting information."

Casper was knocked forward as something grabbed hold of his shoulders. Sharp talons curved around his collarbones and pinched into both sides of his chest. He cried out as he was lifted into the air.

"Casper!" Helix leaped, trying to grab onto his leg, but the distance was too great.

The pain of his weight bearing down on the talons was excruciating. He arched his head back and was horrified at what he found carrying him. Its skin was a muddled gray and leathery and it had massive bat-like wings that were flapping hard to accommodate the extra weight of his body.

Casper screamed and the wind swallowed the sound.

The creature released a high-pitched screech in response. They were high enough that falling would break enough of his bones to kill him. Straight ahead were the residential towers. The *four* residential towers. Jacob must have tele-ported it back into the city. But why?

Air pummeled Casper's head as the creature doubled its efforts, lifting them higher into the air. When they approached an opening in the side of the newly returned tower, Casper realized he wasn't ready to figure out why the tower was back. Dread, thick and heavy in the pit of his stomach, became overwhelming as he saw the dark clouds of aether pouring out of the room they were about to land in.

He struggled against the creature's hold, but the talons only dug deeper into his shoulders. He could feel a warm trickle of blood pouring down his torso. They dipped forward and the creature swung his body, releasing its grip. He heard the slick noise of talons sliding out of his chest just before he tumbled onto the floor, rolling four times before he came to a stop. He heaved in pained breaths, focusing as much as he could on the aether, letting the energy pour into his wounds. He pressed his forehead against the ground, the reflection of the aether's light as it healed his chest illuminating the stone floor.

"I said you weren't going anywhere."

Casper pushed off the ground and sat back into a kneel. Jacob was across the room, which was too close. The creature that flew him there was in a pulsing heap a few arm spans away, the mass of its wings hiding the bulk of its body. The edges of the room broiled with shadows. Casper could feel the corrupted aether like it was crawling on his skin. He searched the room, but there was no sign of anyone but Jacob.

"Where is Agnes?" Casper said, trying to sound braver than he felt. His heart was pounding in his chest. The aether was bringing strength back to his body, but he couldn't will the fear in his mind away. The holes in his shoulder needled with sharp pain as the aether worked on healing him. When Jacob didn't respond, Casper shouted, "Tell me!"

"Or what? You'll beat me up?"

The invisible weight of Jacob's power pummeled into Casper, knocking him over. He couldn't move his arms. He was glued to the floor.

"We've already done this," Casper said. "And I won."

Jacob shook with whispery, silent laughter. The lines of his face were sharper. The shadows under his eyes deeper. Using the aether machine had hollowed the life out of his features. A wave of shadows enveloped his body and then Casper's vision was clouded by black. He was pushed backward, sliding across the floor. When the darkness dissipated, Jacob was stepping on Casper's chest. The force knocked the wind out of him, and he curled under Jacob's hold, trying to pull air into his lungs.

"There's no winner until the battle is over." His eyes were fully aglow with yellow light, his pupils small pinpricks of black in the center.

Casper grabbed Jacob's ankle with both hands and struggled uselessly to push it away. Jacob pressed his heel down harder. Casper's bones ached, threatening to give way to the pressure. A stifled cry hung in his throat with no air to release it on.

"Don't worry," Jacob said as he eased off. He pulled his foot away and stared down at Casper, watching him choke as he finally pulled air back into his lungs. "I'm not done with you, yet."

Casper rolled onto his side, desperately seeking relief from the burning of his labored breaths. The edge of his vision was white. Jacob grabbed the back of his robe and lifted him onto his feet with one swift motion. How was he so strong? How did he aether in ways no one else could?

Jacob stepped directly in front of him. "I want your help."

Casper searched his face for any hint that he was joking. His expression was flat; his yellow eyes were wide. He seemed sincere.

"Why would I help you?"

"Because what we want is not so different."

"You tried to destroy Novilem." Casper gestured at the monster in the corner of the room. "And now you have a monster minion? I know you're delusional, but you do know you're the bad guy, right?"

Jacob smiled, his eyes sparkling as he laughed. "I could see you before. Back on Ouranos. When you were with the Sedrivani."

Images of the tower encompassed in black aether filled Casper's mind. The vision he had after Jacob threw him out of the tower.

"I could feel you," he said sharply. Jacob's eyes closed like he was trying to calm himself down. "You know now that the aether is out of balance."

That is what the voice said to Casper in the vision. It was unsettling to hear the same words from Jacob. Like he really was interested in balancing out the aether. What game was he playing? Where was the trap?

Jacob opened his eyes and watched the creature in the corner as its heaving breaths slowed, and its wings pulled back. "I thought I could do it on my own. The council wouldn't listen. Novilem has maintained the mirage of balance with the help of the Farseers for two thousand years. But it's slipping away, and the council wouldn't take my concerns seriously." He paused for a second before barking, "Brissa wouldn't take me seriously. But with you..."

His yellow eyes locked on Casper, making his stomach twirl with fear.

"I thought I had a chance to take things into my own hands. I thought if I could balance myself out, then maybe..."

A deep discomfort filled Casper seeing Jacob display what looked like real vulnerability. He wanted to punch his lights out, not feel bad for him.

"You killed dozens of people," Casper said.

Jacob's head tilted to the side. "Better than all of us dying."

Casper scoffed. "God, you just don't care, do you?"

"I do care!" Jacob's voice ripped through the room, rattling Casper's chest with its force. He stepped forward, poking a finger into Casper's shoulder, still tender from healing. "You have no idea what is happening. How close we are to losing everything."

Casper pushed Jacob's hand away.

"We've kept the aether separate for too long. It will correct itself back to the natural order. If we don't find a way to control that process, it will take us all with it."

"We?" Casper laughed. "You really think we're going to work together after what you've done?"

"What I've done is try to save my people. What have you done? Accepted their praise? Been a good little boy? You've done nothing but pretend to be their savior."

Casper's eyes fell to the ground, uncomfortable with how close to home that hit. He'd had nearly the same thought about his role in Novilem.

Jacob sighed, clenching both hands in tight fists. "I cannot use the Sedrivani." He gestured around the room. "I thought if I took in enough of the light I would balance out and I could show everyone else how to."

"You use the Kanos?" Casper asked. "That's how you do the things you do."

Jacob hummed an admission, nodding his head.

"Why would you do that?"

"Because no one would listen to me!"

Talk about hot and cold. Jacob's mood was giving Casper whiplash.

"About starting the Ouranos colony?" Casper asked.

"Those fools insist on letting our entire culture die inside this rock."

"How do you know that's going to happen?"

"The Kanos," Jacob said. "It speaks to me."

If Casper hadn't had his own visions, he might have been skeptical that a voice told him to teleport the population of Novilem down to a hostile planet. But Casper had heard a similar voice himself, and he was wildly disheartened to find there was a part of him that believed Jacob. Trust was a whole other issue, but he could find plausible belief that Jacob was telling his truth.

"I am not agreeing to help you," Casper said. "But what do you want me to do?"

A familiar grimace took over Jacob's face. "A child given the power that you have is ludicrous. It seems as the Telos, you alone can create balance through your will."

Casper sighed. "And I suppose you want me to let you teach me how?"

Jacob's brow furrowed. "What? No. I can't teach you how to do something I can't do. And believe me, I have tried. Nearly drained Agnes completely trying."

Casper's stomach leapt into his throat. "Where is she?"

"That doesn't matter," Jacob said. "What matters is that you go to the Farseers and learn from them. They know how to balance the aether."

"What did you do to her!?"

Jacob deflated a little. "The same thing I did to you. Absorbed her aether. Once the majority of the Exoria returned to Novilem, she didn't have enough friends to fight me."

There was no body. There was no scent of blood in the room. "Did you kill her?"

Jacob shrugged. "She isn't dead." He gestured at the creature in the corner. It was still heaving deep breaths. Its face was exposed. All Casper could see was its wide snout and its massive teeth.

Disgust filled Casper. He was so angry that he thought Jacob was still remotely human, even for a moment. He grabbed his astrolabe and moved through his trines. Jacob's eyes locked onto his pendant before flicking over to the creature. Casper latched onto his Libra aether and sucked in a deep breath.

"The balancing is inevitable," Jacob said. "It will happen whether you help or not."

A puff of breath came out of the creature's nose before it released a tiny cry. Casper readied himself, expecting the creature to lunge at him at any moment.

"Dust off," Casper said.

Jacob let his head fall to the side, frowning slightly. "Your choice."

That invisible force punched Casper, and he was thrown backward. His feet dragged against stone until they met open air, and then he was plummeting toward the ground. Casper flailed, trying to spin his body around mid-flight until he could see the ground. He focused on a patch of grass and pocket stepped. He crashed with a thud and groaned. Rolling over, he looked up at the tower. The hole he had been tossed out of was hundreds of feet high. He let his head fall back against the grass.

When will this end?

Talleah searched every room. There was no sign of her mother. Her room was splattered with shiny, red blood. The wall was shattered, chunks of stone and dust blown outward onto the path outside.

Talleah saw the golden bracelet on the creature's wrist in her mind. The mottled gray complexion of her mother's skin. Had her mother really done this?

She leaned against the wall, steadying herself with deep breaths. Anger simmered up to the surface, heating her skin. Her mind itched to bite into the emotion and slip into the ease of rage. It was happening more frequently, this desire to give in to the fury. It was bright and warm and numbing. And now Talleah worried it meant something was wrong.

She jogged through the open hole in the building. A handful of people were running toward the city center. She could see someone helping a poorly figure walk. This thing in her was showing up less and less like grief. It was taking a wild shape. Something with claws. Massive, flapping gray wings flashed across her mind and she leaned forward into a sprint.

It was a middle-aged man gently guiding an older woman. The noise of the city, shaken by the returning of the tower, was echoing down from the dome overhead. The man's eyes were wide with fear when he turned toward Talleah's approaching steps.

"Is it here?" he yelled to her.

"No," Talleah answered. She took in his maroon tunic. A Virgo, as she had hoped. The woman he was with turned to her slowly. Her sunken eyes and sallow skin were too familiar. It took effort to not shirk away from her. "I need you to check me for the sickness."

The man's wide face pinched as his eyes danced around her body. His arm was still supporting the lady. "I have to get her somewhere she can rest."

"I'll help you," Talleah said. "Please. If I'm sick—"

The older woman broke into a deep, shredded moan. The man hissed as her hand clenched his arm too tightly, nails breaking through his skin. Talleah helped pull him away from her grip and the old woman fell to her hands and knees. Her head curled upward as her moan turned into a scream. Then her body began to change.

"Cursed stars," the man said.

Tendrils of dark smoke seeped out of the woman and slithered across her body.

The man looked at Talleah in a panic. "What do we do?"

The mottling of the woman's skin smoothed to a sickly, gray pallor. Her muscles swelled, and with a gut-wrenching crack, her limbs grew in jutting spurts. The woman's robe ripped from her body as wings split away from her back. Strings of dark red blood splattered the buildings on either side of the street.

"How?" It was all Talleah could think. How was this happening?

The shuffling of the man's feet indicated that he was running away, back toward the clinic. The creature turned toward the noise. The features of the old woman's face were still changing. Her eyes looked clouded as her mouth stretched wide to make room for her growing teeth. A bright yellow shimmer filled her eyes as she locked onto the man, then she burst from the ground with incredible speed.

"Shit," Talleah said.

The man cried out a moment later, but Talleah was already running. A small, smaller than she'd like, part of her felt guilt for leaving him to the monster. But she couldn't risk not being able to overpower whatever that woman had turned into. She had just gotten Daphne back...

A wet thud shook the stone beside her while she was in a full sprint. She barely caught sight of the Virgo man's broken body as it collided with the ground. She covered her mouth, stifling a cry in her throat. Gusts of air blew against her as the creature soared overhead. She ducked to the side, pressing her body against the stone facade of a building, but the creature didn't swoop down on her. It was flying toward the tower in the distance.

Talleah rushed back to the man's side, but what little hope she had to help him was immediately squashed. His throat was torn away, and his torso was twisted too far. Dust was still drifting up from his form, sparkling in the air. Her stomach turned.

"May your journey to the stars be swift."

She removed her cloak and laid it over the man's face. It was not enough respect for a man kind enough to help a sickly old woman in a crisis, but it was all she could offer.

Talleah turned from the carnage and prayed to every star

in the sky that whatever happened to that woman was not inside her. And that her family was ok. She sprinted down the road thinking of Daphne. She had to get to Daphne.

SEVENTEEN

The cellblock was empty. Not just David's cell. The entire prison was empty. Casper's awareness floated down the length of the small cave behind the Celestery. In the wake of the chaos, he had thought to check on his father out of instinct. For a moment, he was tempted to say good riddance. To latch on to the relief of his father disappearing.

But he wasn't back on Earth. He wasn't gone. Somewhere in the city, his father was loose. A different kind of monster.

His palms were sweaty, and his heart was pumping at double speed. "He's gone."

Helix brushed Casper's elbow softly. "We should go to the Estellar."

Casper bristled at Helix wanting to go to the council. "I have to find him. I can't leave him out there alone."

"The council is our best chance of finding him. We can't search the whole city on foot."

"We can't run to the council every time something is wrong."

"I need to see Theo."

Casper let the silence hang. He didn't want to go, but he knew the weight of those words. Helix would be worried about his family. Of course he would. But this energy between them was growing sharper. It was frustrating and heartbreaking at the same time. They kept slipping further away.

"What else can we do?" Helix asked.

"I don't know. Find someone more skilled with Aquarius aether to help locate him."

Helix's lips twisted to the side.

"The Aquarius are in the Celestery, aren't they?" asked Casper.

"Come on, let's go," Helix said.

The Celestery loomed overhead. The white pyramid sat perched on the wall of Novilem, all the more bright sitting opposite the returned western tower, cloaked in shadow. Its wide, solid base gleamed, reflecting every bit of light pouring onto it. The opening in the center almost felt like it watched them as they approached. If Casper turned his head slightly, it was easy to picture it as an eye. He shivered, shaking off the feeling of being watched.

The front plaza was a swarm of moving bodies, acolytes rushing inside and pouring out through the gardens into the square below. Casper thought of his isolated days when he was first brought to Novilem. It was difficult to imagine it was the same building. The press of bodies trying to get inside reminded him of the CTA at rush hour.

"How many now?" a passing acolyte said.

"They're popping up all over the city." The conversation

moved with the crowd of people pushing toward the entry of the building.

"Are they talking about those creatures?" Casper hadn't found the right time to tell Helix the creatures were actually people.

Helix was focused on cutting a path through the crowd. "Maybe. We have to focus on one problem at a time."

The city was suddenly too small. The walls beyond the Celestery shifted to a cage, not a massive protective barrier. His shoulders were healed, but he ached where the creature's... Agnes's talons sunk deep into his muscles. How were they supposed to fight monsters? And what would happen when people realized they were their friends, their neighbors... their family?

Helix guided him to the second floor and down a corridor Casper had never been allowed to explore. The usual acolyte guard was not posted at the entry. They passed a few rooms standard to the Celestery's style: ornate curtains and stone furniture. There was a hurried conversation coming from ahead. Helix rushed toward the voices and pulled Casper into a large, crowded hall. Two women wearing the light green capes of an Aquarius looked at them, but they were largely ignored.

The hall was filled with huddles of people. Groups of two, three, sometimes four Aquarius gathered, their hands intertwined, and their eyes closed. The chatter was coming from the center of the room. A group was formed around Preitan Theo.

Helix rushed to him. "Pappous!"

Theo turned and wrapped his arms around Helix as they crushed into a hug.

"What's going on?" Helix asked as he pulled away.

"You shouldn't be here." Theo's face hardened slightly. "Go wait for me in my office."

"We're not going anywhere." Casper said. "My dad is missing."

Theo's expression darkened. "There are more pressing concerns currently."

"I told you this was a waste of time," Casper said to Helix.

"Preitan Theo." Helix stepped back, adjusting his posture to address the Elder preitan and not his grandfather. "Please give us a few moments. I promise we can help. Casper was inside the tower."

The group turned to Casper as one. He bristled a little toward Helix. They came here for help finding his father. Why was Helix offering him up to help the Estellar?

"We can't see into the tower," a man to Theo's left said. "The aether cannot penetrate the darkness."

Casper sighed. It was this or crossing his fingers and walking the streets to find his dad amongst thousands of acres of city.

"I talk and you assign one of these groups to help me locate my dad." Casper pointed at a huddled group of Aquarius.

Theo nodded.

"Jacob is back," he said. "And he has friends."

"Does he have control over the Tektranos?" Theo asked.

He had a name for the creatures? "I don't know if he controls them. But one of them brought me to him." It was Agnes—or whatever Agnes was now—that delivered him to the tower, but he didn't think the Estellar was going to be receptive to that information.

"What are they?" Helix asked.

"A myth," Theo said. "They should be a myth."

"This has gone too far," the Scorpio preitan declared. "We must evacuate."

"Evacuate?" Helix studied Theo's face. "You're considering abandoning Novilem?"

"We have lived here for two thousand years," Theo said to the council members gathered. "We cannot abandon our home without due cause."

"You heard the boy. Jacob has Tektranos."

"He won't keep to the tower. He's back for a reason."

"Pappous," Helix said. "Evacuation?"

Casper had seen the council in many forms of disarray, but he had never seen them look so collectively helpless. They were moments away from crumbling to an every-man-for-themselves parachute. And in spite of every better instinct in his body, Casper found himself thinking about his conversation with Jacob.

He thought of the supposed imbalance in the aether that he needed to seek help from the Farseers to fix. He knew practically nothing about the Farseers, but it was hard to imagine they would be less helpful than the council, who was already halfway to abandoning the city.

"Nothing is decided," Theo said to Helix. "Jacob has only just returned."

As the preitans chimed in, Casper didn't bother paying attention to who was speaking.

"And we have no way to protect ourselves."

"The astrolabes were not built to deal with this much dark aether. It's only a matter of time before we all get sick."

"We can advise the city to use aether sparingly. If they don't take in aether, they will remain unaffected."

"We don't know that for sure."

"Then we can use the aether locks. Since the Gemini were

freed, they aren't in use. Dark aether can't affect us if our channels are closed off."

"There are, what? A few thousand of those at most? It's not enough."

"And we'd be defenseless. There are Tektranos in the city."

The circular arguing would go on for hours. He had spent enough time being lectured by the council to know their pattern. Casper pulled Helix away from their bickering. "This is pointless. They are never going to care about my dad."

Helix was visibly struggling not to give his attention back to the council's argument. "What do you want to do?"

"Will you find him?"

Helix's gaze snapped from his peripheral view of Theo to focus on Casper. "That's what we're doing right now. Trying to figure out how to find him."

"Jacob said something in the tower." When Helix tilted his head Casper said, "I know. But I can't get it out of my head. He said that the aether is out of balance and that I need to go to the Farseers because they know why."

"Why would you do anything Jacob says?"

"Because it's the only thing that might be different than this." Casper gestured at the council. "Something is telling me I have to. The visions I've been having... it's the aether. Something is wrong and if the Farseers know about it, I have to go to them."

"What if they don't know anything? Jacob probably wants you out of the city because you're the only one strong enough to fight him."

"What else is there to do, Helix? Hide? Evacuate? How many people will get left behind? How many will die while we get carted off to safety?"

Helix puffed out a sigh, turning his gaze to the ceiling.

"Will you find my dad? I can't leave him stranded in the city."

"What if I say no? We can still find him together?"

Casper scoffed. "Then I probably go to the Farseers and hope that I can live with myself after I save this stupid fucking city that killed my dad. I don't need to be protected. I need my dad to be safe and out of the way."

A couple council members turned their heads at Casper's raised voice.

"Ok. Yes," Helix said. "I'll find him."

"Great. Thank you."

Casper turned to storm off, but Helix grabbed his arm and spun him around, wrapping him in a hug.

"I won't be able to visit you," he said. "If they let you in the grotto, no one else will be allowed to enter."

The sudden goodbye punched the air out of Casper. He squeezed Helix back. So many unspoken things sat between them. Casper felt like he was back in his garden, running away from the horrible shame that gripped his body. He could feel the glass door sliding shut between them. All he wanted to do was curl up on his couch and cry.

Apparently, Casper had not stepped far enough away from the council. He watched as Theo approached them from over Helix's shoulder.

"I'll send word to the Eye," Theo said. "She will be able to help you. It's a good idea. The Farseers have a way with aether that we do not."

"Thanks," Casper managed to get out before Theo returned to council's circle. He grabbed Helix's hand. "So, I'll go. And come back as soon as I can."

"Yeah." Helix let him go. His eyes were shiny. "Stay safe."

"You too."

The weight of separation sunk in as he turned back to the

door. He was being pulled somewhere completely unknown and leaving Helix in a city under attack by vicious monsters. He kept moving because it was the right thing to do. Or as right of a thing as he could find in the moment. It was better than sticking around only to abandon the people of Novilem with the council.

He had to do something. As much as he didn't want to leave Helix, if it meant he could save the whole city, he had to try. Helix wanted him to let go of feeling responsible for the wellbeing of Novilem. To not accept so much responsibility. The dozen or so fantasies that filled Casper's mind of running away together were all smashed by one thing. He couldn't stop being the Telos. The aether had found him on Earth. It would come for him, no matter where he ran.

"Pappous," Helix said. "Are you really going to have us evacuate?"

Theo didn't fully face him. "Head to the villa and keep the family safe."

A pang of worry for his parents and sister filled his stomach. Had his uncles and aunts made it through the attack? They all were at the festival. But he couldn't bear hiding in the family villa, not knowing what was happening.

Before he could plead his case Theo turned and looked him directly in the eye. "Go home, Helix."

Heat filled his cheeks, and Helix was talking before he had considered the comment. "I won't be dismissed like a child."

Theo's eyes darkened. "Then don't act like one."

"Why won't you let me help?"

"Being safe is helping." Theo's neck was ruddy as he held

back the volume of his voice. "Do you see how I am dealing with you instead of handling the problems of the city? There is nothing for you to do except be safe and check on the family."

"Brissa never kicked me out of a room." It was a petulant thing to say, and he surprised himself by saying it, but his anger had found a point of release, and he was having difficulty choosing to stop.

"A lot of good that did her." The planes of Theo's cheeks were rigid. His nose flared.

He didn't finish the statement, but the implication was a punch to the gut. The guilt of his yiayia's death sat too fresh in his chest to ever forget. Tears filled his eyes. He didn't want to cry in front of everyone, but running off because he was emotional was a hit to his pride that he couldn't abide.

Theo softened, if only a little, as a tear spilled down Helix's cheek.

He closed his eyes and breathed through the remaining heat that filled his head. He couldn't count the number of afternoons he had spent in Brissa's office locked in mock debates, losing his temper as she dismantled his arguments.

Once you've lost control of your temper, you've lost your power. And the debate.

Her warm, melodic voice filled his mind, and more tears fell down his face. He dried his cheeks with his palms. He wanted to say that he missed her. That every day was incomplete. That words couldn't properly encompass the thousand little pieces of his life that had been taken away. That he was scared.

Behind Theo, half a dozen faces openly watched their conversation.

"I'll check on the family." Defying Theo in front of council members would do neither of them any good.

Theo squeezed his shoulder. "Stars guide you."

He did want to know his family was safe, but he had more pressing priorities. If Theo wouldn't give him information, there was another way.

The Celestery library was technically not for general use. It was for historical record and protected by the council for that reason. Helix had only glimpsed the inside on one occasion when Brissa left him waiting in the hall. But Theo said something that Helix could not stop thinking about. He had called the monster that kidnapped Casper a Tektranos.

A myth. One that Helix had never heard of. And he wanted to know why.

So, after meeting Peter in the Celestery garden as they'd previously arranged and tasking him with gathering the crew to start the search for Casper's father, he set his course for the library.

Two acolytes were posted at the library's entry. He didn't recognize either of them.

"The library is off-limits," one said. "Be on your way."

"Here on council business." Helix gestured at his deep blue Estellar robes. Theo may have been keeping him from the Estellar meetings, but he had yet to be denounced as a junior preitan.

The acolytes looked at each other, the question of whether he counted as a preitan clear on their faces.

"I can request a messenger escort from my grandfather if needed." Helix motioned the way he came from. Even though his family name often got things done, it always made him squeamish to use it. "I wasn't aware that would be required."

"If anything happens," the other acolyte said, "it's not like we don't know who he is."

The first acolyte nodded. "Alright, that won't be necessary."

"Two visitors in one day," the other acolyte said, pulling the door open. "Can't remember the last time that happened."

"Two?" Helix asked. "Who else is here?"

Beyond the doors, a giant pillar rose higher than Helix could see. Tendrils of light spun around the large column. A rapid swirl of light around the pillar slowed suddenly, and a book descended a shoot along the pillar's front, landing softly against a pillowed deposit.

A finely dressed man was at the foot of the mechanism. He turned at the noise of Helix entering the room.

"Orrin?"

"Oh good, you're here," Orrin said. "We can begin."

EIGHTEEN

Talleah stopped by her food cart to collect a bag of flour. It was a hard day. Her mood was sour and her patience short. She imagined the storage under the counter of her cart and the staples she had left, worried that food access would become an issue again. The market had already been largely cleared out, but she was sure she had stores of flour, and a bag of nuts left behind for when she returned to work.

The western tower felt like a constant presence in her mind. Like it was watching her. Something was off. She could feel it in her bones. The screech of a monster echoed across the dome above from somewhere in the distance.

Apparently, she wasn't the only one with the idea to raid her stores. The cart shifted as she approached. The door was busted open. Inside, she could make out the shape of a large man digging through the cabinets. Heat bubbled up inside her. She had to hold back the string of curses that sat on her tongue.

He was likely a scared person. Probably also trying to make sure his family stayed fed. *Get it together, Talleah.*

"There's not much here, but I'll split the grain I left behind with you."

The man twisted to face her. The cart was closed up, so he was shrouded in the dark. All she could make out was the yellow glow that shone from his eyes as he stared at her.

"Dust me," Talleah said.

He was sick, and judging from the snarl he released, he was angry. The cart shook from side to side as he barreled out the back. She shuffled away from the door, dodging his swinging arm as he exited.

"I said, I'll share the grain. This is my cart."

The man's voice was strained. "I was here first."

He was a head taller and wide enough to worry her. She knew how to fight, but she wasn't confident she could take him. She should turn away. Let him have the flour. She had food to last them a few days at home.

The man spit on the ground and cursed at her in Greek before turning back to the cart. Talleah's fist was colliding with his kidney before she could process what she was doing.

He fell to his hands and knees, crying out in pain. Her instincts and temper had taken over. She swung her foot to kick him, but he caught her ankle, yanking her to the ground.

"Dust off!" Talleah tried to pull her leg free, but the man twisted her body to the side and shoved her backward. She crashed onto her back from the force. He tumbled after her and the bag of flour slid to the ground, spilling some of its contents onto the stone. She was just about to release the string of curses that had sat on her tongue all morning when she heard the crack of a bone.

The man's skin was turning gray and black. His eyes

smoldered with yellow light. Then he started to grow, his body stretching and bulging with each sickening *crack* until he loomed over her, having grown nearly twice his original size. Talleah cried out, shuffling to her feet as his face narrowed into sharp angles and teeth. Blood and spit fell to the ground as his jaw stretched forward.

A horrible, crackling scream came out of his mouth. When he looked at her, his eyes flared like light gems. Another bone snap, and she shuffled away as his body shivered and expanded in spurts. He was blocking the entrance to the cart and all she could think about was the chef's knife mounted on the wall.

Blood spilled to the ground from the man's mouth as his teeth grew to sharp points. There was no time. He would attack as soon as he could. Talleah had been fighting her anger all day, but now she needed it. She didn't have to reach far for it to surface.

Aether came to her quickly, so her arms were aglow with energy when wings ripped away from his back. He was more creature than person. She approached from behind his crumpled form and inhaled a steadying breath. His head perked up at the sound, taking away the angle she needed to strike. His form rose until his upper body was out of her reach. She stepped backward and tripped on a piece of the broken lock from her cart door. It scraped against the stone, and the now completely creature homed in on the noise, twisting to her.

Wet blood shone around its mouth. Its protruding snout wiggled as it sniffed the air. Its eyes glowed softly behind a haze, like the cataracts of the old woman who lived next door when she was young. Its jaw dropped open and released an ear-splitting screech as it leaped forward, knocking her to the ground. A scream echoed across the square from someone who must have also watched the horror of the man's transformation.

Rolling to the side as quickly as she could, she escaped. She focused her Leo aether into her hands, ready to slice through the creature if it came for her. She should, right? It could kill her. Or go off and kill many others. Was it still human? Did that matter?

No. It didn't. She wasn't going to let it get the best of her. She had a clear shot, and as she prepared herself, she realized how badly she wanted to take it.

The creature's thundering footsteps pounded through the ground and then a massive gust of wind hit her back. She glanced behind her to see the creature had taken flight and was swooping down toward her. She rolled to the ground and heard the swipe of its claws against the stone next to her as she scrambled back to her feet.

Another high-pitched scream filled the plaza and the creature's head perked up. Before Talleah could focus her aether into an attack, it took flight. She hurled her aether into the air, but the creature was out of range. Her beam dissipated as the creature soared out of reach.

Frustrated, she doubled back to her cart and grabbed the bag of flour laying on the ground. The Academy was a couple hundred yards away. People were running into the building. The creature reappeared, kicking a man to the ground as it twisted to face Talleah again.

Should she kill it or run? It was technically human, right? She watched him transform before her eyes. Like her mother must have... She shook the thought from her head, filling her body with aether. The creature was speeding toward her again. It was her or the monster.

A dangerous, seductive energy sat in her chest. Its appearance scared her. What would happen if she let it free?

She dropped the flour, crouched, and leapt toward the creature, cutting through the air with aether shooting from her hand. It pulsed its wings, slowing its movement, and fell to its feet. Talleah's hand sliced through empty air and the creature swatted her to the ground. It released an earsplitting screech as it peeled back into the sky.

A bright beam of aether struck its side and it fell to the ground. Footsteps shuffled out from the Academy. The creature was a couple arm's lengths away from Talleah. They got the first hit, but she couldn't let them get the last. The bubbling heat in her chest summoned a cry in her throat. Her voice was raw. Shredded. Crazed.

Her anger finally had a target. A release. And she hungered for it. She needed the kill.

She was climbing back to her feet when the creature twisted onto all fours and burst from the ground in a blast of wind. One of the men gathered nearby shot a beam of aether after it, but the creature dodged the attack, flying toward the west tower in the distance. Its screech echoed across the dome and beyond, vibrating in Talleah's feet, bright and tinny.

She had to fight to keep another battle cry inside her. She ached to turn the rage inside her on the crew in front of the Academy for sending the monster away. But she held still. It wasn't her seeking blood. Her fits of anger had never blown this out of proportion, but they always passed after a time. The world felt red behind her closed eyelids. Her breath pumped in and out in heavy rotations.

Someone approached her. "Are you ok?" a woman asked.

"Yes," was all Talleah could manage. Her adrenaline was pumping, and her fists ached to land a satisfying punch into the beast that had threatened her life.

"You have a couple scrapes," the woman said. "I can help with those—"

"I'm fine."

Talleah didn't look at her. The heat wasn't leaving her skin. She feared if she laid eyes on the woman the need in her body would react, finding a different target for the aggression built up in her muscles. She walked back to collect the bag of flour. Of course, she found a Virgo just as she couldn't trust herself to be looked after.

The streets were a ruckus as she made her way home. Doors were slamming. Windows were shuttering. The occasional monstrous screech peeled across the dome overhead and any persons also shuffling down the road would freeze, craning their neck to the sky.

It brought back memories of the Turning, and somehow even though the city was in full daylight, it felt more terrifying. Talleah couldn't get the creature's pale gray skin and mouth full of teeth out of her mind.

"You!" a man shouted at Talleah. He was in battle wraps. They were acolyte blue.

Talleah didn't stop. The heat of her fury had simmered down, but she was so tired. She feared if the anger returned, she wouldn't be able to control herself.

A woman appeared in front of her, grabbing hold of her wrist and twisting it behind her back. The sack of flour made a thud when it hit the ground as Talleah was spun around to the man who had addressed her.

"Why are you covered in blood?" the man asked.

Talleah looked down at her tunic, which was indeed splattered with blood. She hadn't noticed.

"One of them killed a man next to me."

The woman holding her wrist let go, speaking over Talleah's shoulder. "Where was it?"

"Four kilometers that way." Talleah pointed the way she came. "Near the clinic. You do know they can fly, right? It's not there anymore."

"We'll send someone to collect the body," the woman said with a furrowed brow.

Heat brushed Talleah's cheeks. Of course, his body needed to be cared for. She had left him there, alone. No more dignity offered than being covered by her cape.

"I covered him," she said. "I have to get to my family…"

"Get inside as soon as possible," the man said. "There are more every minute."

He didn't say so, but the look in his eyes was hard. Like he knew where the monsters were coming from and was also choosing not to share.

"Stars guide us all," Talleah said.

She turned and hustled down the street without waiting for a response.

~

Hector and Daphne were home. She squeezed Daphne, burying her face in curls.

"Are you bleeding, mommy?" Daphne asked.

Talleah pulled away, slipping the tunic over her head.

"Sorry. It's not my blood. I had to help someone who was hurt."

"Where have you been?" Hector asked. "We came straight from the festival. It's been an hour."

"I had to run here." Talleah carried the flour into the

kitchen. "I was visiting Mom. Daphne, baby, would you mind going to your room for a minute?"

"No! I want to know what's going on, too."

Talleah knelt down so they were face to face. "I promise we'll tell you what you need to know. But Dad and I have to talk first to figure out what we can share that won't just upset you. We all need to be brave today, and I don't want to scare you with information we don't quite understand yet. Ok?"

"But I'll be scared in my room alone."

"What about packing your favorite outfit and a stuffy in your bag? Do you think you could handle doing that for me?"

Daphne nodded her head.

"We'll be really quick. I promise."

She walked off to her room, looking back at them before walking through the doorway.

Talleah started in a quick whisper as soon as she was out of sight. "People are turning into monsters. I saw an old woman grow wings and pluck a man off the ground. A man in the main square transformed right next to me. My mom..." Tears she hadn't expected filled her eyes. She brushed them aside. There was no time for tears. "I think she turned, too."

"Stars above," Hector said. "Are you ok?"

Talleah shook her head. She was still crying. The fury had subsided, but the memory of it twisted her stomach. She had wanted to kill the creature. That man who she watched turn. He *was* still a man. And she would have taken his life if he hadn't flown away.

A wave of guilt shook her body with more tears. That poor man outside the clinic had been killed. But all she could feel, the only thing that existed in her mind, was the rage that kept flooding her mind.

"What is it?" he asked.

She was shaking. Her chest was so tight she couldn't get a full breath in. *It's inside me!* The thought was in her head, screaming over and over again. Hector's hands gripped her arms, holding her.

"I think…" Her voice was barely a whisper. "I might be sick."

There was a tiny sniffle from across the room. Daphne was standing there with her bag packed. Her stuffy fell to the ground. Talleah opened her mouth to comfort her, but all she could get out was a strained cry. Daphne ran to her, wrapping her little arms around Talleah's waist, and they cried together.

NINETEEN

The last time Helix saw Orrin was at the tribunal the Exoria held on the Surface to consider Helix's fate. Standing in front of the impressive mechanical structure of the library, he seemed like he could be every bit of the Celestery steward he was a few cycles ago.

"How are you in here?" Helix asked.

"I'm here on Brissa's instructions," Orrin explained. "Which we can discuss." His gaze moved to the closed doors. "But not here."

He placed his hand on the flat surface of a podium in front of the mechanism. It whirred back to life, filling the space with bright light. Overhead, likely to the top of the Celestery, was a massive tunnel of books. As the pillar spun, books floated both from the shelves, into the light, and out to be re-shelved.

A book floated out of the pillar and slid down a shoot, arriving at the podium with a *thunk*. The text on the cover was Greek and read, *Governance and Civil Planning*. Orrin picked it up.

"This is hardly the time for schooling," Helix said. "Jacob is back, and he brought monsters."

Orrin placed the book in a satchel and returned his attention to the podium. "He didn't bring monsters. He made them."

The library whirled back to life, and after a moment, another book slid down to the podium.

"How?"

Orrin faced him and the sharp plane of his cheeks lifted. His dark skin glistened in the low light.

"The sickness that has been spreading since the Turning. It's not a coincidence." Orrin placed a book in Helix's hand, then turned and walked deeper into the library.

Helix looked at the book in his hand. The title read, *Aether and its Limits*. He jogged to catch up with Orrin, who stopped at a table piled with notes. "What do you mean it's not a coincidence?"

"It used to be called the Frenzy. When aether builds up in the body without release, we start to lose the ability to emotionally regulate. Our actions become driven by our base instincts, and our perception of reality becomes deeply warped."

"I thought a buildup of aether would cause a supernova," Helix said. "On the Surface, that's what happened to Casper."

"That is an overuse of aether. This is the opposite. What happens when aether is stored and not used."

"What does that have to do with the monsters?"

"If the sickness progresses, it transforms your body." Orrin took the book on aether back from Helix and flipped through the pages. "Into a Tektranos." He handed the book back. Pictured on the right-hand side was a sketch of the massive, winged creature that had snatched Casper during the festival.

"And the council knows this?" Helix asked.

"The Elders knew when I was serving as steward."

Helix's heart was pounding at double speed. His fingertips were tacky against the book. He closed it.

"Why leave the city in the dark about this?"

"Why worry them with something they believed to be a myth? I've never been able to find record of an actual Tektranos transformation. It's been over 200 years since the last documented case of the Frenzy. Astrolabes have been massively effective at regulating aether use since then."

"What changed?"

"The Enotis broke three central astrolabes during the Turning. They've been repaired, but the damage was done as soon as they were broken."

"I thought the large astrolabes powered the city's machines. The rail. The Split."

"They do." Orrin nodded. "But what do you think happened to all that aether stored in them when they were broken?"

Helix didn't understand. Orrin seemed to expect this because he held up the book on aether.

"We absorbed it. According to this, there are two sides of aether. Dark and light. The aether you're familiar with is light aether. Our astrolabes are designed to filter out dark aether and only allow light aether into our channels. In this way, we protected our people from the limitations of aether. Astrolabes helped stave off the Frenzy by keeping dark aether out of our bodies. And they also throttle aether use so you cannot overuse light aether to the point of a supernova."

Dark and light aether. What would that mean? Was there really a whole facet of the fosergatis that was hidden away?

"Where does corrupted aether fit into this?"

"Corrupted aether is a lie."

Helix felt like the stone below his feet tilted. "The plants on the Surface... I've seen what corrupted aether does to them."

Orrin shook his head, flipping to another passage. "No, you've seen what imbalanced aether does to them." The book described the effects that aether out of balance can have on the natural environment. The overuse of light aether without appropriate balance leaves the imbalanced energy to be absorbed by the nearest organism. The book went on to describe a series of observations of plants and animals falling sick after their ancestors arrived to Ouranos.

Helix pointed at the page. "Wait, this says that we built Novilem because the Ouranos ecosystem was dying out from our aether use. Our history clearly states that the flora and fauna were too dangerous when we arrived."

Orrin sighed. "I'm afraid it gets worse. Come with me. Let's discuss this elsewhere."

Casper spent the entire trip to the grotto rehearsing a speech to convince them to let him inside only to find the guards in front were expecting him when he arrived. One of them guided Casper through a sheet of tropical plants into a small cave. His guide, a man in orange robing, was facing what very much looked like an elevator door.

"You're kidding, right?" Casper said.

The man placed his palm against a stone panel that lit under his touch. The doors slid open, revealing a metal elevator car.

"That's an elevator." Casper pointed at the box. When the man did not respond, he said, "To where?"

The man ushered him into the cube and followed him inside. The doors slid closed, and his ears adjusted to a sudden change in the air pressure. There was a sucking noise like the car had become vacuum sealed, and to Casper's surprise, they started to descend. Because the grotto was on ground level, he assumed they would be going up.

"I've never met a Farseer," Casper said.

The man's tightly coiled hair worn in a natural shape. He had reddish brown skin and wore loose pants. His tunic was made of the same burnt orange fabric as his pants and a multicolor stripe zig-zagged down both of his sides, from torso to ankle.

He said something in a language that Casper hadn't heard in Novilem. His vowels were bright and rounded. The sound was melodic and pretty.

Casper smiled. The man smiled back. Neither of them tried to clarify.

The elevator was still moving, which was alarming. They were likely past even the subterranean level of Novilem. Did they have an entirely separate community? It was hard to imagine the Estellar would allow them to exist outside of their purview.

Casper's feet lifted off the paneled floor. He grabbed hold of the rail lining the elevator car. The man did the same. After observing the absurdity of his companion flipping his body upside down, Casper was looking up at him standing overhead.

"What is happening?" Casper asked.

The man grabbed hold of Casper's arms and turned his body over. For another brief moment he felt like he was in free fall, and then he sank down into what was previously the ceiling.

"You haven't said nearly enough words for what is going on right now."

The man looked at Casper with a furrowed brow. "My English is not so good."

"Of course," Casper said. "I'm sorry for assuming."

The man shrugged his shoulders. "Soon," was all he said in response.

A minute later, the car stopped moving. The doors opened and it wouldn't have mattered if his guide had explained for the full duration of the trip, because he never would have been able to prepare Casper for what he was seeing.

Green. So much green it could be a rain forest. The scent of moist earth and delicious fresh air washed across him with a weight. And birds, he heard birds chirping lightly from somewhere across the way. And that was definitely the sound of a cricket or some kind of bug. The elevator opened into a small cavern of a room, but a dozen paces away was an opening that Casper could swear was a blue sky if he didn't know with certainty that he was inside of a moon.

He followed the man off the elevator car into the room, and for the first time since he arrived in Novilem, he was speechless. He skipped past the guide, jogging into the open, and a laugh of disbelief escaped him. As far as his sight went, he saw trees. A flock of small birds flew in formation over the treetops. Overhead was... well, sky. Expansive, achingly beautiful, deep blue evening sky. The unmistakable heat of sunbaked earth radiated from underfoot.

It was so familiar. So much like Earth that the man could have told him they had jumped to South America and Casper would have believed him.

A woman with deep brown skin and long braids was waiting at the edge of a path leading into the forest. She wore a scarf on her head, woven through the length of her braids.

"Hello, Casper," she said. Her voice was warm and carried the same melodic rhythm as the guard. "I am the Eye. Welcome to the grotto." She gestured to the path and turned. "Come."

As they walked, Casper ached to ask every single question, but the man already explained he did not know much English and the Eye had been commandingly quiet. So, he followed them down a skinny path that switched backed down what felt like a mountainside into the canopy of the forest. They followed a well walked path through the trees, which was teeming with life. Insects familiar and not scurried across the dirt. Casper heard the scampering of small rodents. And then he saw a deer.

"Shut up," Casper said.

The deer perked its head up, looking at him, and then galloped off deeper into the woods.

A mile or so into the serene quiet of the trees, they arrived at a clearing containing a village. Homes were constructed of knotted, pale wood and curved, earth-packed walls with thatch roofs. They varied in size and shape and were configured in concentric gatherings with meandering paths connecting smaller units to the larger community.

His guides walked him past a group of people socializing around a well-equipped outdoor kitchen. The smell of something rich and savory made Casper's mouth water. They approached a woman who bowed gently to the Eye, and they spoke in tones that sounded similar to the language Casper heard in the elevator. It was not the same version of Greek that people in Novilem spoke.

"Thank you," the Eye said to the woman. "A welcome, to the young Telos." She gestured to him as she spoke to the small gathering of people. They all bowed their heads toward him. He returned the gesture, smiling awkwardly.

"This place is incredible," Casper said. "Are we still in Novilem?"

The Eye was already walking away, rounding behind the building in front of him. She spoke over her shoulder. "Not in the ways that matter. We have no time to waste. You can ask questions later."

Casper followed her onto a smooth circle of dirt surrounded by privacy fencing made of what looked like bamboo. She sat on a pillow on the ground and gestured to a second seat across from her. Casper joined her.

"I understand you've had visions." It wasn't a question, but she paused, clearly expecting Casper to speak.

"I've had a couple. Mostly about Agnes. The former Telos. And Jacob on the Surface. And maybe a weird dream or two."

"Awake or asleep, the aether does not care. It seeks balance. Balance is your purpose. The message is always there if you are willing to listen."

"I'm sorry, it seeks balance? Are you saying that aether has a will of its own?"

"A tree seeks sunlight; do you assume it has a will of its own?"

Casper leaned back, admonished. "A tree has never spoken to me."

"Your subconscious spoke to you. Aether is aether. Nothing more. Nothing less." She placed her hands on the mounds of her knees; her feet tucked underneath her thighs. "Get comfortable, Telos. We're going to be here a while."

CHAPTER

TWENTY

Orrin's theory that the council's obfuscation went as far as denying the true nature of dark aether was spinning in Helix's head as he approached the Academy. He spent the night at the Celestery, having fell asleep at Orrin's desk after staying up late discussing the texts. But even sleeping on the new information didn't make it make sense. What could be the purpose of hiding the fact that aether has two sides? Knowing the current council, he supposed it was simply to maintain control. Everything they did seemed to circle back to control.

After far too little sleep, Helix went to inquire after Casper, but the Aquarius he found could only confirm they received word he was received into the grotto. So, he made his way to the Academy hall to their usual training room, hoping to find the crew ready to set off. And in agreeable spirits, because he was going to have to make a stop before joining them.

Peter was alone in the room, sparring with a target dummy. His tunic was hanging from a peg on the wall. Sweat glistened over his back. Helix warmed seeing his friend, brought back to evenings when they were twelve and they would spar against each other while Peter talked a big game about how he was going to be captain of their crew.

"What did that wad of cloth do to you this time?" Helix asked.

Peter landed a blow that echoed through the large room. He dropped his form, breathing steadily as he turned around. "It's paying for old grievances." He smiled and started toweling off his sweat. "You're looking glum. What's wrong?"

"Where is the crew? David is already sick. We can't delay finding him."

"I sent Belen for Gloria and Malia. Faus should be here soon."

Helix felt a flash of guilt at his assumption. "Ah, sorry. Thank you."

"You sure you're ok?" Peter asked. "You seem on edge."

"I don't know if you noticed. But Jacob is back. And he brought friends."

Peter rolled his eyes. "You love a problem you can get overly involved in. That's not what's bothering you." He took a seat on a pile of padded mats and waved Helix over. "Out with it."

Helix smiled to himself. The beauty, and pain, of being intimately known. Peter could always see past Helix's walls. Where to even start? Theo stonewalling him? The constant ache for Brissa in his chest? Casper going off with the Farseers when they were still in the middle of their first fight?

"Everything is different," Helix said.

Peter raised an eyebrow.

"Aren't you bothered by how much they have lied to us?"

he continued. "Sometimes I feel like nothing is true anymore."

"That would require thinking they were ever not lying to us." Peter laughed when Helix glared at him. "What? My family has always carried a healthy suspicion of the council."

"Healthy suspicion." Helix shook his head. "Nearly got all you killed on the Surface."

"Which kind of proves my point. Doesn't it?"

Part of Helix balked at that. The part of him that had been groomed and preened by years of standing at Brissa's side. Still, he couldn't ignore the voice in his head that recognized the truth in Peter's words.

"I don't know what to trust anymore," Helix said. "Is it all lies?"

Peter mussed a hand through his growing hair, pushing the short length of his bangs away from his forehead. "Brissa put a lot of stuff in your head. I don't think you need to beat yourself up over finding out some of it was not true."

He wasn't angry with himself. He couldn't believe that Brissa had lied so much. She had to believe in what she was doing, right?

"Now, do you want to talk about why you're actually here?" Peter asked.

"I'm here to find Casper's dad," Helix said.

Peter nudged him with his sandal. "That's nice. You can lie, too. You told me you needed to check in with your family. And yet, you're here with me. So, what's going on with Casper?"

Helix scoffed. "What makes you think something's going on with Casper?"

"Something is always going on with Casper."

Helix laughed. He couldn't deny that. "He went to the

grotto. To see if the Farseers can help him figure out what's going on with the corrupted aether."

"The grotto? Woah. Cool." Peter rubbed at the stubble on his chin. "And some forced separation."

"It's just a few days."

Peter laid a heavy gaze on him. "You're attached at the hip." He threw his hands in the air when Helix went to object. "Look, I get it. It's new and exciting. I don't blame you."

Again, Helix had the urge to deny Peter's point. They spent plenty of time apart. But it tapped on something that he had not given voice to. The last few weeks had been easy. A reprieve from all the stress of their time on the Surface and the Turning. The ease scared him. It made him feel like he was missing something. That he was ignoring problems because he only wanted to feel the good things.

And they hadn't exactly responded well to their first clashing of minds.

But Casper was leaning in. Through it all. What if Helix was blind to their problems and took that next step unknowingly, walking them straight into an unfixable issue?

"He asked me to move in," Helix said.

"I take it you don't want to?"

"I do." Helix shrugged. "We've just been arguing lately."

"So, things aren't going well?"

"This isn't normal for us. There's a lot going on right now."

Peter watched him, patiently waiting for the explanation that made sense.

"I'm scared." Helix stared at his sandals, feeling a bit naked admitting this.

"Of what?"

"Things with Casper are easy."

Peter narrowed his eyes in confusion.

"Too easy," Helix continued.

"What does that mean? Easy means it's working, right?"

"It does work. We work. But... he's still dealing with a lot of stuff from his life on Earth. Having his dad come to Novilem wasn't easy for him. And like, I'd love for him to not be so blocked around family stuff, you know? But he doesn't put that on me. So, even when he has a hard day, we're still good."

"And that's bad?"

Helix sighed. "No. It's not bad. I'm scared."

"I don't know, man. Casper's pretty cool. He's hot. *And* he's the Telos. I don't see the problem."

The realization came to him as Peter was speaking. "I'm not scared about Casper not being a good fit. I'm scared of losing him."

"Helix. He's obsessed with you."

"Dust me, you're dense sometimes. I don't think he's going to leave me. It's... it's Brissa."

"I'm not going to lie. You lost me there."

"Losing Brissa." Helix's voice caved in. "I've never lost someone before."

"Oohhh. And now you're scared that could happen to Casper." Peter stood up from the mat. "I'm sorry. That's a big thing. You need a hug?"

Helix shook his head, swallowing away the lump in his throat. "I'm good. You're still sweaty."

"But I helped you with a breakthrough!"

Helix grabbed Peter's tunic and tossed it at him. "I'm going to the villa. I'll meet you and the crew in the western neighborhoods to help with the search."

"Oh, ok. Yeah, you're welcome," Peter called after him as he walked toward the exit.

"Thank you," Helix called over his shoulder.

Helix left the Academy hall feeling better. Or at least different. But he, unfortunately, really wanted to hug Casper, and that was not possible. The Farseers would never let him in the grotto. Hopefully, a hug from his mom would do the trick.

TWENTY-ONE

Casper sat across from the Eye the morning after his arrival in the grotto. His legs quickly grew numb from the hours spent folded under each other the day before. The Eye was still trying to get him to clear his mind.

Eman was her name, and it had been no simple feat getting her to share that information. That was practically the only information he got out of her during his first day. So much for the Farseers being more helpful than the council.

Dinner had been unceremonious, but delicious. A stew served over rice. They had rice here, which shouldn't be surprising considering the forest he was sitting in the middle of. This was not the crisp stone city and neatly laid rows of farmland of Novilem.

Eman woke him up before the sky was lit by whatever mechanism granted the grotto's daylight. The majority of his first day was spent in silence, which seemed like a colossal waste of time. Jacob was up, or was it down? Wherever Novilem was, Jacob was there, causing mayhem.

"Your mind is still not at ease," Eman said.

"Novilem is under attack. Like right now." Casper was cracking his fingers one by one. "I don't know how to not think about that."

Eman's eyes opened and fixed on him. "These are things you cannot control. You are here now. What happens there has nothing to do with you."

"I came here to learn about the corrupted aether. Why are we still meditating?"

"You must quiet your mind." She returned to her serene pose.

"Seriously? Why do you want me to learn how to relax while people are being killed by a vindictive narcissist and some giant bat monsters?"

Her eyes remained closed. "Because you will not be able to find the aether with a mind as cluttered as yours."

Casper scoffed. He was already in trine with his Scorpio, so with a thought, he filled their enclosed area with a half dozen copies of his own person. "I can find aether just fine."

Eman held out her hand, her eyes still closed, and each of Casper's Shadows dissipated into dust as they were pulled into her palm. In less than a second, they were all gone.

"How did you do that?"

"You can find the ma'at, the outward path of aether." Her eyes finally opened. "What you need to learn is how to find the isfet, to let the aether in."

"Cool. What does that mean?"

She sighed. "You clearly are not someone who learns by doing."

"Not when I don't know what I'm doing."

Her posture relaxed a little as she leaned back, placing her palms into the dirt. "Let us talk then. The first thing you will need to understand is that there is no such thing as corrupted aether."

"Of course there is. Back on Earth I saw it turn coyotes into demonic teleporting assassins. I fought Jacob myself. He's definitely sick with corrupted aether."

"You saw aether out of balance. Aether is aether," she repeated. "It cannot be corrupted."

"So, this is more lies from the Estellar?" Casper asked.

"This is a truth that Novilem abandoned but the Farseers held onto."

The hairs on Casper's neck stood up. "So, who is infecting everything? If there's no corrupted aether, someone is making people sick. And the Surface? All the plants and animals there are infected."

"It is not one individual, but a result of collective action."

"So, *we* are making people sick?"

"The aether cannot sustain imbalance. It will find a way to balance itself if we do not balance our own use of it. That device." Eman pointed at Casper's astrolabe. "It disrupts the aether. Manufactures connection. Light aether is used and dark aether is left to be cleared. It is unnatural."

"Dark aether, corrupted aether. Why does it matter if you give it a different name? It's still the source of the problem."

"They are not separate. Think of it as directional. You can walk forward, or you can walk backward. The result is different, but in either case you are still walking. It is a cycle. In the day we work, and at night we rest. It is the same for light and dark aether. It can flow out or it can flow in. Either way, it is aether."

"So, using astrolabes has created an excess of dark aether?"

"Centuries of using astrolabes and powering all of Novilem's machinery with light aether has flooded our ecosystem with dark aether."

"Well, damn." Casper sighed. "What am I supposed to do to fix that?"

She leveled a heavy gaze on him. "You learn to quiet your mind."

Casper almost responded that Agnes was a better bet. She had more experience using aether than he did. But Agnes was one of those creatures now. How many people would meet the same fate if he couldn't figure this out?

"But *how* am I supposed to fix the balance of aether?" He waved his hands through the air. "It's aether."

"The grotto has historically helped balance Novilem's abuse of the aether. We have tended to Isfet to maintain balance. That is, we could until the large astrolabes were broken. They released far too much dark aether. And now we cannot keep balance against the Apep."

Casper opened his mouth to ask, but she explained before he could speak.

"Jacob. He is your opposite."

The center of Casper sunk into a void. "Like a Telos of dark aether?"

"Yes." Eman was too still. Like her revealing this was not earth-shattering.

The things Jacob could do were starting to make more sense. "I'm going to engage in this delusion that a dark Telos doesn't change everything. You still haven't explained how to achieve balance. What do I *do*?"

"You must heed the will of Ma'at."

"Who is Ma'at?"

"Ma'at is order. Harmony. The Estellar calls this Sedrivani. Isfet is disorder. Chaos. The Estellar calls this Kanos."

"The visions..."

"Yes. You must listen to the will of Ma'at," Eman urged. "It is the only way to restore balance."

"It didn't tell me what to do. It just said that I needed to mend the severing. Can you actually explain the function of balancing aether?"

"You are fighting what is." Eman sighed while rubbing her brow in frustration. "It is not an action. You cannot force the aether into balance. Aether naturally finds balance. You must listen. Quiet your mind. Find the aether. Let it show you what to do."

She returned to sitting up straight and shut her eyes. Begrudgingly, Casper joined her. Behind closed eyes, he could feel sharp edges. The unfettered energy of the chaos aether. He cringed at the thought of letting it touch him. It was similar to the shadows that clouded his mind when he entered the tower. The oppressive darkness that muddled his thoughts and numbed his body.

Eman's voice was calm as she addressed him. "Breathe. Aether in. Aether out."

With his eyes closed, Casper filled his lungs and released. There was tension in his shoulders as he exhaled. He breathed into the tightness slowly. His neck muscles shuddered as he relaxed. On his third breath, a wave of grief rolled through him. He could smell the piles of old sheets in his parent's linen closet, and he was seven and aching for a hug from his father. A tear spilled down his cheeks.

His chest was lighter when he exhaled, but on his next breath another wave of emotion crashed through him. His arms, backside, and face stung with the memory of his father's aggressions.

Casper opened his eyes, choking for air as he fell forward onto his hands.

"You carry much pain with you," Eman said.

"What just happened?"

She was frowning when Casper lifted his head. "A problem. Your mind is cluttered with things you have been ignoring."

"I'm not ignoring anything. My life on Earth sucked. I don't live there anymore. Why think about it?"

"You cry. You flinch at even the thought of it. This is a great pain, and you have not nurtured it. You must be able to tolerate these emotions."

"Why? None of this emotional stuff happens when I use normal aether."

"It is not normal aether," Eman said sharply. She held up one finger. "It is one aether. Breathe in. Breathe out. Chaos. Order. Not two halves. One whole." She grabbed Casper's astrolabe and removed it from his neck. "No more of this. You must build your tolerance. Dark in, light out."

Casper's eyes dropped to his hands. "But it doesn't feel bad to use aether with my astrolabe."

"It doesn't feel bad to use aether ever. *You* feel bad. The aether shakes that loose."

Casper rolled onto his back, letting out an exasperated sigh. "I'll never catch a break. I need magical therapy?"

"What is therapy?"

Casper lifted his head to meet Eman's gaze. "This."

After an exhausting morning of dredging up horrible memories, they broke for lunch.

"I don't understand," Casper said. "If you know how to keep the aether in balance, why would you keep that from the people of Novilem?"

"We haven't kept anything from the people of Novilem," Eman said.

"Earlier you said the Farseers kept the truth about aether from Novelites."

"I said the Farseers held on to the truth. We keep it. They chose not to. They have known about the balance between chaos and order since before we came to Ouranos."

Casper was unsurprised to learn another way the Estellar had hoarded information and weaponized it against their populace.

"We used to live all together." Eman gestured to the trees surrounding them. "When the Surface showed us hostility, the plants and animals turning violent because of their choice to ignore balance, we sought shelter in this rock. The stubbornness of the council is not a new thing. Our ancestors did not agree about where to settle. My ancestors knew this moon would house us safely. The stars showed them. Eventually, when the Surface had claimed many lives, our people came together to build this ecosystem. Right here where we are standing was the original settlement.

"But as our plants grew and the habitat stabilized, the Novelites grew restless. They wanted buildings instead of trees. This was not enough. They attempted to suppress my people and build their city here. But they never respected the balance of aether. They had ideas of rank and order that did not coexist with our traditions. We wear the colors of our houses, and they tried to imprint their hierarchy on us. Pretending that some aether was superior to the rest.

"We tried to show them that all aether is one. That relying only on Ma'at would create imbalance. They said we were stuck in tradition. Limiting ourselves from having true power by failing to explore the extremes of what aether can do. In the end, they refused to embrace the wholeness of aether and they remained incomplete. They could not overpower us to take control, and we would not relent to their scheming. They left and started over. Built Novilem, and to compensate for what they could not do with their spirits—they built technology. Machines to filter out the chaos, leaving only order."

It was a familiar story. The demand for order regardless of the cost. Casper thought of the many ways progress and greed had been prioritized on Earth. The suffering inflicted on those who were lost to systems that sought profit over all else.

"Why do they refuse to learn?" Casper asked. "If there's a way to stop what's happening, I don't understand."

"Balance requires rest," Eman said. "To sacrifice progress when the season calls for it. The Estellar has never taken their eyes off the future. They demand forward momentum, and it seems now the consequences of that choice have come for them."

"Then why bring me here? If it's their consequence, why do you care?"

"We can no longer ignore the mess they made. Their darkness is on our doorstep."

TWENTY-TWO

Novilem was eerily quiet when Helix left the Academy. An acolyte rushed by him as he was leaving the promenade, but the street ahead was empty. When he entered his family's neighborhood, he found all the windows covered. The echo of his footsteps through the vacant street was haunting. His stomach was in knots by the time he entered the family villa.

It didn't help that he was anxious about seeing his family. He had only been there for a passing hello for more than a cycle. His family's presence made Brissa's absence all the more apparent. So, he was expecting, but not prepared for, the attention he received as he entered the living room. A wave of welcome washed over him as the family noticed him. He did his best to respond as he searched the room for his mother's face.

"In the kitchen," his uncle said to him in Greek, patting him on the shoulder.

Helix kissed him on the cheek. "Thank you."

Two of his small cousins ran through the hallway,

screaming and laughing. The brightness of the home was incongruous with the gloom outside. His family was gathered safely, laughing and playing. Their spirits seemingly untouched. And outside, their people were being ripped apart by their loved ones. Never in his life had the status of his family felt so apparent. The realization stopped him in the hall.

His parents were working side by side on the large island. He watched them knead dough. His father leaned in and whispered something, making his mother laugh. An idyllic image, and he was at war with himself witnessing it. He was so grateful that his family was safe. He could cry for how much relief that provided him. But his heart could not let go of the cost of that safety. The families living on the street that had no place to gather. Nowhere to be safe from the Tektranos.

And yet, his family had such ample space they could all gather under one roof.

"Helix?" His father was watching him as he called Helix away from his thoughts. "What are you doing?"

He was told he favored his father. They had the same wave in their dark hair, but Helix always felt so young compared to the mature edges of his father's features: hard lines that spoke of strength. Though, in the last year or so Helix had to admit he saw more of his father when he looked at his reflection.

"It is good you are here," his mother said when he joined them.

Helix had to suppress the choking cry that begged to escape his throat. His mother favored Brissa so distinctly, it felt cruel. Nearly the only feature that stopped his mind from insisting his yiayia was in front of him was his mother's lighter tone. She had not spent decades developing the commanding voice that Brissa used to fill every room.

"What's wrong?" his mother asked.

He couldn't hold the tears back any longer. She abandoned her dough, and with tacky fingers held up in the air, rushed around the island to embrace him. He cried in her arms as she soothed him, weeks of worry and fear finally finding release in his body.

"Jocelyn," his father called into the main room.

A moment later his sister walked into the kitchen, her eyes going wide witnessing Helix in their mother's arms.

"This dough is ready to rest. Finish preparing dinner."

Jocelyn looked like she wanted to object, but she considered Helix again and then took her father's place.

"Go wait in the room," his mother said, gesturing to the back of the house. To Brissa's room.

Helix's stomach turned sour. The back porch was empty, so he nodded to the deck and said, "I'll be outside."

He heard his parent's start to wash their hands as he exited to the glass doors. He had barely sat at a table off to the side when they joined him. They both had the same look of concern in their eyes.

"Has something happened?" his father asked. "Is Casper ok?"

"Oh, stars. Nothing like that." Helix realized his behavior likely implied something had happened with the Tektranos. More guilt washed over him—his circle remained untouched by the horrors affecting the city. "It's..." His voice gave out. His mother's presence was so loud next to him. He couldn't look at her face and risk seeing her in their shared features. The admission came out as a whisper. "Brissa."

He cried again, staring at the smooth sheen of the deck

behind his tears. Both of them brushed swirling hands against his back.

"I miss her too," his mother said.

Helix's heart smarted in response. He did miss Brissa. Terribly. But the words sat wrong in his chest. And he was surprised to find that it was not her absence that was weighing on him. It was his anger.

"I don't know how to forgive her," Helix said.

"Forgive her for what?" His father's voice was warm and deep. It made Helix feel ten again. They were in his child-hood bedroom and his dad was consoling him after Jocelyn picked a fight.

"This." Helix gestured to the house, then out to the dome overhead. On cue, a screech from a Tektranos traveled across the dome from the other side of the city.

"You blame her for what is happening?" his father asked.

"Yes! How could I not? There are people in the streets being slaughtered by their lovers. Children watching their parents turn into monsters. And what is our family doing? We're hiding in our big house, pretending like nothing is happening. Preparing to evacuate and abandon our people."

"Getting sick with them would help no one," his mother said.

"I'm not upset that you are safe," Helix said. "I'm furious that Brissa served on the council for 86 years and built a city that gave safety to families like ours at the cost of others. We are no better than them. So, why do they have to die in the streets?"

His mother grabbed his hands. "Son, that is not your burden to bear."

Helix ached at how much of his yiayia he felt in that moment. "If it's not mine, then whose is it? Who else will face the truth. That she did this."

Pain flashed in his mother's eyes.

"She always made sure we were taken care of," Helix said. "But at what cost?"

"These are extreme circumstances," his father said. "She couldn't have known that Jacob was capable of this, or that the population would boom with the Exoria returning, the Gemini released, and the slums abandoned."

"It was her decision to displace those people. Order by all costs. Each of those a punishment she designed to demand obedience." It was how she maintained power and was also what ended her life. Helix shuddered, recalling Casper's ascension and the cloaked dealings of the elder preitans.

"She didn't act alone," his mother said. "The council requires a majority vote."

Helix pulled back from his mother's grasp. "And the entire council was controlled by her. Look, I miss her too. The grief is overwhelming some days." He met his mother's teary gaze. "When I look at your face, all I can see is her. But people are dying, and I can't pretend that our family has not led our people to this disaster. We have failed this city."

"You say that you see her in my face. Well, I hear her in your words."

It hurt to hear that. It healed to hear it, too.

"You have always cared so much," his father said. "About everything. Everyone. I think that's why Brissa took to you so strongly. She saw herself in your heart."

Helix sighed. "I was so blinded by her, I never understood what she was doing. How deeply unfair things are."

"You were a child," his mother said. "You're barely not a child now. Beating yourself up for admiring your yiayia won't make anything easier."

"Why?" Helix's voice was too small. Of all the brazen, difficult choices Brissa had made, the one he couldn't find an explanation for sat on his heart. The question fell out from somewhere deep inside. "Why did she do it?" His parents watched him, waiting for him to clarify. He feared an answer could mark the difference between being a strong leader and being cruel. "She was going to let them kill Casper."

There was no one who could answer that question. The center of Helix's grief. Knowing what Casper meant to him, she allowed Jacob and the Enotis to send him to his death. This was the unknowable piece that made his yiayia feel so far away. His parents, to his great relief, did not offer explanation. They closed in and embraced him, their comfort just as unfair as before, but for a moment Helix allowed it. And in their arms, he cried.

CHAPTER

TWENTY-THREE

Using aether without his astrolabe was like trying to ride a wild horse. It was stubborn and stagnant, then bursting through him without warning. Casper breathed in the woody air and tried to center himself. The clearing Eman brought him to was a large space of mulched earth. The sky was blue and crystal-clear overhead. Birds chirped pretty songs from the treetops.

His instructions were to follow the aether. Eman was convinced that if he listened, the aether would guide him on how it should be used. But without his astrolabe, all of his abilities felt too difficult to reach. When he opened his aether channels, all he could sense was a wall of darkness surrounding him.

"There is no light here," Casper said.

Eman spoke from behind him. "Then Isfet calls. You cannot ignore the dark and achieve balance."

Every house supposedly had two powers. As in, a Libra could pocket step with light aether, but could also teleport an object to their person with dark aether. Eman had explained that, as the Telos, he could use dark aether in any house the same way he learned to use light aether. Casper had a difficult time truly believing it. The Estellar hiding trines was bad enough. Hiding the true nature of aether... well, it wasn't surprising that they would try, but it was a feat, keeping their people in the dark for millennia. What wouldn't the council do to stay in power?

He was excited to explore these new abilities, but mostly, his stomach twisted in anticipation of letting in the darkness. He grew clammy as soon as he opened himself to the Isfet. He felt like he was approaching the drop of a rollercoaster. He took a deep breath and leaned in.

A moment before, the clearing was serene and sunny, but he was suddenly preoccupied by the dirt in his sandals and the sound of insects buzzing around.

Focus, Casper.

It was a perception shift. Eman had warned him it would happen. Their work meditating was meant to help him detach from the feelings that came up. And come up they did. He could feel his mind slipping into an anxiety spiral already.

"Stop hesitating," Eman said. "The release will come with using the aether."

Casper locked eyes on a stick a few yards away. He searched inside for his estimation of Libra frequency. The hum in his chest was different, deeper. But he found release, and instead of pocket stepping to the stick, it appeared in his hand. He let go of the aether and the clearing's magical airiness returned like someone turned the volume on his joy back up.

He turned to Eman, presenting the stick with a smile. "I did it!"

"Yes." Her smile looked reluctant, but it reached her eyes. "Now the real work can begin."

Finding the aether reliably took a couple of hours because Casper needed frequent breaks. The weight of the dark aether didn't seem to let up. Eman claimed that in harmony, there was no difference between using dark and light aether. Just like there was no difference between breathing in or breathing out. She explained that there was a pattern. An undulating weave of light and dark that Casper could follow if he listened.

Breathe in, breathe out, Casper said mockingly in his head.

He did eventually notice the aether's pull if he paid close attention. It was difficult to keep track of the weave. And he couldn't even begin to wrap his head around swapping directions. Light to dark aether moved in one pattern, but dark to light aether reversed the pattern.

It became easier when he realized the movement was not house-to-house specific. It was between chakra placements. He was the first Telos Eman had trained, so she was accustomed to working in singular trines. Things got messy when expanding from three houses to all twelve.

"Light aether moves from the ground up," Eman said. "Dark aether moves from above to your feet."

The houses all connected to different energy centers. Body, heart, mind, and soul. So, when Casper filled himself with light Capricorn aether, he was in his body placement. The pattern then tugged him forward. Dark aether through his heart center, light aether through his mind center, dark aether through his soul center. It didn't matter which house or which trine he was in. The movement was a pattern, and much easier to follow than to force.

Once he learned how to listen for the movement, it was not a mental exercise. It was physical and would become instinctual with practice. Eman's meditation work finally started to make sense.

The issue then became practicality. If he was to fight Jacob, how was he going to focus on weaving aether while under attack? He said as much to Eman.

"Balance does not require one-hundred percent obedience. If you exhaust the body, you rest. If you soil your clothing, you wash it. If you exert yourself with aether, you meditate to balance your channels."

"And what about the aether imbalance in the city?" Casper gestured a circle over his head. "I can't meditate that away, can I?"

"Do you know why I am called The Eye?" Eman asked.

Casper shook his head.

"A Telos has never been born to the Farseers. We do not have knowledge of the deeper workings of your connection to aether. But our connection to Ma'at and Isfet goes back millennia. Centuries before we came to Novilem. I was born in the second cycle of the stars. An Aquarius. And in our traditions, the sight is revered.

"It connects us, past, present, and future. A gift beyond measure. As it turns out, I am quite good at it." A rare smile brightened her face. "I do not say this to boast, but so that you understand. I have looked to the future. You will balance the aether. And if you can learn to trust yourself, you will see no harm."

Casper's center caved in. Trust. Not something he was naturally inclined toward. "Great. Super easy."

Eman laughed. She covered her mouth with her hand,

like she could physically scoop the sound back inside. "I apologize."

Casper laughed with her. "People here don't usually laugh at my jokes." His spirit lightened a bit. "It's nice, actually."

Eman was still smiling. "Ok. Enough rest. Continue."

Casper sighed. He was tired. Bone deep tired. But she was right. There was no time. Jacob wouldn't wait for him.

TWENTY-FOUR

"The stars have been kind," Helix said, wrapping his arms around Malia. She stiffened and observed him with a raised brow when he pulled away. His crew was all present and unharmed. They were gathered to the west of the Celestery at Helix's request. "Your families?"

"Bunkered down," Malia said.

"Safe," Faus said.

"For now," Belen added.

"My family made it to the Celestery," Gloria said. "They will be evacuating with my mom."

"Cowards," Belen said.

"Check your attitude, Belen," Malia said. "I don't have patience for your bitching right now."

Before Belen could open his mouth to respond, Helix shifted the conversation. "We have a job to accomplish. Casper's dad is a terrible accident waiting to happen. The faster we find him, the more lives we save."

Belen sighed, but surprisingly didn't object.

Helix continued. "He's sick and doesn't understand anything about Novilem. We need him back in quarantine."

"Because you think Casper will be able to focus better if his dad is accounted for?" Malia asked.

"The Telos is probably our only hope of fixing this," Helix said.

"We could evacuate," Faus said. "If the aether in Novilem is the issue. Leaving makes sense."

Helix crossed his arms over his chest. "David got sick on Earth. Evacuating isn't a long-term solution. If leaving is what you want to do, I won't hold you back. But while there is still a chance, I'm going to do what I can."

"You mean, you won't leave without Casper," Belen said.

He blushed but nodded his head. "I can't leave him behind. And I won't abandon our people. Casper can fix this."

A moment of contemplation hung in the air. Malia and Gloria clasped hands. Belen glowered at the floor. Peter shrugged when he and Faus exchanged a look.

"How do we find Casper's dad, then?" Gloria asked.

Helix's heart was full to bursting. He would have accepted if they chose safety, but he felt more capable having them by his side. "That has proven difficult. The Aquarius haven't been able to locate him."

"Makes sense," Belen said. "He's as much a pain in the ass as his son."

Gloria shoved him playfully, rolling her eyes.

They moved through the streets as a unit. Even though it slowed them down, Helix wanted them together in case they ran into a Tektranos. They started on the outskirts of the

Celestery grounds, moving toward Market Row from the main plaza.

The streets and alleyways were empty. A Tektranos screech rippled across the dome overhead. The crew stopped, crouching lower to the ground. Nothing followed the sound. Their cries had become a terrifying constant since the tower returned.

Before they started off again Helix said, "This feels wrong."

"Probably because we're walking toward the monsters," Belen said.

Helix ignored the comment. "He's from Earth and walks out into an unknown place with two paths. One heads into the city, and one heads into a villa. Why would he choose to go toward the city?"

"You think he would go knock on a stranger's door after escaping imprisonment?"

"He was in quarantine," Helix said. "And I've met a few men from Earth now. They are nothing if not presumptuous."

"So, Casper *is* from Earth."

Helix glared at Belen. Cracking a joke was normal for him, but his constant picking on Casper when he wasn't present was uncalled for. "I thought we moved past mocking him."

Belen shrugged. "He's an easy target."

"So, what?" Gloria said. "Do you want to call on every house in the villa?"

"Do you have a better idea?" Helix said.

The crease in her brow and the curl of her lip said maybe this wasn't worth their time. "It feels less like a good idea now that we're out here."

Helix sighed. "The Frenzy is contagious and somewhere

out here, that man is a bad mood away from hurting Novel-ites. No one else is looking for him."

Peter patted a hand on Helix's shoulder. "Cap is right. There's not much we can do to help right now. But we can find Casper's dad. And if that stops one person from dying, it's worth it. Right?"

"Let's head to the villa," Faus said.

They started back down the street, but Belen stayed put. "It's kind of ridiculous, isn't it? I mean, dust us. Doing the dirty work while he goes off to be the hero." A flush of red showed on his neck. "Why are we putting our lives on the line for him?"

"Lower your voice," Helix said.

"Tell me what to do again." Belen's muscles flexed as he stepped toward Helix.

"What is wrong with you?" Peter went to shove at him, but Belen deflected his smaller frame easily.

Helix went cold as realization washed over him. "Belen, have you been feeling irritable lately?"

"Fuck you," he said before spitting on the ground.

"I'll take that as a yes. Everyone back away."

"Dust off," Belen said, laughing. "You would think I'm the problem."

"How long have you been feeling angry like this?" Helix asked.

"What is going on?" Malia asked.

The group was behind Helix. Belen was alone facing them, his cheeks now red with heat. "Belen, I need you to listen to me."

Shadows fell on Belen's eyes as his head lowered slightly. "I'm done listening to you. All you care about is Casper." Light started to build in his hands and forearms.

"Belen, what are you doing?" Gloria called out.

"Go," Helix said over his shoulder. "I'll handle this."

Belen held out his hands, now blazing with aether. "No, you won't."

There was a shift in the air, then Malia was leaping over Belen's shoulder. She twisted, punching Belen directly in the neck, and the light faded from his hands. He went down to the ground face first.

"I said I'd handle it," Helix said. "Using aether is a last resort."

"Watching you have a limb burned off is a last resort." Malia strolled back toward Gloria.

"Is that the sickness?" Gloria asked. "It was him, but like not."

"I don't know," Peter said. "It's not the first time he's turned on Helix."

"It's the first time he tried to burn a hole through him," Faus said. "Belen's not that hot-headed."

"What do we do with him?" Gloria asked. "We can't leave him in the street."

"No," Helix said. "We can't."

Belen was the biggest of the crew, so it took Helix, Faus, and Peter to lift him. They carried him back to the plaza and had to take a breather before starting up the stairs toward the Celestery. Inside, Helix explained the situation to an acolyte and handed him over to be held in quarantine. He was promised that a Virgo would see to him as soon as possible. Hopefully, it was early enough to be cleared out of his system.

The crew looked haunted when he returned to the garden outside.

"I'll do this alone if you want to go to your families," Helix said.

Malia and Gloria didn't budge. Faus folded his arms

across his chest. Peter tilted his head to the side and smiled coyly.

"Don't think so little of us," Peter said.

Helix held his hands up in the air. "I wouldn't blame any of you."

"Belen will be fine," Faus said. "But if you're right about David, some family is in big trouble not having Malia around to save them."

Helix scoffed. "I said I had it."

Peter patted him on the back. "Sure, you did."

TWENTY-FIVE

The villa was quiet, lifeless except for the occasional figure crossing a window and a woman pacing her front garden. Nothing to distract from the eerie, vacant atmosphere. The crew split up to knock on doors, asking after David. They made quick work of it until they came upon a house nestled into the wall of Novilem not too far from the entrance of the villa. The homes were stacked on top of each other where the space had run out but the want for prestige had not.

Helix knocked on the door. The silence returned, like the air around him retreated on a held breath.

The door opened slowly, and a woman peered out. Her eyes were dark under a concerned brow, but they brightened when she recognized Helix. Before he could address her, she turned to the inside of the house, disappearing from view.

"Hello?" Helix said in Greek. "I'd like to ask you about a man."

The door opened wider, and David came tumbling out of

the home as if tossed. Helix caught him by the arms to stop him from falling. The door shut quickly.

"That... doesn't feel good," Faus said.

Malia's stance subtly shifted, like she was ready to jump at any moment. Gloria stepped forward and helped Helix hold David up.

"David," Helix said, bending over to try meeting his eyes.

David's head lulled further down. His jaw was slack, and he was hot to the touch. He looked on the verge of sleep, until his eyes met Helix.

"You." His voice was a croak. Low, gravelly, and filled with hatred.

"I think he's sick," Helix said.

"Duh," Peter said. "That's why we're here."

"With fever."

Gloria's hands began to glow, but Helix pulled her wrist away from David gently.

"The aether," Helix said. "You can't use it around him."

"His fever is too high. I can't let him die in our arms either, can I?"

"This is how the sickness spreads," Helix said.

"It's my choice."

"He's too far gone," Malia said. "Gloria, please."

Gloria didn't face Malia. Her brow set harder. Her hand started to glow again, but David retracted his arms. His body vibrated, as if shaken from the inside. Then he fell to his knees, crying out in a terrible moan.

"Back up!" Helix called out as he hopped back.

The crew shuffled down the path, eyes on David's hunched figure. Dust on the walking path around him pulsed out on puffs of air. His spine rippled in an unnatural way. He shouted again, but it was cut off in a pained grunt.

"He's turning," Peter said.

"Yeah, dust for brains," Malia said. "We know."

"We have to go." Peter's voice was shaking.

"What if we knock him out right now?" Gloria said.

That wasn't the worst idea that had passed through Helix's mind. It was worth a shot. He nodded.

Faus stepped forward. His tall frame towered over David. Helix followed suit, approaching David from the other side. A horrible sequence of cracking bones started. Helix could see them shifting under David's skin. Faus met Helix's eyes, and they nodded.

Faus swung a heavy kick toward David's head. David's hand shot out, claws at the end of his fingers, and grabbed Faus's sandal. The sharp ends of the claws bit into flesh and he hissed as David shoved, throwing him onto his backside.

Helix rushed in, but David twisted on the ground, rearing up toward him. The shock of gray skin and protruding teeth stunned Helix long enough for David to leap at him. He pinned Helix to the ground, clawed hands clasped around his forearms. He tried to struggle, but David was too strong.

His teeth grew in size, jutting out of his too-small mouth. Blood dripped onto Helix's face. One of the crew was beating against David's back, but it didn't faze him. His eyes were locked on Helix, their yellow glow intensifying with every breath. The sound of rending flesh and something wet hitting the buildings on either side filled the air and David howled. His grip on Helix's arms threatened to crush bones.

Helix cried out in pain.

That rippling vibration rolled through David again. The skin of his face stretched as the bones underneath protruded. His jaw opened as his mouth became too large. More blood dripped from his face onto Helix.

More Tektranos than human, David's weight shifted, releasing Helix's arms enough that he was able to pull away. Something knocked the creature off balance. Helix scurried from underneath the monster. Peter helped him to his feet.

Two massive wings filled the path around the creature. It pushed back onto its hind legs and the wings stretched out in shuttering movements. It reared its head toward the dome and screeched. Helix crushed his hands against his ears, wincing at the pain from the sound.

The air pulsed as its wings began to flap in a lazy rhythm. Then Faus jumped onto the creature's back. He grabbed hold of its wings, hands aglow, and they crashed to the ground.

"What are you doing?" Gloria yelled.

Faus went to work, draining the creature's aether, and it was noticeably affecting the Tektranos.

"Knock it out!" Faus yelled.

Helix skipped forward and planted the side of his foot into the Tektranos's head. It collapsed to the ground, face in the dirt.

Faus rolled off of it, staring at his hands. His face was pale.

"Are you ok?" Gloria rushed to his side.

Helix bent down, placing a hand on the monster's back to check for breath. His hand rose slowly and then lowered. It was alive.

The crew was huddled, Gloria kneeling beside Faus. He looked awful, his eyes red-rimmed and his skin clammy.

"I took its aether," Faus said.

"That was impulsive for you," Malia said.

"It worked," Peter said.

Gloria looked up at Helix with wide eyes. "I don't know how to clear dark aether."

"Help him get up," Helix said. "Peter, Malia. Grab its legs. I'll carry the front."

"What?" Malia gestured at the Tektranos. "It could wake up at any moment."

"Exactly. There's no time to waste." Helix squatted low and lifted the creature's chest with difficulty. This was going to suck. It was heavy. "We're not going to waste Faus's efforts. If we can get it back to the Celestery... we can have a Tektranos to study."

"Or we'll be delivering death right to the Celestery's door." Malia wasn't moving.

Helix twisted, pulling the bulk of the creature onto his back. "If we leave it here to wake up, it will start killing people in the villa. That doesn't sound like a better option to me."

Half of the back weight lifted. Helix heard Peter grunt as he hoisted the creature onto his shoulder.

Gloria and Faus were making their way down the path, Faus's arm draped over Gloria's shoulders.

The creature shifted again as Malia silently took her share of its bulk.

"Slow and easy," Helix said.

And as they took heavy steps to follow toward the Celestery, Helix kept telling himself it was the right thing to do.

Talleah spent the entire day cooking. She prepared a large stew that would keep well enough and made a double batch of flat breads. She said it was to prepare for whatever would happen now that Jacob had returned to the city. But it was really the only way she knew how to take care of her family —now that she knew it was no longer safe for her to stay.

"I have to go," Talleah said.

Hector's arms rubbed against her back. They were in bed, and she was so tired.

"You can't." Not an argument. He said it as a simple fact.

"I'm going to infect both of you."

She could not get Daphne's soft curls out of her mind. The need to go to the next room over and cradle her in her arms consumed her. To protect her baby girl. Except she was the one Daphne needed to be protected from.

Hector's lips pressed against her forehead. She was crying. It felt like she never stopped crying.

"We will get through this," he said. "You're the strongest person I know."

"I don't feel strong." Her voice was small with the admission. "It's in me and there's nothing I can do about it." She pumped a fist against her chest. "When it takes over and I lose myself. The hate..." She sucked in a breath. "It's so angry."

"You sure that's the sickness?"

Talleah slapped his stomach, but they both giggled.

"The things I saw today." She pulled her head back to meet his eyes. "I don't want to become that."

"Maybe Casper can fix it. He's been with the Farseers for a couple days now."

Helix had sent word to them and all but ordered them to shelter in place. Talleah hummed an agreement. She didn't say how worried she was about time. Time she didn't have. The thing inside her clawed from the inside even as they lay together. But she wanted to pretend.

"You and Daphne should go to your family in the morning."

"We're not leaving you alone."

"I need to go into quarantine. It's the only hope I have of holding it off."

His hand slipped to the back of her neck, pulling their gaze together. "I can't lose you."

"You are the best thing that ever happened to me," she said.

"Stop it." His eyes were red with tears. "This isn't goodbye."

She didn't answer with words. She melted into him, memorizing his shape and the temperature of his skin. She wouldn't sleep. Tonight was for savoring Hector. Her beautiful, incredible man.

CHAPTER

TWENTY-SIX

A crowd of people were gathered at the stairs leading up to the Celestery from the promenade. They dispersed quickly, and loudly, when they saw the Tektranos being dragged by Helix's crew. The guards posted at the entry to the stairs rushed forward.

"It's unconscious," Helix said. "For now. We need help bringing it up to the cell block."

"We should kill it while we can," one of the guards said.

"You will not," Helix said. "There is a person in there."

The guard was not convinced, but they took the weight of the Tektranos all the same.

"To the cells. If I find out he's been harmed, I will hold you both accountable."

Helix turned to his crew. They looked exhausted. Faus looked three shades paler than Helix was comfortable with.

The screech of a Tektranos arced overhead. Instinctively, they all crouched and looked up, but it came from somewhere else in the city. They turned back to the stairs and Helix took over Gloria's spot, shouldering Faus.

When they reached the Celestery garden, Helix spotted an acolyte and traded places with Peter.

"Get him inside to a Virgo," he said.

"You're not even going to say goodbye?" asked Malia.

Helix swallowed a pinch in his throat. Things were bad. Faus was not doing well, and Belen... There was no guarantee the council could get this under control. But there was also no space in his heart for that word. Letting it move across his tongue would break him into a million pieces. How could he survive that kind of shattering?

"Stay alive," Peter said.

Helix cleared his throat. Without raising his head to meet their gaze, he said, "See you soon."

A shift of wind moved his bangs, and Malia punched his right arm. Before it started to ache, she crushed into him, hugging his middle. He closed his arms around her, wincing at the pain when her cheap shot registered in his body. She let go and shoved off him to help carry Faus away.

He turned and skipped off to catch the acolyte he saw before more emotions could overwhelm him.

"Where is Preitan Theo?" Helix asked.

"The preitans are preparing for the evacuation."

Already? The cowards. How many people would inevitably be left behind? If Helix hadn't heard the evacuation was ordered, thousands of others also had not.

"Where is he?"

"I believe the council retired to their offices."

Helix turned from him without comment, rushing inside and to the back stairs that lead to the upper floors. The Celestery was lined with anxious people. A woman grabbed Helix by the arm. Her fingers dug into his skin.

"Please! Take my daughter with you."

She was crying, her grip relentless as she shoved a young

girl toward him. He removed her hand from his arm and was about to ask the woman about her drastic action when he noticed the crowd around her angle to encircle him. They yelled over each other, shoving to get to the front. His heart dropped to his feet.

"I'm sorry." His voice was thin and tight.

He turned and ran past the acolytes standing guard at the back. He heard the thuds of bodies colliding as they closed in behind him and stopped the people from following. When he made it to the stairs, his immense relief made him hate himself. He hated that he was able to pass those guards and that he was glad he could. That when the moment arrived, he chose to hide, just like the rest of his family.

At the third floor, he was warm and breathing heavily. Theo's office was in view, but the thought of confronting him made his stomach twist. Down the hall, he found himself in front of Brissa's office. His chest ached and his cheeks were wet with tears. He couldn't go in and not find her there. He also couldn't stop himself.

The door swung open easily. The air was starting to stale. He soaked in the memory of her as he walked inside, absorbing whatever phantoms of her presence were held by the walls. Then he noticed someone laying on the leather couch.

"Pappous?"

Theo shifted, his head turning at an extreme angle to meet Helix's gaze.

"Nothing smells like her anymore," Theo said, relaxing back into the couch.

Helix swiped the back of his hand to clean his cheek. He looked around, but the room immediately blurred behind a new rush of tears. Crouching beside the couch, he reached out and held Theo's hand. His grandfather's grip was firm, holding Helix as much as asking to be held.

"You're evacuating the city."

Theo's chest rose and collapsed with a sigh. "We must, before it's too late."

"How can you give up?"

Theo released his hand and slowly sat up. "The evacuation plan was designed to preserve our culture. Too many are dying. We cannot get messengers out safely to gather those in hiding. Jacob has won."

Helix shifted to join him on the couch. "Why not go to the Surface? Use the Enotis caves to shelter while we figure out a way to stabilize Novilem?"

"The Surface is not safe."

"The Enotis survived. So can we."

"Helix—"

"We can't give up. I won't accept it." Theo's pitying look filled Helix with heat. "Do not look at me like I am a child."

"You are not a child. Though you are filled with the vigor of youth. I envy that."

"We have the aether locks. We can use them to protect us from the dark aether. The Academy and the Celestery are both defensible. We can establish a scouting team to collect those in hiding while we find a way to stop Jacob."

"There are not enough aether locks."

"It can work. It's better than abandoning the city *and* our people to Jacob's monsters."

"We can do nothing to stop Jacob."

"Casper can."

Theo pressed his lips into a thin line.

"You don't believe in him?"

"I think this is beyond the abilities of a Telos. Jacob has wrought something evil in this city."

"He is not the cause of this. *We* are. Orrin showed me the texts from the library on the Tektranos."

Theo's expression remained flat. "Did the texts explain how best to send our people out to kill their infected brethren? Their partners? Their children? We have lost so much. We won't survive hunting down our own fallen."

Helix thought of Belen, infected and likely soon to be transformed. Would he be able to take his life now when he was a monster? Was that the merciful thing to do? He would prefer to be killed rather than left as a creature hunting his own kin. But was it right to make that choice for all the infected?

"There is no easy way out of this." Theo cupped Helix's cheek. "But it will not be the end of Novilem."

"This is our home. Without it, there is no Novilem."

Theo's thumb brushed away a stream of tears. Helix leaned into his touch. "Cities can be built. But only if we are not dust."

His words were sensible. Preserve as much as possible. Helix was reminded of an unusual blight that effected the wheat fields when he was small. The council burned over half their yield to stop it from spreading to the remaining crops. He could follow the logic, but it hinged on a point Helix could not support. Theo didn't believe in Casper.

He grabbed Theo's hand and kissed his knuckles.

"Keep the family together," Helix said.

Theo's eyes widened. "Please. Come with us."

"I won't leave him behind. He can fix this."

"Helix—"

Helix turned from him and headed to the door. "I love you, Pappous. Stars guide us both."

"Helix!"

He shut the door behind him, heart pounding, and tried

to slow his breathing. Staying was the only choice he could stomach, but that didn't stop him trying to recall his last moments with each of his family members. He moved before the grief could weigh him down to the floor. He would see them again, but he needed to make sure there was enough city for them to return to.

CHAPTER
TWENTY-SEVEN

Casper settled on the floor of his room. Knees folded in and hands in his lap, his lower back ached from the long hours sitting with Eman, pretzeled in on himself. But he missed Helix, and if there was a chance he could talk to him, he wanted to try.

His aether channels were clear from his work that day, so he went straight to find his Gemini resonance. The heady, vibrant ring of energy was there but he had to sit and wait to find the lower thrum of dark aether. He concentrated on Helix. The weight of him. The fullness of his muscles. The honeyed smell of his long hair. The way he was quick to offer a half smile but always made Casper work for the real thing.

Then he let the dark Gemini aether in. His consciousness shifted and the ache of his back and legs faded away. He could feel Helix immediately. His mind was sharp and focused.

"Helix," Casper said. Thought? It felt enough like speaking, even if he was disembodied.

"Casper?"

Helix's body froze. He was somewhere in the Celestery, settling onto a cot to sleep. Casper could tell something was wrong, but he didn't dig out of respect. If he pressed further into Helix's mind, he wouldn't be able to control what information showed up.

"How are you here?"

"Learned some tricks today." Casper wanted to sink into him. To feel the warmth of his skin. "I miss you."

"I miss you, too. Are you ok? I was going to get a message to you. Your dad—" Helix stopped talking suddenly.

"What is it?"

"He... well, he turned."

Casper was grateful for the disconnect between this experience and his body. It made the news less overwhelming to not have to deal with the full brunt of his emotions.

"Oh." It was all he could get out.

"We brought him back to the Celestery. At least we can stop him from hurting anyone."

"Ok."

"I'm sorry, Cas."

He couldn't tell if it was shock or the aether bond, but didn't know how the information made him feel. Horrified? Sad? Relieved?

"Yeah, me too."

His dad. A Tektranos. What did that mean? Was he gone? Casper's head spun, realizing his last moment with his dad was walking away from him as David screamed his name.

"Hey, we'll figure this out. Yeah?" The care in Helix's voice was so inviting.

He tried to believe him. To hope. "Yeah."

He focused on the Gemini connection. It felt more like lying next to Helix with their eyes shut. Much less all-encompassing than the full mind connection that happened with light aether.

"How bad are things?" Casper asked.

"About as bad as you'd expect. You talk first, though. What's the grotto like?"

"Would you believe me if I said there is a whole rainforest down here?"

"Down?"

"It's like an entire other Novilem. They took me on an elevator, but we went so far down that gravity like swapped. I think we must be on the other side of the moon's center? I don't know. But there are trees. So many trees. And animals. I saw a deer. There's birdsong all day long. And the sky looks so much like Earth. It's kinda crazy."

"That sounds beautiful."

Casper could feel the smile in his voice. "I wish you could come here, and we could pretend like nothing was happening."

"That sounds nice." There was weight in Helix's words.

"What's going on?" Casper asked.

"Today was a rough day. You know how Belen has been more ornery than usual?"

"Hard to tell. He's never exactly softened to me."

"Well, apparently, he's been sick for a while. We had to put him in quarantine."

"Fuck."

"Faus also got infected helping us contain your dad. He's being looked at now."

Guilt washed over Casper. "Helix, I'm so sorry. We should have just left him on Earth."

Helix didn't respond for a moment. "Do you think they're still in there?"

It wasn't too crazy of an idea. They were now living in a

world where people grew wings and fangs. Why couldn't it also be a world where those wings and fangs could go away?

"I don't know."

"How's the balance thing coming along?"

"It sucks." Casper sighed. "Turns out balancing aether requires a stable emotional landscape."

"Ooph." Helix laughed.

"Not funny."

"It's a little bit funny."

"It's ironic that in order to save Novilem, I have to get over all the trauma they've caused me."

"Is it ironic? Kind of seems like that's the way of things."

"Why can't I just hurt in peace?"

"How could I forget your core identity of wounded soldier?"

"I'm gone for less than two days and it's like I was never there."

Helix let out a hearty laugh. "I miss you."

"I miss you, too."

"When do you come back?"

"Soon, I hope." Even though the thought of leaving the green sanctuary of the grotto to return to the chaos of Novilem was daunting. "Eman has been a bit standoffish about timelines. But I'm finally making some progress."

"Good. We need you." There was a pause and Casper felt like Helix was trying to figure out what to say. "I need you."

The weight of Helix's grief sank into Casper's chest through the aether bond.

"We're going to get through this," Casper said.

"Are we?"

It hit Casper how scared Helix was. Strong, reliable, unflappable Helix. He had been the most steadfast support Casper had ever experienced, even when they were abandoned on the Surface. So, it was only fair that Casper returned that support in his time of need.

"We are," Casper said. "I'm going to fix this. I promise."

"Cas, just... be safe. Okay? I need you to be safe. I can't lose you, too."

"I will. I'll see you soon."

He let the bond release, and his awareness returned to his body lying on the mat in his room. He was running out of time. If he didn't get back to Novilem, there wouldn't be anyone to return to.

CHAPTER
TWENTY-EIGHT

Later that day, Casper was walking down a path, enjoying the sound of the evening breeze through the trees, and the next his mind was swept away to the astral plane. Eman had explained it was a place that was both real and not real. Made of the mind rather than physical matter.

"Come on!" Casper said. "You can't keep doing this without warning."

But the Sedrivani didn't answer. The world around him was dark. Panicked, Casper searched for any sign of danger. There was a figure watching him. Too still. He noticed the long gray hair first.

"Who's there?"

When there was no answer, Casper approached slowly. He found Jacob smiling, sitting on a high-backed throne of black stone. His body was restrained by braided tendrils of black, smoky aether.

"Has the savior come for me?" Jacob's voice was gravelly.

"Hello!" Casper yelled out into the aether. There was no light to be found. Where was the Sedrivani?

"There's nothing there to answer you, I'm afraid." Jacob rotated his hands, demonstrating how trapped he was. "The Kanos has already chosen its vessel."

Casper tried to pull in aether and immediately fell to the ground. There was nothing but chaos here. The dread that filled him was immense.

Jacob laughed. "A pity, really. For you to be as broken as you are."

Casper clutched a hand against his stomach. "I'm not broken."

"You can't fool me." Jacob's glare was heavy, and more present than Casper had ever seen it. "I know what the aether does. I have lived with it for years. It touches your shame. Makes your grief vibrate in your bones to the point of breaking. If you can't handle a moment of its presence, then you are exactly as weak as I thought."

Casper raised off the ground. "Says the man who has completely lost himself."

Jacob's brow lifted. He hummed a small agreement. "You aren't wrong. I was naive to think I could control the chaos."

Something felt off. Jacob was reasonable. His presence was steady. Stable. The quick flash to righteous superiority was missing. There was a resignation in his posture, like he had accepted his fate and was simply awaiting the end.

"You're really here, aren't you?"

Jacob smiled again. "Where do you think here is?"

"We're in the astral plane."

"Wrong." Jacob's voice rang out into the empty black surrounding them, the sound going tinny and hollow as it traveled away into the seemingly endless nothing.

Coils of black latched onto Casper's feet, wrapping up his legs. He tried to pull away, but he was already locked in place.

"It seems you figured out how to pay a visit to my mind."

Casper's heart stuttered.

"And I'd love to have a chat."

The dark energy wrapping around his body formed into a chair, sliding Casper across the ground until he was sitting face-to-face with Jacob. The planes of his cheeks were hollow. Dark circles bagged under his eyes. He was a man dragged to the end of the line. Every drop of life sucked out of him.

"You look awful," Casper said.

"I see Brissa didn't break your habit of speaking your mind." Jacob smiled. "That's nice. Might be the only part about you I enjoy."

Casper pulled at his arms, but they remained bound to the chair. "I suppose now's the part where you tell me none of this is your fault?"

"The Kanos brings out the darker parts of us. Intensifies things some of us try to suppress. But it's still us."

Casper's stomach clenched. He couldn't help but think about the lives that Jacob took. The damage he caused to innocent people.

"Hate me all you want. I told you; this was inevitable. Had it not been me, it would have been someone else."

"What do you want, Jacob?"

"Exactly what I said. A chat. What do *you* want, Casper? You're the one who came here."

Not by choice, if it was his doing. Casper didn't believe Jacob wasn't playing one of his games. "I want you to stop the Tektranos from killing people."

"Rather nasty, what happens when people's base instincts are laid bare, isn't it?"

"You're turning them into monsters."

Jacob shrugged. "There's a monster in all of us. Most are just afraid to let it out."

"I don't understand. You said you were trying to save Novilem. To preserve the culture by forcing them to colonize the Surface. Now you're fine to let the city rip itself apart?"

"Sometimes, you're so dull," Jacob said, making a show of shaking his body to display how stuck he was. "I thought I could force the balance by leaning in. I was wrong. Or right in an unexpected way, the aether is balancing itself."

"And no one will survive to see the end result."

"Well, that's what our dear boy savior is for. You get to save the day. Have effigies carved in your honor. They'll probably put a mural of you on the Celestery walls."

Casper rolled his eyes. "Jesus Christ, you're exhausting." He shut his eyes and tried to wake up. If he was the one who started this, he should be able to finish it.

Jacob cleared his throat. "I'm… not out there anymore. Not really. I haven't been for a while." His hands rotated, gesturing to the darkness. "It's all shadows and silence these days. When it comes time… could you—"

"End it?" Casper scoffed. "Are you seriously asking me to mercy kill you right now?"

"You get everything." A bit of the Jacob Casper knew came back to his face, his upper lip pulling into a thin sneer. "Give me this."

"Whatever happens"—Casper laid a heavy glare at Jacob, holding his gaze—"you deserve worse."

He pulled his awareness back, searching for the corporeal. Finding a hint of the real world, he ran toward it like waking from a bad dream. The world blurred around him, his eyes struggling to adjust. But there was light, and Jacob, thankfully, was gone.

On his third day in the grotto Casper woke to birdsong. Beams of warm sunlight sloped through the slats of the windows of the small hut he was given to sleep in. He dressed and opened the door, taking in the fresh open air. It was tropical, weighty with humidity, and filled with the scent of earth and floral plants. So completely opposite of the thin metallic edge of Novilem.

He would have lessons with Eman later in the morning, so he had some time to wander and find something to eat. English was not nearly as popular amongst the Farseers. Even so, the people greeted him with warm, open smiles. As Casper walked through the village, he didn't need to understand the language to observe how communal their lifestyle was. Their shared open kitchens fed many. Babies were passed freely to those with open arms.

Casper approached a woman serving meals from a large pot over an open fire, and she handed him a wooden bowl. He accepted it and gave a bow of thanks since she wouldn't understand his words. It was a porridge of sorts with sliced berries and a drizzle of honey. It was delicious.

The constant dread Casper held in his body about what Jacob would do to Novilem next was still there, but he could almost pretend it was a world away. Something for other people to worry about. That was immediately replaced with an intense wave of guilt that he would even consider the thought. He noticed others washing their bowls in bucket of water. He followed suit and returned his bowl to the kind woman before making his way to the meditation circle behind Eman's home.

She was already seated on a small cushion, legs folded in, and eyes closed.

"I have to go back," Casper said.

Without opening her eyes Eman said, "You are not ready."

"I'll never be ready. But the longer I stay down here trying to force myself to feel things I don't, the more people get hurt up there."

Eman met his gaze, her deep brown eyes measuring him. "You do not feel because your fear overwhelms you. If you remain afraid there will be no balance. When your mind lives in extremes, so does your spirit. Open yourself to the aether like this and the pendulum will swing. You must find your center."

"What does that even mean?" Casper asked. "How can anyone experience peace when the universe is crashing down on us? People are turning into monsters!"

Eman rose to her feet and strolled past Casper. Over her shoulder she said, "Come."

Casper sighed, turning to follow her. They walked through the village following a path that led into the forest. Days in, and the towering trees and full canopy still made the grotto seem like a different world. The skittering of small rodents filled the bushes bordering the trail. Casper smelled cedar and pine and oak. The sound of needles and leaves crunching underfoot made his heart ache with fullness. He wanted to stop and bask in the stillness of the forest. To pretend that he was back on Earth. It felt so impossibly close.

The trail widened into a clearing where a group of people faced them. They greeted Eman happily, clasping arms and smiling through words that Casper didn't understand. She gestured for him to stand beside her as the five people returned to a staggered position.

"This is the balance." Eman nodded at the group.

Two of the five stepped forward and gave each other a

salutation Casper recognized from around the village. When it began, it looked like a martial arts movie come to life. His untrained eyes struggled to focus on their quick motions.

The woman created a Shadow, but before she could use it, her opponent gestured in a smooth circle and the Shadow was pulled into his hands. Casper recalled Eman performing the same action on his Scorpio aether. The man pulled back his hand to his chest and his opponent teleported into his arms. She was off balance from being transported. He grappled her, twisting her body over his shoulder and onto the ground.

The man helped his opponent off the ground, and they stepped back, patting each other on the shoulders. The next pair stepped forward. In the time it took the tall woman on Casper's right to shoot a beam of aether at the man across from her, her opponent knelt, scooping glowing hands into the dirt. A wall of earth rose with his hands, blocking the beam. He then punched out his palm and the hardened earth hurled toward her. Her bare foot glowed bright orange as she flipped over in a back handspring, slicing through the projectile. It fell on either side of her in two pieces.

A third woman blurred into thin air and reappeared atop the taller woman's back, knocking her forward and pinning her to the ground. The man hung back, giving them space to duel. The reality of this being a mock fight crashed back into Casper's awareness. It felt so real.

The taller woman could not wrestle her smaller counterpart off. The woman's tiny frame was strangely immobile. Her arms and legs were rigid as the woman underneath her struggled. It looked like she had turned herself to stone.

Placing a glowing hand on the smaller woman's arm, the tall woman closed her eyes in a look of concentration and her attacker's body melted from its rigid pose. They rolled together and the taller woman rose to her feet as her opponent tried to recover on the ground.

"What was that?" Casper asked, unable to understand what aether they had used.

"Aries and Sagittarius." Eman pointed at the smaller woman still recovering. "She used Aries in ma'at to ambush. Aries in Isfet immobilizes one's body and makes your skin hard as metal." She gestured to the taller woman. "Then she used Sagittarius in Isfet to deplete the aether in her opponent's body."

"The things they can do... it's incredible. Why didn't you show me this earlier?"

"I underestimated how difficult it would be for you to make progress without a frame of reference. A mistake, I'm afraid." She sighed. "So, I arranged these duels so you could see what I've been trying to explain to you."

It was helpful to see. Casper managed to withhold comment about how they should have started with this display. Mistake or not, it was refreshing to hear an adult express regret and admit their fault.

The duels continued for a time until Eman called for them to rest.

"How are they using so many different kinds of aether?" Casper asked.

"You call it a trine," Eman said. "With Ma'at and Isfet, a trine becomes six. Everything has it's opposite."

It was incredible, but Casper still didn't understand where to begin. "How do they let the chaos in without being overwhelmed by it?"

Eman touched his chest with one hand and his temple with the other. "You are disconnected. Fragmented. Just like the aether. You must come back together."

"And if I can't do that?"

Eman lowered her hand from his temple to cup his cheek. "Then we will all die."

TWENTY-NINE

"Why are we going to the Gemini quarters?" Orrin asked.

Helix led the way to the occluded path on the side of the Celestery garden. He'd barely slept after talking to Casper, his mind preoccupied with his tense goodbye to his pappous. He replayed the conversation in his head, wondering what he could have said to change Theo's mind. In the end, he decided he would have to take matters into his own hands. "The corrupted aether can't affect us if our bodies are blocked off from the aether."

"That would leave us defenseless."

"We will gather at the Academy. There are plenty of weapons."

"And very few people trained to use them."

"There won't be people left if we don't do something. The sickness is spreading too fast. This can buy us some time. Do you know how many aether locks we have?"

"Without records in front of me I can't be exact, but I would estimate somewhere in the range of three thousand."

"It will have to be enough."

Orrin grabbed his arm, stopping them before the door at the end of the tunnel. "Helix, there are nearly two-hundred thousand people in Novilem. If less than two percent of them can be protected, it will cause a riot. We should continue holding out for Casper. He is with the Farseers learning how to fix this."

"We don't know what the Farseers are doing with Casper. And until he's back, we can't assume anything. If we don't do this; there might be no one left for him to come back to."

The Gemini quarters was a large structure built behind the wall of Novilem, resting behind the Celestery. When they entered the large, open room, disarray was apparent immediately. The place had been ransacked. Cushions were tossed from the benches along the central area. Debris from the residential chambers was strewn along the walkway.

"I guess it was a bit foolish to assume this place would be left alone because it sits behind the Celestery," Helix said, surveying the area.

"Yes, well, it wouldn't be fair to judge how people go about surviving apocalyptic disasters."

Orrin was on Helix's left tinkering with a panel in the wall. There was a click and a hiss, then doors opened to a storage room. Inside were neat rows of countless aether locks.

"Thank the stars," Helix said.

"What did you find?"

Helix turned toward the voice. It was a young man, maybe a few years older than Helix. He had warm eyes and short hair.

Helix stepped closer to him, blocking the view into the

storage room. "Some materials for the council. What happened here?" He pointed at the mess throughout the hall.

The man shrugged. "It was like this when we got here."

"We?"

The man went rigid, on guard. He studied Helix for a moment before responding. "You might still follow their orders, but don't get any ideas about trying to clear this space. We aren't going anywhere. The streets aren't safe."

Helix's stomach turned. How many Novelites hadn't found a safe place to hide? "We aren't here to clear the space," Helix assured the man. "Just here for the materials."

"What materials?"

The doors to the storage room clicked shut and Orrin spoke from behind Helix. "That's council business."

The man scoffed and gestured at the entrance. "There are monsters ripping us apart. And the council still keeps secrets?"

Helix turned to Orrin, who shook his head. It wasn't safe to let information about the locks out until there was a plan on how to distribute them, but it went against every fiber of Helix's dignity to withhold the information. He could hear Brissa's voice in his mind. *The people need leaders to make difficult choices. Not to tend to their feelings.*

The man was glaring at them. He and Orrin were representing the government that had failed the city, and he was understandably angry. Well, Helix didn't have to play a part in disappointing him.

"How many of you are there?"

The man didn't answer, his body going rigid again.

"I'm going to help you. I promise." He pointed at the storage room behind him. "There are aether locks inside here. They will protect you from the corruption sickness."

"Helix—"

Helix turned to Orrin. "Open it."

"I'm not sure that's a good idea."

"I don't care if it's a good idea. It's the right thing to do. They are here and they need to be protected."

"So does all of Novilem. We need to find the most effective way to use the locks."

"You may be comfortable turning him away, but I am not. His life doesn't mean less than anyone else's."

"That is not my point. The locks are needed to safeguard the Academy."

"And a few less locks won't change anything. Now, are you going to open the storage room, or do I need to figure out how to open it myself?"

Orrin sighed, but he turned back to the wall and placed his palm against the stone. The stone lit under his touch, and with a click and a hiss, the doors popped open.

Helix addressed the man. "How many of you?"

"Five."

Helix collected five aether locks from Orrin and handed them to the man. "You won't be able to use aether with them on. You're welcome to join us at the Academy. My people will be here soon to transport the locks. We could use all the help we can get. Otherwise, stay put and find a weapon you can defend yourself with."

The man nodded and hurried away.

"I'm not sure that was wise," Orrin said.

"If it saves their lives, I don't care."

"They might talk. If people find out the aether locks can protect them and they are here, they will come for them."

"Then stay and guard them."

"I am one man."

"I'll have acolytes come help."

Orrin looked unsure.

"What other options are there?" Helix asked. "Jacob is winning."

"Fine. I will stay."

Helix patted him on the shoulder. "I will be quick. Stars bless us both."

"I'm not sure which of us needs the stars more."

Helix laughed, the statement too true for his comfort.

THIRTY

Talleah woke with a start. Her heart was pounding in her chest. An intense, pinching ache stretched across the sides of her skull. She felt like she might throw up. The light from the window hurt the back of her eyes. She heard Daphne laughing from the other side of the house, the trills reaching her like they were being filtered through a dream.

A chill shook through her body and yet sweat broke on her brow. She felt fine the night before. She stood from the bed and immediately fell to the ground, catching herself on trembling arms. This wasn't just a fever. The shadows that had been plaguing her mind were distinctly louder. The cold rage too present in her belly, threatening to come out of her mouth in a strangled cry.

Hector stepped through the doorway and dropped to her side.

"Tal."

His hands were on her shoulders, their heat overwhelming. She shrugged away, holding back the sound of disgust that wanted to escape her.

"What's wrong?" he asked.

Everything. Her body was revolting. Her mind was rioting. It took monumental effort to not scream.

"Mommy." Daphne was in the hall, staring at her on the ground with tears already in her eyes.

"I have... to go... outside..." Talleah managed to say on broken breaths.

Hector's hot hands grabbed her sides, and she suffered the touch long enough to let him help her up. Then she pulled away and walked past Daphne. She tried to smile at her, but Daphne shrunk back and began to cry openly. There was no time. Daphne couldn't see her like this. She had been through enough.

"Tal, wait," Hector called after her as she shuffled out the door of their apartment.

She stumbled into an elevator car. She heard Hector running, calling her name as the doors slid shut. The stone wall of the car was cool against her back, supporting her as she took labored breaths through flashes of heat. She exited onto the ground floor, hurrying across the lobby, and burst outside. When she made it to the grass, she fell to the ground, immediately sick and emptying her stomach. A chill rolled through her, raising her skin with a prickly ache. The constant thrum of aether pouring out of the western tower had become a background noise over the past days. But it became blindingly loud in her mind. Each wave crashed into her like a physical punch. The scream she had been holding back finally made its way out, spit flying from her mouth as her voice strained her vocal cords.

She felt the first crack of a bone. Her vision went white from the pain. Then everything turned black.

Hector watched in horror as Talleah thrashed against the ground. He called out to her, and she motioned for him to stop. The skin of the palm she held out toward him turned gray and black before his eyes. Then a wing ripped from her back, flinging blood across the ground. A second wing followed, accentuated by a horrible screech.

"Fuck," Hector said.

Tears blurred his vision.

"Mommy!"

He turned and Daphne was standing right behind him.

"I told you to stay in your room."

"What's wrong with Mommy?"

Hector lifted Daphne into his arms and started walking back toward the tower. It felt like ripping a piece of himself from his chest to turn away from Talleah. She needed him. But he had to get Daphne to safety.

"Daddy no!" She wriggled in his arms, trying to get down. "What's wrong with Mommy?!"

"I don't know." Inside the lobby, Hector set her down and wiped the tears from his eyes. "We'll figure this out, but it's not safe to be near Mommy right now."

Daphne disappeared from between his hands. He spun around and she was back on the lawn.

"Daphne! Stop!"

Through the doorway Hector could see that Talleah, or whatever Talleah was now, was taking off in flight. Daphne was running toward her. Hector rushed back outside. A chorus of screeches echoed through the air. He winced at the volume as he scooped Daphne back into his arms. Crying, they watched Talleah ascend into the sky and join dozens more creatures flying toward the tower on the horizon.

"Mommy!" Daphne yelled after her.

Hector squeezed her tightly.

"It's going to be ok," he said. And he repeated it to himself over and over again, trying to convince himself as much as Daphne that he was telling the truth.

Daphne's cry pulled at her, but she couldn't turn around. She couldn't risk hurting them. Even with the wind rushing by, her hearing was sharp enough to pick up Hector telling Daphne it was going to be ok. A rattling screech burst from her throat at that.

Nothing was ok. There was no ok anymore. No going back to how things used to be. Things used to be bad. Why did everyone seem to forget that?

Anger had always been a defense. A way to protect herself against a world that did not nurture her. But it had transformed. The bluntness of it. The heat of it. She realized those were her own barriers, but now the rage came quick and cold.

It slipped through her like cool air, soothing her mind. The world felt clear. She was powerful. More powerful than those who had caused her harm. They were an easy problem to solve.

She pivoted in the sky and, like the fury in her heart, she cut through the air.

THIRTY-ONE

The two books that Orrin gave Helix were on the table in front of him. The Academy didn't want for useable rooms. It was packed with people sheltering, but Helix managed to find an empty corner in the cafeteria to occupy. He'd successfully convinced two acolytes to gather the aether locks from the Gemini quarters without confirming with the council first—another boon from his family name. He instructed them to distribute the locks to those with enough training to protect the others first, then by need. When he was satisfied his instructions were being carried out, he retreated here to look for more permanent solutions. He couldn't wait around while Casper was with the Farseers. He needed to do something.

He pushed *Governance and Civil Planning* aside. He flipped open *Aether and its Limits*. It was an old book. There was no table of contents. Reading Greek wasn't an issue for him, but he frequently found words that he had to focus on to understand. So, the book was old enough that it was closer to Earth's Greek than theirs.

Like most moments when Helix slowed down these days, he found himself missing Brissa. He could hear her admonishing him for taking materials from the library. *You seek knowledge you are not yet ready for,* she would say. And he would be annoyed, even if a non-insignificant part of him would find comfort in Brissa having the knowledge he desired. Because she would be able to handle the issue. Whatever it was.

Soon he was flipping through the pages haphazardly, hoping his eyes would land on something important. His frustration mounted with every page flip that revealed what felt like more useless information until he couldn't make out the words from the tears that filled his eyes. He pounded a fist into the table.

What was he doing? Belen and Faus weren't going to be healed by a book. The Frenzy was so unknowable. The aether, something that had been an integral part of his every day, became insidious. Knowing it was all around him, waiting to enter his body, made his skin crawl. His mind raced thinking of the past days, trying to remember if he used aether.

It was second nature to dip into his Capricorn aether to refresh his muscles after a hike up the stairs or a night of not enough sleep. Had he been mindful enough to stop himself? He raked over moments where he could have moved into autopilot, letting his mind wander. Knowing it could have happened when he wasn't paying attention was terrifying.

He wiped his face dry when he heard footsteps enter the room. He turned to find Orrin facing him.

"Apologies for the interruption," Orrin said.

"Clearly, I wasn't getting much done." Helix gestured to the books on the table.

"May I?" Orrin nodded toward the table.

"Please. I don't think I'm capable of focusing on the words right now."

Orrin sat on the bench opposite of him. He gently lifted the open book and placed it in front of him. "Books are many things. They rarely offer the exact answer you are looking for. Though, if you're lucky, sometimes they provide the perfect context needed for you to sort something out."

"This isn't a time for books," Helix said. "Truly, I don't know what I'm doing here. Two of my crew fell to the Frenzy today. I have no time for reading."

"That sounds like the perfect time for books." Orrin was scanning the pages of *Aether and its Limits*. "What else is there for you to do? Play hero in the streets until you also contract the sickness?"

Helix dropped his face into his hands and released a frustrated grunt through his fingers. "I don't know how to fix this."

"You don't know how to be unable to fix it." Orrin was watching him with soft eyes when Helix peered through his hands.

His frustration doubled being seen so pointedly. Helix's face flushed.

"It's normal." Orrin returned to flipping through the book. "Human nature is to pretend at being a god. You are not alone in fretting when your efforts are deemed insufficient."

"Why are you here?" Helix asked.

Orrin peered up from the book, his eyes quizzical, but he didn't reply.

"You betrayed the Estellar. You helped Jacob stage a coup. Brissa exiled you. And you're back here in the Celestery spouting the same philosophical quips. It doesn't make sense."

Orrin settled back in his seat. The dark planes of his face showed no sign of his nearly eight decades. It was easy to forget the wisdom that existed behind his youthful appearance. But every moment of his experience felt present as he held Helix's gaze.

"You are free to judge my actions as you like. But if you have questions, ask them."

"Why?" Helix's voice came out as a whisper. He had to look down at his hands to get the words out. "Why did you do it?"

Orrin hummed, setting the book down on the table. "Jacob was always self-interested. Jealous and vindictive. He joined the council decades after Brissa, but that didn't stop him from envying her status. It was an obsession. Even before his time as an elder he would undermine her, never pushing far enough to be punished. When she couldn't keep the council from voting him into an elder seat, it was clear the day would come when he would outright challenge her.

"As steward to the Celestery, I was a valuable asset. So, in order to get behind Jacob's lies and machinations, Brissa assigned me to align myself with him."

Helix's stomach was in a knot. He couldn't keep the remains of Brissa's body out of his mind, splayed on the rocky beach of the Surface, wet with too much blood and boiling rain. He remembered finding out that Brissa and Theo had known Jacob was going to attack at Casper's ascension festival. Theo had even admitted it when Helix confronted him.

"Jacob had too many allies on the council," Orrin continued. "Brissa's control over the table wasn't as widely accepted as it seemed. Jacob offered the idea of a balance against her. Someone willing to counter her wishes."

Traitors. All responsible for her death. For what was

happening outside. How many seats sanctioned it? "Name them," Helix said darkly.

"Inconsequential."

"Dust off. It matters. They helped kill her."

"What good does knowing do you?" Orrin asked. "Give me an answer that isn't rooted in revenge, and I'll give you names."

Heat radiated from Helix's chest. His palms were clammy. He was all the more angry for knowing Orrin had a point. The fury swirling inside him just wanted something, someone to aim at.

"Brissa spent years in political battle with Jacob. He was smart. There was never enough evidence to depose him. But she knew that he was building toward something dangerous. So, I worked my way into his circle. To garner access to his plans. Only, I found that his network was far larger than anticipated and the issue had become untenable. When Jacob began his campaign to collect the Telos, Brissa saw an opportunity to expose his intentions."

"Let him think he was winning, so he would finally push far enough to cross the line."

"Precisely."

"You haven't answered my question." It was a clean story. The loyal steward who was willing to cross political lines. His actions directed by those more powerful than him. "Why are you here now? Brissa's gone. Jacob is attacking the city. Again. What's your angle?"

Orrin brushed his long fingers across the pages of the open book in front of him.

"Books have always been the focus of my life. Even as a child I was enamored with them. To experience the lifetimes of adventures and information they held. To know things I couldn't know from my own mind. What was life on Earth like? How civilizations rose and fell. What was it like to be in love?"

Helix perked up at the admission. He'd known Orrin had never been coupled. But given his natural aloofness and handsome features, Helix figured he preferred a casual approach to relationships.

"I found myself in books. And my love of books led me here. And this place, for better or worse, was run by Brissa. A stubborn woman. A force of nature."

Helix smiled. He could hear her voice in his mind. He could imagine her standing over his shoulder, smirking at Orrin's comment. Her presence was so tangible, he looked over his shoulder to see if she was there.

"It's nearly impossible not to fall into the gravity of someone like Brissa. She was a friend as much as she was my superior." He paused, taking a deep, steadying breath. "It was difficult to manage the tasks Jacob required of me. To know the damage I was helping inflict on the people of Novilem. But I believed in Brissa. I wanted her to be right. To believe that ousting Jacob would help swing the public back toward a more stable future for Novilem."

Helix waited patiently. Orrin still hadn't answered his question, but it was clear he needed to tell his story, to unburden himself. Selfishly, Helix didn't want him to stop. Because in his words, there was a time when Brissa was still with them. When Helix could find her pouring over documents at her desk. He could nearly smell the aroma of her favorite cup of tea sitting next to her.

"When I discovered Jacob's plan to assassinate Brissa, it was finally the moment she had hoped for. Actionable offense that she could use against him."

"He had you orchestrating an underground Ramal distribution inside the Academy," Helix said. "How was that not enough to use against him?"

"He would have pinned it on me," Orrin said. "And he had enough support on the council to back up the claim. Brissa needed him to air his intentions publicly. And the ascension festival was the perfect opportunity for that. But she also knew there was a chance he would be successful."

We hadn't considered your feelings for the boy. Theo's words replayed in Helix's mind with a whole new context. She was willing to bet Casper's life because to her, it meant gaining control of the city again. It meant ridding Novilem of Jacob's malicious intent. Instead, she paid with her own.

"So, before she exiled me, she instructed me to continue your education."

"From the Surface?"

"I was never going to remain on the Surface." Orrin smiled softly. "I don't think she ever imagined you would be successful in having the Exoria returned as a whole. But she and Theo were to exonerate me after Jacob was handled."

There were three completely different worlds resting in the space between them. The plan that Orrin explained. The weeks of coming back together after the Turning. And the hollow, monstrous streets of Novilem that currently existed outside the Celestery.

"I miss her," Helix said. "Every day."

"Her absence has left a massive hole for all of us."

There wasn't much conversation left in him, but he wasn't ready to return to the issues outside. He was so tired. He ached for Brissa. He wanted to bury his face in Casper's chest. To drown in the comfort of him. To pretend even for a moment that there was some normalcy to be had.

"It never stops falling apart," Helix said.

"No, it doesn't."

"So, what do we do now?"

Orrin inhaled deeply before sighing. "I wish I could say I know the answer to that question."

"Nothing in those books of yours?"

Orrin closed the book with careful hands. "Not today."

Helix stood from the table. "Yeah, I didn't think so."

"Helix."

He turned back to Orrin.

"Thank you," Orrin said. "For listening. I know it was of no small effort on your part to hear that."

Helix nodded. A swell of grief, anger, and disgust still spun around his center. But he was glad to know what Orrin shared. There was a time beyond this day when Helix could find understanding. But in the moment, he turned away without responding. He had done enough.

The Academy was swarming with people. The noise and movement felt like a constant reminder that at any moment one of them could fall sick. Hector knelt and squeezed Daphne's small frame between his hands.

"How are you doing?"

She sniffled, but her eyes grew steady like she was daring him to a game of hide and seek. "We have to find Mommy."

His stomach pinched. They had an agreement to not placate or lie to Daphne. Their main priority was building her trust back up after being separated for so long. "I'm not sure that's possible. She could be anywhere, and it's really important for us to find a place to be safe."

Daphne visibly fought back more tears. She went rigid in Hector's hands. "She's out there alone."

"You saw what happened, right? That Mommy got really sick and flew away? We don't know how to help her get better yet." Or *if* she can get better. Hector felt like he could throw up. "People who turn into Tektranos aren't safe to be around. They seem to always want to hurt us."

"Mommy won't want to hurt us."

"Of course not. But she might not be able to help it. They call this sickness the Frenzy because it makes people unable to control their bodies. They can't stop themselves from hurting people."

Daphne put her little hand on Hector's arm. "It's Mommy."

There was a hole in Hector's chest. A giant empty space that seeing Talleah transform had created. He had busied himself getting them to the Academy and making sure Daphne was ok. But her gentle touch and the fierceness in her eyes, so much like her mother's, pulled every ounce of Hector's awareness to Talleah's absence. He nearly crumbled onto the ground in tears. If Daphne wasn't watching him so intently, he would have.

"You're right," Hector said. "It is Mommy."

More importantly, it was Daphne. Their little fighter. If he doubled down and tried to hide her away, she would be gone, looking for Talleah on her own, in a heartbeat.

"After we talk to Uncle Helix, we need to rest for a while. It will be dark outside soon, and we won't be able to find Mom in the dark. But as soon as we wake up, what do you say we get some food and extra clothes from home?" Hector said. "We'll need to be ready to be away for a while."

Daphne nodded. "Ok."

Hector grabbed her hand and led her into the hall of the Academy, racking his brain for any way to convince his daughter not to run after her monster mother.

Stars guide me. But he wasn't sure the stars could save him from this one. Daphne wouldn't wait for the stars.

A Virgo checked for the Frenzy and cleared them. Daphne was crying. Hector hugged her against his body. He wanted to put her somewhere safe so he could talk to Helix, but the thought of not being next to her filled him with a surge of desperation.

When they found him in the middle of the main hall, Daphne hugged his legs, hiding her face in his pants.

"Hector!" Helix said, stopping in his tracks when he took in Hector's expression.

"It's Talleah—" Hector's voice broke. His eyes itched, like he had never stopped crying. They filled with tears again as Helix rushed to him, pulling him into a hug.

"Where is she?" Helix asked.

"She turned"—Hector sucked in a wet breath—"into one of those things."

"Dust me," Helix said.

"I don't know what to do." Hector's skin itched at the thought of hiding while Talleah was somewhere out there, but protecting Daphne was his priority. He ached to ask about the Tektranos. To find out what Helix knew of where they went and what the council was doing about them. One thing was for sure; the acolytes were hunting them in the streets. He pushed the thought away. He didn't have the strength to consider that.

"Stay here," Helix said. "It's well guarded. There's food and water."

"She's out there. Alone—"

Helix grabbed his forearm, gentle but locking them

together. "Daphne needs you here. This is where Talleah would want you to be."

He tried to greet Daphne, but she buried herself into Hector.

"She'll be ok," Helix said. "It's Tal."

Hector nodded, tears filling his eyes.

THIRTY-TWO

On the morning of his fourth day in the grotto, Casper fell into a vision before waking. He was in the sky. The edges of Ouranos behind him and the vast openness of space waited to welcome his warmth. He tried not to think about this moment. The feeling of completeness that consumed him when the aether took over. How close he was to giving in.

The Sedrivani spoke to him. "You are afraid."

The voice pulled him out of his body. Weightless and hanging in the sky, he observed himself. His eyes shined with tears. His hand was stretched out to the stars. It was painful to remember how fulfilled he felt as the supernova neared.

"I am."

"You were incomplete then."

The astrolabe lodged in Casper's chest glowed bright. The expanse of Ouranos below faded behind a massive shroud of darkness. Tendrils of black smoke reached for his body; held back like he was protected by a shield.

"You were nearly there, but the Kanos could not reach you."

"Hold on," Casper said. "You want me to supernova again?"

"The aether will find release. If you cannot let the dark in, the light will take you."

"Why? If I'm so important and supposed to help balance the aether, why would you do this to me?"

"This is balance."

"I don't understand."

The astrolabe in Casper's chest faded away, leaving behind his smooth chest, unmarred. His body began to vibrate with energy. Light burst from him, starting at his fingertips as his form dissolved into energy. A stream of aether so concentrated it was practically a laser blasted away from Ouranos into the expanse of space. Particles of energy drifted away as the beam traveled.

"You will return the balance."

The vision started to fade.

"No, wait!"

Casper sat up on the bedroll in his guest hut. He heaved in deep breaths. "Shit."

He dressed and made his way through the village. Eman wasn't in the usual meditating spot, but he found her in conversation with a serious looking man on the path to the elevator.

"I have to go back." Casper didn't wait for them to finish talking.

"No," Eman said.

"What do you mean, no? Are you going to keep me here against my will?"

"It isn't safe. Novilem has fallen to the sickness."

"What does that mean?"

Eman walked back toward the village. Casper had to follow to get answers.

"Are they ok?" he asked.

"We are out of time."

"What does that mean?"

She stopped, pinning him with a serious glare. "It means that you won't like what comes next."

"What comes next?"

Eman started back toward the village.

"What comes next?" Casper called after her.

The room smelled like warm spices and mud. Casper was seated on a soft pillow on the ground. Eman was seated across from him. He was nervous even though he wasn't the one about to ingest a hallucinogenic tea.

"Lay back," Eman said. "Relax your mind as much as you can. Flow like a stream. Drift like the breeze. Connect to your breath and ease into the ground."

Casper's muscles melted a little with each breath. He heard the tap of the cup touching the ground, indicating Eman had drank the tea. He kept his eyes closed, concentrating on his breath moving in and out. She moved behind him and placed her hands on his temples. He heard her exhale.

"Your mind cannot touch what your body has locked away," she said. "We must find the release."

He could smell the earthy, herbal aroma of Eman's tea. A thread on the pillow was poking his neck, making it itch. The sunlight coming in through the window lit the back of his eyelids. Eman was humming, the warm alto of her voice filling the room. Slowly, he worked on letting go of the thoughts bouncing around in his head. Per usual, new thoughts came at a quick pace to grab his attention, but he let them float along the river he was visualizing. He didn't grab onto them.

But the worry wouldn't let go of him. Eman said Novilem had fallen. His friends were in danger. Helix was in danger. They needed him and he was laying on the ground, trying to meditate.

"Calm your mind," Eman commanded.

"It's not that easy."

Eman gripped the back of his neck and placed a palm on his forehead. "Yes, it is."

The outside world slipped away. His attention was pulled to parts of his body that were tight. Muscles wound in knots he hadn't noticed. Both of his pectorals were clenched, rounding his body upward. The energy coming from Eman gently touched on that feeling.

An image of his father screaming flashed in his mind. Instinctively, his muscles clenched tighter. His ears rang as his jaw ground shut.

"I am here." Eman's voice was warm. "You can let go."

With the tension in the forefront of his awareness, Casper was able to slowly find a release. He trembled slightly as he worked on relaxing. More memories of his father appeared in his mind. The first time he hit Casper. The first time he threatened to kick Casper out. The first hole he punched in the wall.

As the memories surfaced, Casper noticed Eman's warm energy envelop them. The recollections were clear and bright, but their sharp edges were shaved away. Behind the terror and shame, he could feel a younger version of himself, cowering. Still beaten down by his father's tantrums.

Casper started to cry, seeing this part of himself that had

been left alone. Forced to live with the memory of his father. He felt the distance between his current life and his life back on Earth. He never reckoned with how eager he had been to pretend none of it mattered anymore.

He visualized the presence of his younger self, and approached him slowly, because he knew how deeply both versions of himself wanted to run away. Young Casper's gaze was locked on his feet. Floppy bangs covered his eyes.

"Hey," he said to himself.

Young Casper didn't respond.

"You've been in here a long time, haven't you?"

He willed his smaller self to look up. To speak. To give him some indication of what he needed. But that wasn't what Casper had needed in the wake of his father's abuse. He didn't need someone to listen to him. He needed someone to care.

"What you've experienced is really hard," Casper said. He could feel more tears stream down his face. "And I'm really sorry I left you in here to deal with it alone."

Young Casper lifted his head.

"Our dad is an angry man and he... how he treated us was wrong. Our whole family failed us. And I failed you."

He looked young Casper in the eyes then and the depth of his sadness became overwhelming.

"I didn't want it to be true," he said. "I didn't want to believe that it happened to me and that no one was there to help. But it did. And I didn't realize that pretending meant I left you here. Alone. Just like everyone else left us alone."

Even saying this, Casper could feel the urge to turn away. To seal it back up and go back to pretending. To fight his way back into Helix's arms and send his father back across the universe where he couldn't hurt Casper anymore. Monster or not, he wanted him gone.

"I'm sorry. That I left you alone. That I made you deal with this by yourself."

Young Casper reached out and Casper stepped toward him, pulling his younger self into a hug. It hurt deeply and it was relief. His heartbeat throbbed in the corners of his chest as the tension rolled away. Eman removed hands from his neck and forehead and cool air filled the spaces where she had been touching him.

He opened his eyes and immediately curled in on himself, weeping as the grief overtook him. Eman rubbed his back as he let the waves crash out of him. She waited for him to let go first, which he appreciated.

He was raw around the edges, but he also felt a deep solace, like he had been waiting to shed those tears for too long. Then he noticed the aether. Light and dark both, drifting through the room. It was similar to the thrum of energy he found on the Surface of Ouranos when Jacob launched an assault on the Exoria. But less bright. Less intense. Instead of the aether threatening to rip through him, it was simply there, like an endless ocean of energy he could tap into.

His body felt unlocked. Where there had always been a gripped, sluggish feeling in his chest, there was a sense of openness. And beside it, a new feeling. Something else. Something more relaxed. Like rest after a long day of work.

So quiet it could have been his imagination, he heard the voice of Sedravani whisper, "You are whole."

He knew he could never be more ready. He met Eman's gaze and found her smiling.

"It's time for me to go back."

CHAPTER

THIRTY-THREE

She felt strong. She was free. Land and sky were hers. The fury she struggled to bridle for so many years burned through her. It itched along every inch of her awareness. It was so intense she fell in and out of consciousness. The world slipped away for long periods. She was aware of how easy it would be to let it go.

Small memories came to mind when she fought her way back, but never for long. The only thing that mattered was finding release. The fury had awoken a bloodlust. Something had to die.

Her vicious flesh threatened to nosedive into the streets. She could hear the petulant breathing of a dozen people below. Weak. Selfish little people. They had ripped her family apart. They deserved to be crushed.

No.

There were people responsible for taking her daughter from her hands. If anyone should pay for her suffering, it was the council. If she let the world slip away, she might find the nearest person to tear into. The itch was unbearable. Too much longer and it might drive her to rending her own flesh.

Her vision was hazy, but one thing shone bright enough to capture her focus. The white marble of the Celestery was so bright it was painful to observe. She soared through the doors. Screams filled the large rotunda. She shoved a man out of her way. He flew through the air and landed in a *thud* against the far wall. Through the back hall, she could feel the pulse of them.

The doors were right there. She smashed them open and let go.

It only took moments for the itch to subside. She could have come back to awareness then, but she was scared of what she would come back to. The screams reached her in the unknowing place. She was almost ashamed that they didn't bother her. Almost.

Then pain. Searing heat that was going to cut her through. The world came back like she had been dunked in cold water. Every inch of stone before her was stained red. Two men faced her. The closer one's hands were glowing. He was going to attack her again.

It was instinct. It was him or her. But more importantly, it felt good. He screamed as her talons sliced through him. The sound stopped as he fell under her weight. The crunch was satisfying.

She faced the last preitan. His silver hair and beard were speckled with the blood of his peers. His hands were held out toward her. He was pleading. Something familiar tried to tug at her mind. It made her pause even though she could not reach the part of her that knew why.

That's when the wound came alive. A gash running from chest to hip bled too freely. She screamed from the pain. The preitan fell to his knees, covering his ears. Bodies crashed into the room. There was light. She couldn't die here.

She leaped into the air, gliding through the crowd. A woman fell to the ground to avoid her. She pressed against her wound, trying to hold herself together as she galloped through the building. She didn't need to look down to know she left a trail of blood behind her.

Free open air. The pain went in and out. That was a relief, but the faraway part of her worried that not feeling the pain was bad. She aimed herself at the towers. There was a safe place for her there. She could rest. There was nothing else she could do but rest.

Glass shattered and she fell to the floor. She went back to the empty space for some time. It wasn't dark and it wasn't light. It was nothing. The pain was enough for her to know what laid in wait if she tried to push through again. It wasn't the worst way to go.

Then she heard his voice. Panic gripped her in a vice. Was she with him? Were they here?

The world returned with fire. She had no breath to scream. The gash on her torso rippled with agonizing, hot pain. She dragged her hand against the ground. She managed the smallest, shallowest breath.

They were right there. His footsteps were coming through the hall.

Please!

It took an eternity.

Please, help.

There was a gentle pressure against her wing.

The pain slipped away, and her mind filled with joy and love so bright she could cry.

"It's ok, Mommy," came a whisper. "We found you."

When they returned to the residential tower, the power was stuttering, and the lobby was empty. Most people had evacuated the towers to avoid being near Jacob. Hector ushered Daphne upstairs to the darkened apartment. The light gems wouldn't turn on. Hector crossed the living room slowly, navigating by memory and outstretched hands, and drew the curtains. It was early morning, and the Split had barely begun to rise, but enough light came in from outside to make out the shapes of their furniture.

"Alright, do you need anything? Are you hungry or tired?"

Daphne crossed her arms. "I'm not staying here."

He knew trying to get her to stay put was a losing battle, but he had hoped to maybe coax her into a few hours of rest. Passing the night in the crowded Celestery brought precious little sleep and it was all Hector could do to keep Daphne indoors until the first rays of sunlight appeared.

"We won't stay. But we need to make sure our bodies are fed and feeling strong."

"I am hungry," she admitted.

"I thought you might be." Hector moved into the kitchen and opened the cooler. It was room temperature inside. The aetherflow had been cut off for at least a few hours. Talleah was in the habit of batch cooking so she wouldn't have to come home from work and continue cooking. Hector had tried to learn, but his food never compared to hers. He prepped as many ingredients as he could for her, but they landed on her making large portions of dishes they could throw together.

He placed his hand on the side of the container of what Talleah liked to call chickpea mix-up. It wasn't cold enough. On a normal day, he would probably say it was fine. But they couldn't afford food poisoning when the city was besieged by Tektranos.

"How's a nut butter wrap sound?" he asked.

"Yeah!"

His heart melted a little hearing her excitement. Talleah rarely let her have simple food. He opened the pantry cabinet, and his hand froze on the cloth-wrapped flatbreads. Talleah had made them mere days before. They gathered in the kitchen after waking and she started making bread to keep her hands busy. His heart ached. She had been here. He wanted to sit on the floor and let the horrible moan residing in the back of his chest out.

He pulled out a piece of bread and wiped his eyes with his other hand. While he was spreading nut butter on the flatbread, Daphne cuddled into his side. He put the wrap down and returned the hug.

"We'll find her," she said, almost whispering.

He squeezed her tight against his middle. "We will."

A sharp clack sounded from the hall. Their two bedrooms were in the back of the apartment and the noise came from one of them. Hector moved Daphne into the corner of the kitchen. He held a finger to his lips, commanding her to stay quiet. He mouthed *stay here* and pointed at her feet. He grabbed a large kitchen knife from the butcher block and slowly moved into the hall.

There was another clack. Bright and coarse like something scratched against the stone flooring. It was nearly pitch black in the hall. All the light from the drawn window bled out behind him. His heart thumped in his chest as he took careful steps, guiding himself with one hand against the wall on his left.

He paused at his and Talleah's room, listening. The sound didn't come again. He stepped inside and tried to see, but he couldn't make anything out behind the wall of black. He shouldn't, but he didn't have a choice. He pulled in a deep breath and used just enough of his Leo aether to set his arm aglow, casting the room in warm, orange light. It was empty.

He released the aether and turned back to an even emptier darkness in the hall. His steps were painfully slow. He didn't want to give his position away by bumping into a door or the wall. When his hand found the threshold, he turned toward Daphne's room.

There was another clack, followed by heavy breathing. Too heavy. His heartbeat pounded in his ears. He made it to the next door, and something crunched under his step. He froze, biting his lip. If someone or something was inside, he should rush in, right? Use the element of surprise to his advantage. Or he could grab Daphne and get out of the apartment.

That was probably the smarter choice. But he was already facing the noise in the dark. Turning his back on whatever it was felt more dangerous. He took one smooth-as-he-could-manage breath and pushed aether into his arm as he held his knife in a readied position. He stepped into the room, ready to swing as the edges of Daphne's belongings were lit by the orange light of his aether.

In the middle of the room, taking up the entirety of the floorspace, was the collapsed figure of a Tektranos. Hector's instinct to attack was only stayed by the silhouette of Daphne's little body. She was standing directly over the Tektranos.

"Daphne!" He grabbed her with his left hand, brandishing the knife at the monster with his right. "I told you to stay put."

"Daddy, it's ok!" She struggled against his grip, trying to move toward the Tektranos. "It's Mommy!"

Hector went rigid.

"She's hurt," Daphne said.

The Tektranos wasn't moving. One of its massive wings was folded, covering the majority of its body and hiding its face. Its leg twitched, a sharp talon clacking against the floor. The room filled with the noise. Then he noticed blood.

He was about to ask Daphne why she thought it was Talleah when Daphne's hand clasped his arm. The light from his aether faded away and his mind slipped into a memory. He was in Daphne's body; she was touching the Tektranos. Its skin was leathery and warm. It hissed but didn't move. She reached inside with her Gemini aether. There was blinding pain. Heat in her chest that she didn't understand. The feeling of soaring through the air. Then she found Hector and herself. Almost too much love to bear. Then anger clouded the images and darkness pressed in, erasing everything.

Daphne let go of Hector's arm. "See? It's Mommy."

He squeezed her hand. Their little girl wasn't so little anymore. She was brave and bold and strong, just like her mother. His chest went hollow thinking of the time they lost with her and how, even though they were separated, he could still see so much of Talleah in her.

Hector lit the room again. The Tektranos pulled its wing closer against its body. The red pool on the ground had grown bigger. It was actively bleeding.

If this was Talleah...

"Daphne, stay back. Ok? I'm going to check where she's hurt. I don't want her to lash out at you."

She nodded, her loose curls bouncing with the motion.

He cautiously moved forward, kneeling next to the Tektranos. He set the knife on the ground next to him. Easily accessible, but not in hand, ready to accidentally maim himself or kill the monster. Talleah? She was inside, but it was impossible to see the creature before him and think of it as her.

"Talleah?" he said. "I'm going to move your wing. I need to see where you're bleeding from."

The creature didn't respond. He gently grabbed hold of the bony ridge running the length of its wing. The skin felt exactly like Daphne's vision had shown him. Rough and leathery, but it wasn't quite so warm. That was worrisome. He lifted the wing and moved his arm, filled with aether, underneath.

He flinched when the Tektranos hissed, its cavernous mouth showing finger-long fangs. When it didn't follow through with the threat, Hector turned his attention to its body. There was a long gash along its torso. Blood flowing too freely. The wound didn't look terribly deep, but the Tektranos would likely bleed out soon. There wasn't time to find a Virgo.

"I can heal her," Daphne said from behind him.

Hector cursed under his breath. Daphne was trined. Born a Libra, but she also had Gemini and Virgo aether. She could heal the Tektranos. Heal Talleah. But using aether around the monster was dangerous. The more corrupted aether they took in, the more risk of getting sick themselves, and Daphne had already used Gemini aether.

They were cleared by a Virgo that afternoon. But she was so little. He couldn't let her take on that kind of risk. But if she didn't...

Talleah would likely never forgive him for taking the risk, but Daphne shouldn't have to lose her twice, especially knowing she could have done something to save her.

"Come here."

Hector gently lifted the wing higher to let Daphne in.

When she hunched underneath with him, the Tektranos didn't hiss. Instead, it hid its face, turning away from them. Daphne held her hands out and they lit up with aether as she gestured over the long gash on its torso. When she dropped her hands to her side, the wound was gone. A dark line ran the length of the creature's stomach where the gash had been. Most importantly, the bleeding stopped.

Hector ushered Daphne away and removed himself from under the Tektranos's wing as it pulled its limb back. He moved them toward the door. The creature lifted itself off the floor, sitting in a crumpled position. With its tough, gray skin cast in orange light it looked like it could be made of stone instead of a living, breathing monster.

"You're going to be ok, Mommy."

Hector realized he left the knife on the ground. There was no way to reach it without stepping into the creature's reach. His heart kicked in his chest. He slid Daphne behind him as casually as he could.

"Tal, if you're in there..." His voice broke. "We'll get you back. We'll find a way to fix this."

The creature turned and leaped through the broken window. Its wings stretched out, flapping hard as it soared over the city.

"Mommy!" Daphne cried.

Hector lifted her, crushing her into his embrace. They were ok. Daphne shook in his arms, crying. But they were ok. He carried her back toward the kitchen, repeating the small comfort in his mind.

CHAPTER

THIRTY-FOUR

All of Helix's extended family were gathered in Theo's home by the Lakefront. They were evacuating to Earth, and as infuriated as Helix was that they were abandoning the city and those who would inevitably be left behind, he couldn't bring himself to not say goodbye.

He found Theo on the patio, holding a glass of wine.

"Pappous."

Theo set his glass down and wrapped Helix in a hug.

"Thank the stars you are here," Theo said. "The family should be together."

"I'm here to say goodbye. Not to hide."

Theo patted Helix's shoulder. If he felt any sting from Helix's words, he didn't show it. "You should rest. There's nothing to do."

"Of course there is. Why are you giving up?"

"What is there to give up on? The council is no more."

Helix froze. "What happened?"

"A Tektranos." Theo was staring blankly over the water. "Broke into the Celestery when the aetherflow stuttered.

Headed straight into the Estellar chamber. The entire council is dead."

Helix fell to a seat on the bench, the world spinning around him.

"I... couldn't do anything but watch. It was so powerful. It happened so fast. When it turned on me, it stopped. I think it recognized me. Its eyes. For a moment they were human."

"Dust me," Helix said.

"The loss..." Theo's lips trembled as he watched the still waters of the lake. "Everything we have known. Everything that she—" He had to force in a rattled breath. The glass in his hand shook to the point of spilling.

Helix took the glass, setting it on the table behind them. "I think about her all the time."

Theo's eyes were closed. A tear ran down a deep line in his cheek. He covered Helix's hand on his arm with his own and the world slipped away.

They were still on the patio, but it was filled with their family. Beads of light strung overhead were aglow. Helix's small cousins were squealing on the path below the deck that led to the lake. And in front of them was Brissa. Surrounded by her three daughters. Laughing.

A deep, sharp ache filled Helix's gut, and at the same time a tension in his chest melted. She was smiling so brightly. The length of her silver braid hung down her back. Helix's mom and Brissa bound their arms together as they shared a private moment. Brissa's eyes lowered as she listened. When she opened them, she looked directly at him. A jolt surged through his body. She smiled softly and winked.

Theo patted his hand, and the shared memory slipped away.

Helix's face was wet with tears. He nearly begged for the vision to continue. The intensity of being known by her was so tangible. So real. The emptiness of the patio swallowed him whole as the warmth of that evening dissipated.

"I am never not thinking about her," Theo said.

Helix embraced him. The weight of their grief came together to make something greater than their two parts, as if the missing piece of her became more for the different things she meant to each of them.

Theo pulled away first, saying, "Come with us to Earth."

Helix's head was fuzzy, but the change in subject sharpened his mind. "Pappous, no. Casper is still with the Farseers."

"We are beyond the help of the Telos. Tektranos attack in the streets. More and more of our people are falling sick with the Frenzy. Jacob has won."

"We have the aether locks. People are gathering in the Academy. We can't give up."

"Half-measures," Theo said. "Novilem is lost. A few thousand safe is not enough. We cannot fight against them."

Helix looked at his grandfather. His age showed more than ever. Losing Brissa had taken any semblance of vitality he had left. The years caught up to him over the last months. He seemed so tired.

Inside their home were dozens of Helix's relatives. Many of them children. Too young to really comprehend what was going on.

"Go," Helix said. "Start the evacuation for Novilem. Bring the family to Earth. I'll wait for Casper and fix this."

"You are too young to give up your life," Theo said. "If the boy can do anything, he can do it alone. Come with us."

"None of us do anything alone, Pappous. You taught me that."

Theo grunted. "There will be no stopping you, will there?"

Helix leaned in and kissed his cheek. "No, there won't."

Helix made another round through the villa, hugging every member of his family. He was near to breaking down in tears by the time he left. He prayed to the stars it was not the last time he would see them.

The council was dead. He could barely believe it was real.

CHAPTER
THIRTY-FIVE

The stillness of Novilem beyond the cave opening was unsettling. Casper had braced himself for chaos in the streets, like that before the Turning. He waited to hear shouts, but it remained quiet. He exited the small cave that housed the Farseer's elevator and was hit with an intense wave of homesickness. He wanted nothing more than to rush to his villa with the hopes of finding Helix waiting for him.

He could smell him. The warm honey and salt of being wrapped in his embrace. His chest ached. Dealing with Jacob was the priority, but he couldn't walk in completely blind. And he wasn't sure he could manage the task without seeing Helix first. Making his way down the path, his head spun thinking of how long it would take him to cross the city on foot, enduring the emptiness of the streets.

He felt naked without his astrolabe, but it was a boon to not have to think about his trines. He pocket stepped down the street, planning to make short work of the distance to the western villa. Checking his house, then Helix's family home was the best place to start. When he made it to Market Row, he could sense he wasn't alone. That unnamable feeling of being watched flared on the back of his neck.

He spun around, scanning the street. Empty. The storefronts were closed up, stools turned over at the tea shop. The hanging lanterns in a cute dessert shop Helix showed him were turned off. Casper turned to continue on his way and saw a head duck behind a building across the way.

"Hello," Casper said.

Long waves of hair swung as a young woman poked her head back out. Her dark eyes were wide as she took Casper in. She waved him over with vigor and moved her finger to her lips. He crossed the street to join her.

"Where is everyone?" Casper whispered.

"Gone." Her eyes lifted to the dome overhead, frantically searching.

"Gone where?"

Her hand rested on the swollen mound of her stomach. "To Earth." A tear spilled down her cheek.

"Are you alone?" Who would leave behind a pregnant woman?

She shook her head, nodding out to the street. "My family stayed behind. I am too close to birth for the jump."

The sound of flapping entered the small alley from above. The woman's head shot up and she began to tremble. She put her finger to her lips again. Casper scanned the strip of open air, a sharp terror filling his mind at what might appear. Something landed on the building next to them. The woman grabbed his arm, her fingers digging into his skin.

Heavy steps fell against the roof of the building. Large huffs of air resounded as something sniffed. When Casper saw the talons poke over the rooftop, he held his breath. He pulled the woman back toward the street, ready to pocket step if needed. She looked at him with steely eyes and shook her head, releasing his arm from her grip.

What was she doing? That creature was going to jump into the ally any moment now. She leaned against the wall, covering her mouth. Her eyes were shut. Casper stayed put, slowing his breathing as much as he could. His eyes were locked on those talons. They tapped against the stone twice, then the creature leaped off the building, flapping its wings to take flight. Casper's heart was racing wildly in his chest. He remained silent for a few moments, but the creature didn't come back.

"We have to go," he said.

She shook her head.

"I can't leave you here alone."

The woman cried openly again. "That is my husband."

Casper balked at her claim. Eman had explained that a buildup of dark aether in the body would have a transformative effect. Regardless, the creature was on the hunt. They weren't safe. He urged her forward. "He's gone."

"No!" She collapsed on herself.

It must have been so painful to know her partner was a monster. He imagined Helix—no, he couldn't. He also couldn't leave her there to be mauled by her monster husband. If only he could turn back time, he would go to the grotto earlier and learn how to balance the aether before people started morphing into murder on wings.

I can't reverse the flow of time... but I can reverse the flow of aether.

If the creature's transformation was a problem of too much aether stored in a person's body, that also meant he should be able to reverse the aetherflow. *What if...*

"Stay here," Casper said. "Do not follow me."

The woman looked concerned, but he didn't hear her

footsteps after he turned and entered the street. He pocket stepped a few hundred yards away, then lifted his head to the open air and whistled. A screech echoed across the dome and a few moments later he heard the flapping of wings.

The creature came swooping in, talons first. Casper teleported a few steps away and the creature pummeled into the ground, beating its wings to regain its balance. With a controlled breath he took in Sagittarius aether and released it, sending a wave of energy at the creature as it ran toward him. It dodged the blast but caught some of the beam on its wing. It twisted, losing its bearings, and plummeted into Casper.

He clamored underneath the weight of the creature, getting free just as it swiped at him. Its claws caught his bicep, tearing through his robe. The cut burned bright with pain. He flared his aether to heal the wound. He needed both arms for what came next.

The creature fumbled with its large wings to get upright, screeching with earsplitting volume. Casper pummeled an energy wave down on it, holding it to the ground. The creature crashed against the stone like gravity had intensified. He wouldn't be able to hold it down and work on reversing its aetherflow at the same time. So, he beat it into the ground a few more times, hoping to exhaust it long enough to get to work.

When he released his hold, the creature stayed put. He placed his hands on its leathery skin. It was hot to the touch. He pushed the sensation out of his mind and focused on his breathing. His arms broke out in goosebumps as he found the dark aether inside. It was loud. Ripping through the creature in quaking waves.

The creature bucked under him. He climbed on its back,

attempting to pin it down. Peace of mind was hard to locate when face-to-face with a real-life monster.

"Fuck!" Casper said.

The creature scrambled off the ground, tossing Casper aside. He rolled against hard stone a few times before catching himself. He fought back to his feet quickly, but the creature wasn't coming after him. It was walking down the street. Toward the woman.

"No!" he yelled.

He caught the whites of her eyes as she tucked back into the alley, but it was too late. The creature fell to all fours, running toward her. There wasn't time to figure this out. But he also couldn't kill the woman's husband right in front of her. Casper didn't want to kill him at all. Somewhere in that creature, the man had to still be there.

The creature made it to the alley and the woman screamed. Casper pocket stepped behind it and placed a hand on its back.

"Please work," he said.

With Cancer resonance, he started pulling aether out of the creature. He became nauseous. The creature halted, shaking under Casper's touch. He had to actively work on not throwing up as the dark energy poured into him.

But it was working. The tips of the creature's wings started to break way into ash. The mottled gray tone of its skin warmed to a light brown. Casper was reaching the limit of what he could handle, but the creature was becoming more and more a man. He held on until the last visible piece of gray skin was gone, and then he immediately threw up.

The man crumpled to the ground. Casper heard the woman cry out his name, but he turned away, stumbling back into the street. The woman spoke to him, but he waved her away. He needed to create some distance between them.

The edge of his vision was fuzzy, the dark aether he had absorbed distorting the world around him. He let the rage that was building in his mind pour into his body. Holding up his hand, the aether poured out of him in a beam of pure light aether. The stone street ahead of him was scorched from the ambient heat nearly to the end of Market Row.

He collapsed to the ground, exhausted. Moments later the woman approached with her husband stumbling next to her, arm hooked over her neck.

"Thank you," she said, crying. "The stars bless you, always."

Her husband was naked, shivering as he more hung from her neck than leaned on her for support.

"Here," Casper said.

On his knees, he shrugged out of his robe. Lifting his body with great effort to remove it from his waist, he handed it to the woman. He still had on a light tunic and his pants. The woman accepted the robe, hanging it over her husband's shoulders.

"Stay safe," Casper said.

"You saved him," the woman said. "You will save us all."

And although Casper was bone tired and unsure he could physically handle doing that again, he tried to believe her.

THIRTY-SIX

Helix was with Malia and Gloria in the Academy offices when a woman in Aquarius robes sprinted through the door.

"He's back," the Aquarius said.

"Where?" Helix asked.

"Market Row." The woman was nearly out of breath. "He turned a Tektranos back to a human."

"Sounds like Casper," Malia said.

"Careful, that sounded like a compliment." Helix was grinning ear to ear. He was back. "Grab whatever supplies you need. We're moving out."

"He didn't turn all of the Tektranos back," Gloria said.

"And he won't be able to if they overwhelm him because he's alone," Helix said.

Gloria pursed her lips, shaking her head.

"He's one of us," Helix said.

"He's the Telos," she said. "And your boyfriend. I'm sorry, Helix. But you can't think straight when it comes to him."

"Ree," Malia said, grabbing her hand. "We can't leave him out there alone."

Gloria went stiff. "My mother is dead. Faus is sick, Belen is in quarantine. He's probably changed by now. How much more do we have to lose?"

Gloria's mother was the Scorpio preitan and was killed in the Tektranos attack. "We'll lose everything if Casper dies," Helix said.

"He's not a god," Gloria said. "He's a boy."

Helix felt heat rise in his chest. "Did you not hear? He changed a Tektranos back."

"Then let him change them all back. What does he need us for?"

Malia sat next to her, placing a hand on her knee. "We're going to make it through this."

"Don't go," Gloria said. "I can't lose you, too."

Malia's hand squeezed hers. She turned her head but wouldn't meet Helix's gaze.

"It's fine," he said. "I'll go alone."

"We can find a way to get a message to him," Malia said. "He can come to us."

"Keep yourselves safe," he said.

He didn't wait for an answer.

Novilem felt small. Closed in. Caged. As Helix moved through the city, its massive walls seemed like they might fall on top of him at any moment. The emptiness made the stone buildings feel more like a graveyard than a city. For the first time in his life, he wasn't certain this is where he belonged. The heart of Novilem had been ripped out.

When he was five years old his parents took him to a park. After the third time they were stopped, he asked his mother who the strangers were that kept speaking to them. He learned then that his family was important. Respected.

The first thought he had when he saw tiny feet scurry past an open door was that his important family was safe on Earth and they had left people behind. Those with power should serve. What good was having resources if they weren't used to make sure the community was taken care of?

Helix made his way toward the small home. In the shadows of the room beyond its open door, faint light caught on hands waving at him. A few more steps and he realized they were not welcoming waves; he was being waved off. The street around him was vacant. Why would they be wary of him?

Unless... his head snapped to the dome above. He scanned the roofs of the buildings. Shivers ran down his spine. That bothersome feeling in the back of his head was screaming at him that he was being hunted.

Where is it?

He continued walking down the street. If a Tektranos was nearby, he could at least lead it away from the family. How he would manage to overtake a creature that could scoop him up to the sky, he had no idea. Then he heard a shout ahead. Where the street opened to a crossway, a man stood. Helix watched as he took a nasty swipe of sharp claws across his forearm.

Helix ran toward them but stopped when the Tektranos froze in place. Its mouth hung slack as the man held a hand against its chest. His dusty brown hair billowed in a wind that Helix didn't know the source of. Helix walked closer until the shape of him was almost familiar. His heart leapt into his throat.

When the creature collapsed to the ground and its grotesque shape began to melt away, Helix found hope. He sprinted toward the figures. The man fell to ground just before Helix came upon him.

"Stars above," Helix said, grabbing his body, pulling him close. It was Casper. His eyes were closed, and his breath was shallow. Whatever he had done took a lot out of him. "You're here." When Casper didn't stir, he continued smoothing his hair back. "You figured it out."

Casper's eyes slowly opened. A drowsy, drunken movement of heavy lids. "Hi," he managed to say.

Helix laughed. Tears filled his eyes. "Hi."

Casper's eyes fell back closed. "I just need a minute."

"Take as long as you need."

The creature in front of them was gone. A woman was sprawled out on the cobbled street. Her chest rose and fell in steady breaths. He could turn them back. This changed everything. Casper could actually do it. He could save the city.

He waited until Casper could bear his own weight, then Helix carried the woman to the hiding family down the street. He asked them to look after her until she woke, and they agreed. Then he and Casper made their way back toward the Academy.

"You figured it out," Helix repeated as they walked.

"Barely," Casper said. "I should have been here sooner." Casper winced as if in pain.

"Are you ok? That seemed to take a lot out of you."

"I'll be alright. That was the third Tektranos I found. Too many back-to-back, I think."

"I missed you." Helix squeezed Casper with the arm that was half supporting him while they walked.

Helix's touch on his arm was a comfort he'd been craving. Casper smiled. "I missed you, too." There was more to say, but the words were buried too deep.

"There's some shelter under the walkway over there." Helix grabbed his hand and led him under the arch of a bridge created by a walking path overhead.

Casper felt a whirl of emotions, fresh, bright, and unfettered thanks to his recent work with Eman. He was so, so grateful Helix was alive, and they were together. He was surprised his idea to reverse the aether flow had worked, and... proud of himself? But he still felt the weight of how much damage had been done. He could easily be swallowed whole by guilt about how long it took him to get past his own shit so he could be helpful.

But when Helix grabbed his hand and thumbed a circle on his palm, he mostly felt shy. He was more open, more raw, more himself. Would Helix see that when they met each other's gaze? Would he know what Casper had to do without Casper having to say it? Helix had lost so much already. Casper couldn't bear taking anything else away from him. Even if he was doing it to give Helix his home back.

"Do you think life after this is going to be too boring for us?" Helix asked. "We keep finding ourselves in dire situations."

Casper smirked slightly but didn't respond.

"Hey, what's up?"

He took a deep breath and decided to be brave. He tilted his head to face Helix, but his eyes remained on the ground. "I'm not sure there is an after for me."

Helix's heart sunk to his feet. A cold sweat broke out across his chest. He was going to be sick.

When he didn't respond, Casper continued. "I have to supernova to balance the aether."

"No." It was a plea. It was a command.

Casper winced. "It's the only way."

"You don't know that. We'll find another way."

Casper reached out for his hand. Helix grabbed onto him like he could physically hold him there.

"You know those visions I've been having?"

Helix nodded.

"The Sedrivani showed me. Novilem is flooded with dark aether. The balance is millennia off. If we want to fix it now, I have to do this."

"We'll go to the Surface."

"The Surface is no better." Casper shook his head. "Remember? It's also flooded with dark aether."

"We'll go to Earth."

"Helix." Casper rubbed the back of his hands with his thumbs. "It's your entire culture. We can't let it die."

"They did this to themselves. You don't have to fix their problems."

"I want to."

Helix pulled him into a hug. A shaking cry fell out of him. "I don't want to lose you."

Casper squeezed him back. "Maybe you won't."

He kissed Casper's neck. He wondered if maybe was enough. He admired Casper's resolve, his willingness to risk his life for a people that had used and abused him. But mostly he felt selfish. He wanted to hold on to him. To steal him away and keep Casper to himself. But then he'd be no better than his family. And Helix didn't think he could live with that. So, the question was, could he bare to live without Casper if the supernova took him?

He squeezed Casper tighter and hoped he wouldn't have to find out.

THIRTY-SEVEN

The Celestery grounds were nearly empty. It was the first time Casper had ever seen the place when it wasn't bustling with life. It made the stairs leading up to his father feel that much more ominous. But he had to see him. There was a possibility he wouldn't survive attempting to balance the aether in Novilem, and the only way he could mitigate that chance was to go in with a clean slate. He couldn't carry the baggage with his dad into the supernova. It was too risky.

"Will you wait for me?" Casper asked.

Helix looked pained. "I can come with you."

Casper kissed him, giving no care to the acolyte standing nearby. "I think you being there would be distracting."

"I'll be here," he said. "I love you."

Casper pulled their hands to his mouth, kissing Helix's fingers before letting go and turning toward the stairs.

~

The cellblock was full of people in differing stages of sickness. Guilt, slick and achy, filled his gut as he passed them. He had the power to help them, but not the strength to do it now. Ahead, he could make out sharp, scraping noises coming from his father's cell.

His breathing shallowed and the fist of energy in his center shivered brightly. He skipped the last few steps and jumped as the Tektranos lashed out at the bars of its cell.

"Dad..."

Casper's back was against the wall. Spittle dripped from the monster's mouth as a rumbling growl built in its throat. Its wings were expanded against the edges of the cell. He filled up the entire space, blocking the dim light gem in the upper corner. He was shadow and flesh and teeth.

It was a nightmare made real. Casper's hand shook as he covered his mouth. The creature... his father? He didn't know how to think of it. Fear was splitting his thoughts in half. It gnashed its mouth in the air. The snap of its jaw sent a jolt through him.

Why was he here? He couldn't go in the cell to try healing him. He'd be mauled before he could start.

A familiar heaviness was rising in his chest. It felt like the night before a week of standardized tests in eighth grade when his father had been laid off and the house turned into a one-man show of his fury. It felt like the drive to select team tryouts for soccer when his father spent the entire journey yelling at someone on the phone. It felt like getting dressed for prom and having to watch videos on how to tie his tie because his father was giving him the silent treatment that week.

How long had this monster been in him? Or had he been the monster the whole time?

The Tektranos raised its head and released a piercing

screech. Casper clasped his hands to his ears, trying to block the sound, but the ringing pain brought him to his knees. The sound died out and a puff of its breath shifted Casper's hair.

He got back on his feet. "I don't know if you're somewhere in there, but I guess in a lot of ways talking to you has always felt this way more for me."

The Tektranos watched him, pulsing with slow breaths. Its eyes, softly glowing yellow, were locked on him. Casper's gaze fell to the floor. He couldn't look at the creature and say what he needed to say.

"I blamed myself for a really long time. It felt like it was my fault that you would get so angry with me. You told me it was my fault. Over and over again." Casper brushed tears off his cheeks. "Nothing was good enough. You were always disappointed. Always. But I was a kid. Your kid."

He glared at his monstrous father and a decade of resentment poured out of him. "It wasn't my job to make you proud. It was your job to fucking love me."

It might have been coincidence, but the Tektranos's wings collapsed then. The light gem cast the cell in clean white-blue light.

Maybe it was the fact that his father couldn't talk back. Maybe it was the absurdity of the creature in front of him being the man he grew up with. Maybe Casper was finally strong enough to stand up to him. Or by some combination of it all, he found himself wanting to lay it all out. He stepped toward the cell bars.

"I won't carry this with me anymore. You were a terrible father. Selfish and mean and vindictive. The thought of you fills my heart with dread."

The Tektranos snarled.

"No," Casper said. "You made your issues our entire

family's problem. Sickness or not. I don't care. That was yours to bear. But you treated us like punching bags. This"— Casper gestured at his claws and teeth and leathery skin— "this fits. I hope you remember how this feels when it's over. Because you deserve that."

The creature growled, but it wasn't sharp. It was muffled, like a dog throwing a fit.

"You're going back to Earth. And I want you to know how much relief I feel that I'll never see you again."

Casper's tunic was wet from his crying. He dried his face with one of his sleeves.

"I deserved better than you. And you never deserved me."

He turned from the cell and the world blurred behind more tears. He winced when a screech filled the cellblock again. The sound of claws crashing against stone filled the hall.

Something inside his chest felt different. Not lighter, but like the weight had shifted. Like he had been holding a heavy boulder for too long, and his aching arms could finally rest for having set it down on his lap.

Now he just had an entire city to save. Again.

CHAPTER
THIRTY-EIGHT

Casper had no more excuses to delay the inevitable as he left the Celestery. He knew what had to happen. And unfortunately, he had already explained it to Helix.

"It's time," Casper said.

"I can't—" Helix choked on a cry.

Casper cupped the side of his face.

"I can't lose you," Helix repeated. "I don't want a life without you."

"We can't choose us over all of Novilem."

"Then take me with you."

"It doesn't work that way."

Tears spilled down his cheeks over Casper's fingers. "Why you?"

"I don't know. But I'm glad it is me. Because I never would have met you if it wasn't."

The tower was impenetrable. The Libras couldn't jump in. Taurus couldn't carve their way through. Whatever Jacob was doing to pulse dark aether through the city seemed to also affect the tower itself. Casper didn't have to work to hear Jacob's thoughts anymore. If he opened his mind, Jacob was there. The hatred seethed so loudly he felt like he might lose himself in the screaming void of Jacob's chaotic thoughts.

Dark aether pulsed off the tower like a heartbeat. Casper tried to bring his center to balance, but as the waves of energy passed through his body, the weight in his chest was undeniable. For the thousandth time, he wondered if he could do this.

The screeches of multiple Tektranos filled the air. He had been noticed. He could turn around and jump back to safety. He didn't feel ready. But when does one feel ready to release control? To risk their life and the lives of an entire civilization?

The screech vibrated against his back. He was out of time.

"Don't fuck this up, Casper," he said to himself.

Then he opened his aether channels. Immediately, he felt sick. He fell to the ground, his arms barely catching him. A gust of air blew against him as a Tektranos swooped past where he stood a moment before.

The dark aether overwhelmed him. He couldn't stop himself from trying to resist. He cried out. The sound of his voice echoed, coming back to him as a shredded, broken thing. Shadows pooled around the ground, gathering where he was touching the stone. The aether was trying to enter his body.

There was too much. He could feel the vastness of it. Like the dark expanse of the universe was trying to funnel through him. Somewhere in his mind he recognized that the Tektranos was coming toward him. His eyes could see, but his mind was so full it was hard to pay attention. The creature screeched and Casper felt his mind go sharp. Wrath. Pure, vicious hatred cut through him. He lifted his right hand, and the creature was thrown backward, slamming into the tower. It fell to the ground with a deep thud.

He hoped it was dead.

And then he was awash with hot shame. That was a person. Fear quickened his mind. The dark aether was winning. If he couldn't figure out how to balance the dark with the light, it would take over. He closed his eyes, trying to find the calm Eman taught him. Novilem was shrouded in loud, oppressive darkness. Like the black expanse of outside after a bad nightmare.

But if he stretched his awareness, he could sense the light. It was timid and elusive as he pulled it to him. The two halves felt to him like pools of water. One hissing, hot and angry. The other cool and still in the way that indicated depth. They were less like two halves than opposites.

His body was slammed into the ground. Fingers closed around his throat. He opened his eyes and saw Jacob crouched over him. The strings of his thin hair tickled Casper's face.

"I knew I should have killed you," Jacob said.

The pressure on Casper's throat was unbearable. His body fought for air, but he could not pry Jacob's hand away. The corners of his vision started to go black.

"Let's correct an error in my judgement, yes?"

The voice of Sedrivani spoke in Casper's mind. "Stop fighting."

A difficult ask when he was being choked to death.

"Let the aether in."

He was moments away from losing consciousness. It was now or never. So, Casper did the scariest thing he could think of. He let go.

The world around him faded away until there was nothing but a spark of light.

"Rest," a deeper voice said. "It is time."

And Casper, or whatever he was in this place of light and not light, began to free fall. If he still had a stomach, it was twisted tight.

Clouds of aether, light and dark, surrounded Casper. Jacob was blasted backward by an invisible force. Helix's chest felt tight as he watched him float into the air. His face was pinched in concentration, or in pain. Helix's heart was in his throat, a clawing, desperate panic threatening to take him over. He needed Casper.

The warmth of his skin when they were lying in bed. The way his eyes crinkled when he laughed. His curiosity and the way he cared for others. Casper was his person. And Helix had already lost so much. He couldn't stand to lose Casper, too.

"I love you," Helix said, looking up at Casper. "Come back to me."

Something smashed into him. He tumbled to the ground. When he finally stopped rolling, Jacob was in front of him, scowling. With a flick of his wrist, the stone below Helix broke into shards that reached out like fingers, crusting over his body, locking him in place.

THIRTY-NINE

With his aether channels still completely open, Casper's body reacted with little effort. One moment Jacob was pinning Helix to the ground and the next moment Casper pocket stepped and punched Jacob in the back in a single motion. Jacob slid forward from the impact. Casper was trying to listen to the direction the aether pulled when Jacob blasted him with an energy pulse.

The hit threw him, flipping him over as he flew across the clearing. He couldn't manage aether cycling while fighting. Eman had said there could be periods of imbalance, and there was so much dark aether. His only chance was to fight fire with fire.

"And we're back to this." Jacob gestured to the open field and the western tower looming beside them.

Casper pushed past the nausea as dark aether filled him up, pulling energy in until he felt the anger start to build.

"I'm done talking to you," Casper said.

With dark Taurus aether he dragged Jacob across the field. A wave of inky black aether streamed out of Jacob's hands, but Casper waved it away with dark Leo aether. It was like erasing a picture.

Jacob was still on the ground, but his eyes grew wide with surprise. "You've learned some new tricks."

Casper dug deep, and through the dark aether, found the bright ring of light. He filled his body with Aries aether as he bent over and grabbed Jacob's tunic.

"I said I'm done talking."

With a twist, he hurled Jacob into the tower. The crack of his body crashing into the stone was satisfying. It echoed all the way up the dome. Casper pocket stepped to the base of the tower. Jacob was already climbing to his feet.

"Fine, let's play." Jacob wiped blood from the side of his mouth.

Shadows plumed out from his hands and the world disappeared behind an opaque wall of black. Casper swiped at them, but it didn't make a dent. Where he absorbed the aether, more shadows filled in. Anger flared inside him. The inky black surrounded them, and Jacob was visible only by the purple shade of aether reflecting off of him.

He smiled. Then smoke surrounded his body until he was shrouded. It stretched away from him as he multiplied. With dark Aries aether, Casper planted himself in place, his body immobile and invulnerable. Let Jacob do his worst.

The many forms of Jacob rammed into him. Casper felt pressure where they sank into his skin, but there was no pain. When there was only one Jacob left, Casper released his aether.

Jacob scowled and dug his hands into the ground. Shards of stone emerged from underneath the grass, spinning violently before him. From the little tornado Jacob shot stone projectiles at Casper.

With dark Taurus aether, Casper latched onto them,

twisting them around his body and sending them right back at Jacob. He dodged, but a large piece lodged in his left arm.

He screamed out in pain, clutching his arm. The shard of stone stuck out between his fingers. "It seems I've become outmatched."

"You always were." He let the fury build. Jacob was at his mercy and the aether was begging Casper to let go.

Why was he holding back? Look at what Jacob had done to the city. How much pain and loss he had brought to the people of Novilem. Surely, to end that suffering was worth the life of one man. Casper had ruminated on this choice hundreds of times. Imagined this exact scenario when he could finally face Jacob again and stop him.

So why did killing him still feel wrong? Dangerous. He wasn't sure what it would unlock in him to push past the wall. What did digging into that kind of hate do to a person? The heat of his anger dissipated. His stomach turned again as he backed away from the dark aether.

Blood was dripping through Jacob's fingers as he grasped his wound. "Please." The flare of yellow in his eyes was muted. Was the real Jacob breaking through? "End this."

Casper winced. It was the right thing to do. He positioned himself to gather aether and still found his hand unwilling to raise.

Get angry, Casper. You can do this.

He killed Brissa. Orchestrated a rebellion that nearly killed Casper and Helix. He turned so many Novilites, including Talleah, into monsters. And still, selfishly, Casper couldn't get past the fear of what kind of guilt he would feel upon taking his life.

Jacob was on his knees. The yellow glow of his eyes faded in and out as he stared at Casper. Soon whatever lucidity Jacob had fought for would slip away and he would attack again. Casper raised his hand. He started pooling aether into his arm. Bile rose in his throat. Was he really going to do this?

Jacob smiled. He closed his eyes. And a Tektranos crashed into his body.

Casper jumped away, falling onto his back as the sickening rip of flesh being torn from bone filled the air. He rolled back onto his feet as quickly as he could to find that Jacob's body was splayed on the ground, his head laying several feet away. He had to fight back the urge to be sick because the Tektranos was facing him, bloody teeth bared. Its screech blasted into him.

The walls of shadows disappeared, and as the world came back into view, Casper was horrified at what he saw. Too many Tektranos to count swirled overhead, like vultures waiting to swoop in after the kill. The smell of blood was pungent in the air. Then he heard Helix cry out in pain.

He was wrestling a Tektranos to the ground. Red was smeared across his upper body. Casper couldn't tell if it was his blood or the creature's.

"I can't hold it off much longer," Helix called out.

"Dust me," Casper said to himself.

Because of course, Jacob was not the end of this. The aether was still out of balance. These people needed to be healed. And there was only one way Casper was going to be able to do that.

He raised his hand to blast the Tektranos so he could concentrate. But it lowered its head, and folded its wings, covering their bodies. Helix cried out in pain. There was no time.

Casper pulled at the aether, dark and light, desperately filling every part of himself to force the process. It didn't take long. When he felt the tug, he released control and the aether lifted him into the air.

You are complete.

It was the voice of Sedrivani. Casper felt a tear fall down his cheek.

Now rest.

One moment Helix was struggling to keep the Tektranos's head pinned to the ground with his one good arm, and the next the creature's gray form stopped struggling and it began to shrink in on itself. He pulled away and the body morphed back into a man.

Helix held his mangled right arm against his side with his working hand. A dozen meters away, in the middle of a swirling ball of light, Casper was floating into the sky. The Tektranos circling the field fell to the ground, changing back as they crashed. The heavy shadows blocking the West Tower from being visible grew fuzzy, like they were being cleaned away.

Helix's breathing grew shallow. He recalled seeing Casper float into the sky on Ouranos. Watching him fade into the clouds and not knowing if he would come back. But if he lost control here, it would destroy the entire city.

That fearful voice screamed in the back of Helix's mind, begging him to call to Casper. Wanting him to stop this. But Helix had to trust him. He looked at the countless people laying in a ring around the field. Casper had healed them. The balancing was already working.

Helix pooled aether in his core and focused on the gash the Tektranos had opened on his arm. The burn of the healing was enough to white out his vision. He fell to his knees. Somewhere in his mind he was aware that he screamed, but maybe he imagined it.

Casper was encircled by rings of light and inky shadow overhead. They were swirling around and into him, gusts of wind blasting his hair to and fro.

In the center of the field, just below Casper's storm, Jacob's body was splayed out next to a woman. She was stirring, struggling to lift herself off the ground. Helix hurried toward her, crouching slightly as gusts of wind blasted him.

Wavy red hair. It couldn't be. She turned toward him, and their eyes met. Helix's heart leapt, a laugh nearly escaping his mouth.

"Talleah?!"

She was crying. She reached out to him, and he helped her to her feet. They crawled away from the air beating down into the grass until there was enough calm to set her down to rest.

"It was you," Helix said. "You killed Jacob." Helix shrugged off his cloak and draped it over her shoulders.

"Long overdue," she said.

"How were you still aware?"

She shrugged lazily. "Guess I got angry."

Helix laughed. Then a blast of energy knocked them both off balance. A brilliant light was pouring out of Casper, now halfway up the height of the tower. Panic bit at Helix's mind. He was glowing. The aether was building.

"Stars above," he said. "Please be ok."

Casper could feel the city. The bones of it started to vibrate in frequency with him. There was a give and take to what the aether was doing. It wasn't quite like the Surface supernova.

Back then, he felt out of control, that incredible brightness trying to pull him into its warm embrace.

This was like breathing. Exhilaration, then rest. It had a rhythm. Brilliant Sedrivani would flow into him and grounded Kanos would flow out.

He could feel where the frequency was off in the stone below. The deep warbling of Kanos and the overly quick chirping of Sedrivani. Both left alone for too long, building on themselves until they became beacons of unbalanced energy.

Casper's mind was brought to his dad. It wasn't forgiveness he started to feel, but maybe an understanding. Of how his anger and his beliefs had built on themselves for years, and how that could lead him to treat Casper the way he did. A smile broke on his face when he realized how difficult it would be for his dad to reconcile what happened here with his religious beliefs.

His attention moved back to the city. As far as his awareness could reach, the vibrations blended seamlessly with his own flow of aether. And for maybe the first time in his life, Casper trusted himself.

The task was done.

"Thank you." He spoke to the aether, but there was no response, which he took comfort in. Balanced, it had no reason to communicate.

Feet back on the ground, the weight of his own body nearly made him fall over. Helix and a partially dressed Talleah were waiting for him. Helix grabbed onto him and held him upright, smashing a kiss against his cheek.

"You did it!" Helix said.

Casper warmed at his words. Not quite sure how to handle Helix being proud of him, he diverted to Talleah. "You're back."

She offered a small wave.

"She took out Jacob," Helix said.

Casper gaped at her.

She shrugged. "You were hesitating."

"I was going to do it!"

"Yeah, yeah. Sure." Helix pulled him forward. "Come on, let's get you somewhere you can rest."

"I was literally gathering aether to do it."

"Of course you were," Talleah said.

"I can't believe you're ragging on me right now," Casper said. "I just saved the entire city."

"After choking *so* hard," Talleah said through a laugh.

"Oh my god! I can't believe you two!"

Helix leaned in and kissed his cheek again, whispering into his ear. "I'm so glad you're ok."

Casper grabbed his arm and squeezed.

Ok. They were all going to be ok.

CHAPTER

FORTY

Talleah wouldn't delay to see a Virgo, so Casper gave her a once over with his aether to make sure she was in working order. Then, wrapped in Helix's cape, she crossed the field to the eastern tower. She wished to run, but she was too tired.

Inside her chest, the near constant pulse of heat was gone. The bite in the back of her mind had finally released. She could fall to the ground and weep from the relief of it. But she needed to find Daphne. To hold her and know that she was safe.

The lobby of the tower was vacant. The elevator ride to their floor impossibly long. The hallway to their apartment painfully quiet. And then the apartment was dark when she opened the door.

Her eyes adjusted slowly. The blinds were open, letting in enough light to make out the shape of their living room. She was still weak, but she collected enough aether to fill her hand with light. The apartment was cast in orange hues as she turned toward the kitchen.

Hector was standing there, brandishing a large knife. He set it on the counter as their eyes met. He rushed forward, collected her in his arms, and every part of her melted as they lowered to the ground. They shook together in silent cries. His hands were searching her body.

"I'm ok," she whispered.

"You're here." The disbelief was thick in his voice.

She cupped his face in her hands. "I'm ok."

"When you came back, I hoped. But I really thought you were gone—"

"I'm ok," she repeated.

His eyes were nearly bloodshot. The long, hard days showed on his face.

"Where is Daphne?" she asked.

"Daph!" he called out. "Come here!"

The tiny patter of her footsteps broke Talleah's heart. She wept with hope and grief and joy. When Daphne's honeyed curls came into view, they were all Talleah could see for how much she cried.

"Mommy!"

Daphne jumped into her arms and Talleah squeezed her. Breathed her in. They were ok. Through blurry eyes she held Hector's gaze. Daphne was in her arms. They were ok.

"I knew you'd come back," Daphne said as she pulled away from their hug.

Vague, faraway images of Hector and Daphne tending to her wounded body flashed in her mind. Most of her time transformed felt like a bad dream. But she could recall that.

"All thanks to you." Talleah brushed at her hair.

"Mommy, why are you naked?"

Talleah and Hector both laughed.

"I didn't have any clothes after Uncle Casper changed me back."

"Come on," Hector said. "Let's get you cleaned up."

Hector was buzzing. Daphne stood beside him with the biggest grin he'd ever seen her wear. His knee was aching slightly by the time Talleah came into the living room. She stopped in her tracks when she saw him kneeling. Her hand floated up to cover her mouth.

"We've had enough adventures," Hector said. "What do you say we settle down?"

From the pocket of his tunic, he produced a small satchel. The fabric was smooth and intricately patterned with a rope tied into a neat circle. A symbol of binding.

"Hector." Talleah's breath escaped her. She reached a hand to his cheek, her eyes swimming with tears. "Really?"

He nodded, crying himself.

"Will you marry me?"

She smiled, her tears flowing freely as she looked into his eyes. "Yes." She leaned in and kissed him. "Yes," she said more loudly between their lips.

His heart was so full. His body felt lighter than air. Like the only thing keeping him on the ground were Talleah's arms wrapped around him.

"Yaaaaay!" Daphne's little voice filled the room.

She was skipping in a circle beside them.

And that felt like the perfect description. He would be Talleah's husband. She would be his wife. And that was the most yay Hector had ever felt.

Casper gripped Helix's hand tightly as they approached the jump pad outside the Celestery grounds. A ring of acolytes were gathered and with them, looking healthier than Casper had seen him in years, was his dad. He smoothed the front of his cape and seemed shy to meet their gaze.

A part of Casper called to be familiar. To push past the pain that lay between them and remember that this was his father. The same man who played soccer with him in the back yard. Who read him books every night when he was little.

"David," Casper said.

His father's eyes slid up to him, then immediately to Helix. "You're not coming back, are you?"

Casper shook his head. He was never going back to live on Earth. But knowing his father had some hope that he would sucked the air out of him.

"I heard about what happened." David gestured to the acolytes. "What you did for these people. I'm proud of you, son."

Casper tightened his grip on Helix's hand. He didn't want to fight. He wanted a clean break. But his father had no right to have pride in him. Not after how much shame and abuse he had poured into Casper's life.

"I came to say goodbye," Casper said. "So... uh. Goodbye." He turned his back on his father.

"Cas, wait."

Helix turned away with Casper, leaning in. "Are you ok? You said you wanted a simple goodbye. We can go."

Casper leaned into him, laying his forehead onto Helix's shoulder.

"You don't owe him anything," Helix said. "Don't give him more than you have."

Casper kissed Helix on the cheek. "Thank you for being here." He turned and stepped closer to his father, giving him space to speak his mind. He wasn't sure if it was hope or morbid curiosity that moved him. But he wanted to know what his father had to say.

"The way I felt when I was that thing..." David's hand was rubbing the back of his neck. His eyes were on the ground. "The rage that filled me from head to toe." His cheeks were flushed red. "It was a familiar feeling. I know I haven't done right by you. That I tried to control you. And uh"—he wiped a tear away from his cheek—"I took my anger out on you."

Casper's breathing was shallow. Adrenaline pumped through him. This was so close to what he'd always wanted to hear his father say. He nearly stopped him from continuing. The pain of him sneaking past Casper's walls just to stab him in the side would be too much.

"This place," David said. "These people... your magic. I don't know how to make sense of it. Father Bryant has never given sermon on the expanse of the cosmos."

He laughed. Casper winced; afraid his father was about to shove old beliefs back onto him.

"I heard you," David said.

Casper's body froze. His heart thumped heavy in his chest.

"When I was that thing," he continued. "I wasn't always aware. But when you visited, I was there."

"Good," Casper said.

David looked past Casper to Helix. "Does he treat you well?"

Casper stared down his father. He wanted him to feel the words. "I've lived my whole life with this tightness in my chest. Like I had been punched in the throat. The ache never went away. Until him. When I'm with him the tension disappears. He is kind and strong and true." And because the way David was speaking presented the tiniest hope that maybe he would go home and work on himself, Casper didn't say, *I would choose him over you every time in any situation.*

"I'm glad to hear that," David said. "You deserve to be happy."

They were the right words, but they landed hollow on Casper's ears. He chose not to respond.

"I think you're about to apologize," Casper said. David's wide eyes let him know he was correct. "Not yet. Neither of us are ready for that."

David hugged his arms across his middle.

"Go home," Casper said. "Fix things with mom. Get your shit straight. If you do that, we can talk about what an apology looks like."

David looked awash with relief. He also looked like he wanted to hug Casper, but that wasn't going to happen.

"Bye, David." Casper stepped back to Helix's side.

"I love you, Casper."

Tears rolled down Casper's cheek, but he didn't reply.

The acolytes joined hands in the jumping circle. David hesitated a moment, then joined as well. Casper's gut twisted tight as he felt the aether flow into the circle, and then, with a flash of light, his father disappeared. Where he stood a moment before was nothing but air.

Casper was dressed, with the help of a tailor, in a nice double-breasted jacket and a matching pair of deep green trousers when he showed up at the clinic to visit Agnes.

"You dressed up for me?" Agnes asked. "You shouldn't have."

Casper smiled as he entered the small room where she was recovering. There was a soft blue rug on the floor. A window in the corner let in the late afternoon light. She was lying in bed, covered with soft, white bedding.

"How are you?" he asked.

"Better," she said. "Thanks to you."

"I'm sorry I didn't get to you before—"

"Casper." She placed a hand over his. "You stopped him. You changed those of us who transformed back. Whatever guilt you carry, absolve yourself of it. You did enough. More than enough."

"That might be harder than saving Novilem."

She rolled her eyes but smiled, nonetheless. "You know, I wasn't much younger than you when this all started. I know what the pressure feels like. You don't give yourself enough credit. You bear it well."

To Casper's surprise, her words reached his core. They touched a part of him that had longed to be seen. It was such a comfort, and he felt aglow with pride. Everything had been difficult, and scary, and more often than not dangerous since he was brought to Novilem. And through it all, in spite of his mistakes and struggles, he managed to save them. Hundreds of thousands of lives. It was genuinely difficult to comprehend.

She squeezed his hand before pulling away. "You clearly have somewhere to be. Thanks for stopping by Casper."

"Of course," he said. "Thank you."

"You've got nothing to thank me for."

"You see me," Casper said.

She gave him a once over before lying her head back on the pillow. Casper smiled to himself and let her rest.

The house was filled with chatter. Conversations loud and small filled the space. There were more faces than Casper could count. The Novelites that evacuated to Earth had returned. A forum was held to make plans for repairing damages to the city. Helix was pretty chuffed that his idea to have the Gemini communicate information and gather consensus was implemented. It had expedited the process considerably and the city was already brimming with movement and life again.

No definite plans had been made for the future governing of the city. By a large majority the people of Novilem voted for the council not to be dismantled. So, they would need to come together to choose a new form of leadership.

Casper was taking a breather, people watching when Talleah poked her head out onto the patio. She was followed by Daphne and Hector.

"You came," Casper said as he wrapped her in a big hug. Daphne pushed against their side, joining in.

"To support you?" Talleah said. "Of course."

Casper smiled, understanding the discomfort. He felt some of that too. He started to sign the Trine at Hector, but Hector pulled him into a hug.

"Keep your formalities." Hector pounded a heavy palm against his back. "Thank you for everything."

"Where's Helix?" Daphne asked.

"Stuck in a conversation somewhere in there." Casper pointed inside the family home just as Helix approached the open door. "I needed some air."

"Hiding away?" Helix said as he joined them.

"Ran out of things to say," Casper answered.

"And I don't really want to be here," Talleah said.

Helix chuckled, knocking her shoulder softly. He smiled at Casper. "It's time. I was hoping you'd come with me?"

Casper took his outstretched hand. His stomach flittered with butterflies. He didn't know why he was nervous.

"Yeah, let's do it," Casper said.

"Stars be with you," Hector said.

"Thanks," Helix said. "See you in a bit."

Helix guided Casper back inside. Faces turned to them with reverent smiles as hands folded in salutation. Wherever they walked bodies parted for them. Helix offered soft thanks to the remarks of strangers. Casper tried to keep his eyes on the ground to avoid making eye contact. He didn't know what to say if someone tried to address him. He was here for support, not as the Telos.

They made it through the living space into a den, warmly lit with light gems. Theo was standing up front. His eyes were red, but dry. It had been a long day already. He pulled Helix into a hug and then patted Casper on the shoulder.

And then they faced Brissa. A large and beautifully rendered painting of her seated near a garden scape was positioned at Theo's side. Her hands folded in her lap next to the length of her long, silver braid. Helix shuddered. Casper squeezed his hand a little harder.

Helix was whispering, but Casper didn't try to listen. Whatever words he had to share were for him and Brissa. Casper tried to remember the warmth he glimpsed in her. The few and far between moments where he saw the wholeness of her, not just the ambition. He wasn't sure what one did at a wake. How one said goodbye to someone once they passed. There was a sadness, but it didn't feel entirely like his own. There existed a collective grief among those gathered that Casper was helping carry by being present.

Helix wiped at tears before turning back to Theo.

"Pappous," he said with a broken voice. They embraced again.

"She is with the stars," Theo said, his red-rimmed eyes once again dewy.

Casper looked away, feeling like he was encroaching on their privacy.

When they returned to the living room Casper squeezed Helix's hand. "Hey, we can talk about it later. But there hasn't been a good time to mention it. The moving in thing? I'm ok with waiting."

Helix's brow creased. "Are you sure?"

Casper nodded. "I haven't had a home, like a real home, in a long time. And somewhere along the way I got it in my head that you moving in would make this real. But I was..." Casper had to look away. "I was just scared of losing you."

Helix gently placed his finger under Casper's chin, nudging him to meet his eyes. "I'm not going anywhere."

Casper smiled. "Me neither."

"Ok. Good." Helix pulled him away from the corner of the room they had nestled into. "Are you ready?"

"For what?" Casper asked.

"Now we celebrate."

Before Casper could respond, the heavy beat of drums filled the room. As one, the people gathered cried out in a joyous whoop and broke out in dance. Helix was still crying, but he grabbed hold of Casper and together they moved in step with the crowd. Casper reached out and dried Helix's cheek. He was laughing, so Casper laughed. The spirit of the home lifted immediately and all at once.

"I love you," Helix said.

And deep in Casper's heart, he felt it. The bond they had

built. The dangers they had faced. The trials they had overcome. He had never known an intimacy like this. And he would never let it go.

"I love you more," Casper said.

And they danced.

Acknowledgments

This book wasn't supposed to exist, and it honestly wouldn't without the love and support of so many people. I set out on this intergalactic journey hoping to write a stand-alone for my debut novel. But when I finished A Circle of Stars, I could feel there was more story to tell. Casper and Helix hadn't finished their journey. So, I did the scary thing. I promised a sequel.

Sophomore books are notoriously difficult, and A Sky So Hollow gave me a bit of an understanding as to why. I've been incredibly blessed with the reception of my first book, which of course placed some pressure on my shoulders to deliver with book two.

I'll start off the gratitude train by thanking the readers that have been so kind and enthusiastic when showing up to these pages. Your love for the space boys and this story has been a dream come true. I can't thank you enough for giving my work a chance and spreading the word. Books, especially indie books, live and die by word of mouth. Y'all really did the thing and I will be forever grateful.

Thank you to my husband, Luke. I'm so glad you pushed me to take the chance; to chase the dream. I could not hope a more perfect partner. I love you.

Thank you to Cee M Taylor and Sarah Sanders. Your editing efforts and emotional support are entirely to thank for me making it across the finish line on this novel. It was a privilege and a joy to work with both of you.

Thank you to the online bookish space. It's a weird world sometimes, but it has also enriched my life in many ways and introduced me to so many wonderful people. Bookish friends are the best friends.

Thank you to my parents, who have cheered on and cherished my imaginative ways my entire life. I'm so thankful I never let go of the spark, and that's in no small part because you allowed me the space to keep it alive.

Thank you to my sister, Karen, for showing me what it means to be loved and to love. You are and incredible human, a fighter, and the best role model I could have had. Your generosity of spirit and tenacity are the stuff of legends. The affection and care that the characters show to each other on these pages are a tribute to the way you have showed up in my life.

Until the next time, may the stars bless and guide you all.

About the Author

Craig Montgomery lives in Central Illinois with his husband and their two cats. He enjoys long walks in nature where he can dream up other worlds. And ice cream, he really likes ice cream. Make sure to sign up for the newsletter!

www.craigmontgomerybooks.com

facebook.com/craigmontgomerybooks

instagram.com/craigmontgomerybooks

tiktok.com/@craigmontgomerybooks

Also by Craig Montgomery

A Circle of Stars